THE FINAL RECKONING

Also by
Chris Bishop

The Shadow of the Raven Series:
Blood and Destiny
The Warrior with the Pierced Heart

Published by RedDoor
www.reddoorpublishing.com

ISBN 978-1-910453-72-8

A CIP catalogue record for this book is available from the British Library

Cover design: Patrick Knowles
www.patrickknowlesdesign.com

Map design: Joey Everett

Typesetting: Tutis Innovative E-Solutions Pte. Ltd

Printed and bound in Denmark by Nørhaven

THE FINAL RECKONIN

CHRIS BISHOP

For Millie, Jo,
Charlotte and Nina

A glossary of some of the terms used in this story can be found at the back of the book

THE FINAL RECKONING

CHRIS BISHOP

RedDoor

Published by RedDoor
www.reddoorpublishing.com

ISBN 978-1-910453-72-8

A CIP catalogue record for this book is available from the British Library

Cover design: Patrick Knowles
www.patrickknowlesdesign.com

Map design: Joey Everett

Typesetting: Tutis Innovative E-Solutions Pte. Ltd

Printed and bound in Denmark by Nørhaven

A glossary of some of the terms used in this story can be found at the back of the book

For Millie, Jo,
Charlotte and Nina

Know that your fate follows you like a shadow
for all the days of your life

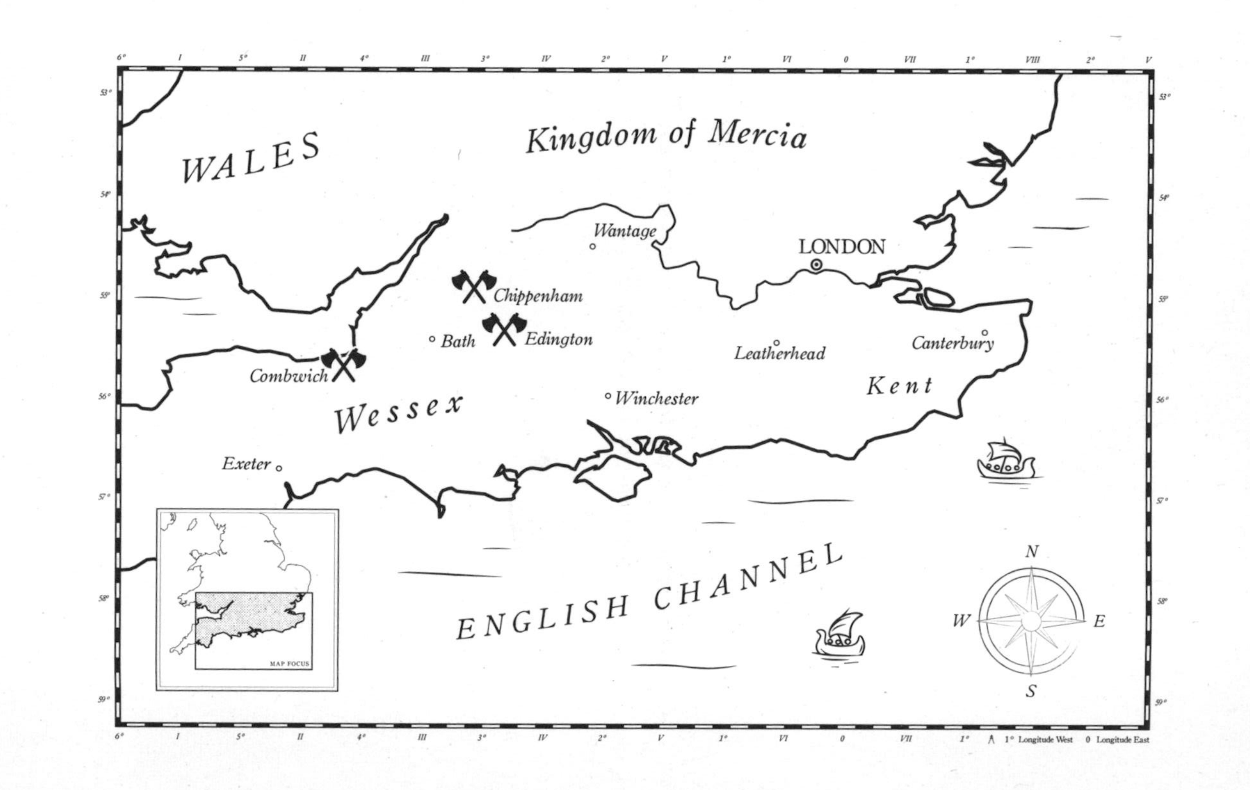
WALES
Kingdom of Mercia
Wantage
LONDON
Chippenham
Bath
Edington
Combwich
Leatherhead
Canterbury
Kent
Winchester
Wessex
Exeter
ENGLISH CHANNEL
MAP FOCUS
N
W
E
S
1° Longitude West
0 Longitude East

Prelude

Whilst I'd learned much since being a novice at the Abbey near Winchester, the lesson I found hardest to accept was that duty is not a matter of choice. Certainly for me it was more like a disease which, having settled itself upon me, riddled every fibre of my being. Thus infected, I could no more refuse my King, Lord Alfred, than I could deny my birthright or my blood, even though what he asked of me went against every tenet of my fragile faith.

Even with the wound to my chest scarcely healed he would have me return to Leatherhead with just one man to aid me, there to train and properly arm the fyrd in anticipation of an invasion by Jarl Hakon's Viking horde which had gathered on the southern banks of the river at London.

Whilst in Leatherhead I was also to call to account all those suspected of treachery, not by bringing them to trial but rather by dispensing justice by whatever means I considered fit. Such was the weight he placed upon my young shoulders; and all that whilst I waited, desperate to know whether the child which Emelda carried in her womb was that of my blood or the wretched spawn of another man.

Chapter One

'What's wrong with the name you already have?' asked Aelred as we rode towards my former Abbey.

Once there, I intended to renounce the vows I'd sworn as a novice monk, something I felt I'd been remiss in not doing before. I was determined to set matters right before embarking on the mission for Alfred – and was hoping to persuade Aelred to be the one who would come with me to Leatherhead. Although not of noble birth, he'd more than proved his worth in helping me to escape from the slavers as well as with all that which had since befallen me. So much so that I'd come to regard him as a true and trusted friend.

'The name "Matthew" was bestowed upon me when I first joined the Abbey,' I explained. 'I was named for one of the Apostles in the hope that I might emulate such a Holy personage. Once I leave the order that may no longer be appropriate especially given the role I'm charged to perform. By rights, I should now revert to my given name.'

'What, and be known as Edward?'

'Exactly. As I told you, that was the name with which I was christened. It was derived from that of my father, Lord Edwulf.'

'Yet I've never heard anyone call you that,' he said. 'You're known to all as Matthew. Either that or by your reputation as the so-called warrior with the pierced heart.'

'I wish that were not so,' I mused. 'A reputation such as that isn't always welcome.'

'Why, when it means that your enemies fear you?' asked Aelred. 'Surely that's an advantage given the troubled times in which we live?'

'Perhaps. But anyway, appropriate or not, I'm minded to remain as Matthew for, as you say, it's the name that everyone knows me by. At least, all those who matter.'

'Well, whatever name you choose to go by, you never did tell me how you got away from that bastard Torstein.'

'Have I not?' I was surprised as I seemed to have been telling that particular story so often in the few days since arriving back at Winchester. Yet it was true that Aelred and I had not had much chance to speak since meeting up again. 'Well, like you I made it to the shore when the boat capsized,' I explained. 'But I ended up on the Vikings' side of the river. I was so weary that all I could do was rest and, whilst I did so, was taken captive then marched back to the Viking encampment to stand before Jarl Hakon himself. There I was accused of having upset the boat on purpose…'

'Which sounds fair enough given that's exactly what you did!'

'Yes, but I convinced them that it was Torstein's fault as the man he let manage the steering oar was drunk.'

'And the fools believed you?'

'It made no difference whether they did or not. They were afraid I'd tell Alfred about the longships we'd seen being built beside the river and resolved to silence me. However, that little runt, Arne, told them that I'm known to the King so rather than risk his displeasure by simply killing me, they decided to let Torstein do it for them. Their plan was that if I died fighting him over some personal grievance, no questions would be asked afterwards.'

'Phew! Rather you than me, that's all I can say. That Torstein was a bloodthirsty bastard if ever I saw one. He'd slaughter anyone – man, woman or child – and he'd do so without cause or compassion! How the hell did you get away from there?'

'I didn't. Or at least I did but I had to fight him first.'

'What? You actually managed to better him?'

'Yes, thanks to you I did.'

'Thanks to me? What the hell did I do? I wasn't even there!'

'I remembered that story you told after we'd escaped from the slavers – the one about the small man in the land of giants. Like Hereric, I refused their offer of a mail vest so I could move more freely and instead fought stripped to the waist so that Torstein could see the scar on my chest. Because he was so in awe of that, he chose to fight whilst dressed in full mail, the weight of which made him tire more quickly. When he did, I slew him, just as Hereric did in your tale.'

Aelred looked surprised. 'And Hakon then actually freed you?'

'Yes, but he sent a man to guide me back to Winchester who I was certain had orders to kill me along the way.'

'So you slew him as well? No wonder you feel the need to make confession given how many men you've now killed!'

'Actually, I didn't kill him, I let him live. And I'm not going to the Abbey to make confession; you are. I'm going there to renounce my vows.'

Aelred gave a snort of derision. 'What's the point of me confessing anything? I'm bound to commit a few more sins sooner or later so why waste time on it now?'

'Because you need to absolve yourself of all the things you've done, then mend your ways,' I explained.

'I will,' he said. 'But I plan to do it just before I die. That way I'm not wasting God's time any more than I have to.'

'Well, there's good cause for you to do it now,' I offered. 'If you make confession Lord Alfred has agreed to pardon all your past transgressions.'

'What, all of them?' pressed Aelred, sounding almost incredulous. 'Why would a great man like Lord Alfred be prepared to do that without even knowing what I've done?'

'Ah, well there's a little bit more to it than that,' I admitted. 'You then have to come with me to Leatherhead and there help me to train the fyrd.'

He shrugged. 'That doesn't sound so bad. Why does the fyrd need more training?'

I could see that he was going to press me hard on the real nature of our mission so decided it was time to tell him all. 'It needs more training because parts of the Shire suffer many raids and yet the fyrd has not once managed to intercept them. In fact it's proved so inadequate that we suspect there may be those who profit from the raids in some way.'

'A traitor you mean? So who do you suspect?'

'Well, the son of the Ealdorman for one.'

Aelred reined his horse to a stop and stared at me. 'The son of the Ealdorman! God's truth, Matthew, you certainly know how to choose your enemies! First you slay Jarl Torstein, a man known to Hakon himself, then you want to accuse the son of an Ealdorman of treachery!'

'Yes, but I'm afraid that's not all we have to do,' I continued. 'Whilst there we have to fortify the settlement as well.'

Aelred was quiet for a moment. 'Why does the settlement need to be fortified?' he asked, clearly sensing there was even more to it than I was saying.

I decided to choose my words with care. 'You remember all those Viking ships we saw at London?'

He nodded.

'Well, Alfred fears that Jarl Hakon is planning to launch an attack on Wessex and will march his army south to meet those ships once they've sailed around the coast so they can then be used to supply his army and...'

Aelred was already ahead of me. 'And he'll need to march right through the settlement at Leatherhead to do it! So how many warriors were in that camp?'

'Whilst I was there I estimated about two hundred, but all those ships he was building probably mean he's expecting more.'

'And you expect the fyrd at Leatherhead to fight them off?'

'No, not fight them off, just delay them.'

He looked very doubtful as he considered what I'd said. 'Delay them? For how long?'

'Just till reinforcements arrive,' I assured him. 'Possibly for just a few days or a week at worst.'

'A week! Why so long?'

'Alfred has set spies to watch Hakon's camp but it will take them at least a full day to ride to Leatherhead to warn us if the Vikings start to move. It will then take us two days to get word to Winchester, another day or so for Alfred to muster enough men, and then two days more for them to come to our aid.'

'Do you really mean to hold off two hundred Viking warriors for almost a week with just a handful of poorly trained men and a makeshift fence?'

'Hakon won't attack until his ships are ready. Even then it's unlikely he'll risk them putting to sea until he can be certain that the winter storms have abated or there's a gap in the weather. We can use that time to properly train the men. Besides, reinforcements from the neighbouring settlements should reach us more quickly.'

'Oh, that's all right then. For a moment I thought you and I were going to fight them all ourselves!' he teased.

'So will you come with me or not?' I asked.

He shrugged as though it made no difference one way or the other. 'Why not?' he said, pressing his horse forward to continue as we'd come. 'You've nearly got me killed so many times now that one more won't make much difference.'

* * * * *

Alfred had assured me that there was no need for me to go in person to see my abbot in order to renounce my vows as he could have others deal with it on my behalf. Even so, I'd made it clear that it was something I felt I needed to do for myself.

As we approached the gates to the Abbey, I recalled how the abbot, Father Constantine, used to say that there's no rest for the wicked in this world nor precious little for the righteous. For me that surely seemed to be the way of it for, having spent so long wrestling with my conscience whilst desperately trying to survive all that which befell me, I longed for the chance to rest and restore myself and thereby determine whether all the changes forced upon me were indeed for the good. Yet, barely having had time to catch my breath, I was charged by Alfred to set forth once more on what promised to be a hazardous and extremely dangerous mission. Thus when Aelred and I passed through the Abbey gates I was looking forward to a chance for some quiet contemplation in a place where, as a young and innocent novice, time for such reflection had been a part of my daily routine.

The Abbey was just as I remembered it, looking more like a fortified farmstead than a religious enclave. It comprised various buildings, all formed from timber and thatch, surrounded by a stout fence and with a pair of sturdy gates to the front. It had been founded by a group of committed monks who sought to form a community wherein they could worship according to their own particular creed. As their number grew, they'd added more buildings to provide dormitories, a chapel and various stores, workshops and shelters. They also had the benefit of extensive pastures, a large and well-stocked pond and, like most Abbeys, access to a nearby river. Despite the fortifications, it was a miracle it hadn't suffered unduly from Viking raids, perhaps having been spared only because it was so close to the major settlement at Winchester.

As Aelred and I approached, a man came forward to greet us. I recognised him at once as being a lay brother who had been in service there for many years.

'Seth?' I said when I saw him. 'So you're still here?'

'Aye my Lord. But then I've no place else to go but the grave. Besides, they couldn't manage without me if I had.'

As a lay brother, Seth was indentured to serve at the Abbey in whatever capacity was needed but was not sworn to a life in orders. In return he was granted board and lodging and, more importantly from his point of view, the promise of salvation in the life to come. Whilst we were never told what he'd done to be so much in need of redemption, he was much liked by all, having a cheery manner which seemed to find humour in even menial tasks. Even so, I found it strange that he should defer to me as befitted my station beyond the Abbey precincts rather than as one of the brethren, though assumed that word had reached even him regarding the purpose of my visit.

'So has much changed since I was last here?' I asked as we dismounted so that he could take our horses to be fed and watered.

'Nothing changes here, my Lord,' he said. 'All is much as it was before, though some members of the order come and others go.' He then mentioned two brothers who had died and named another who had recently joined the order. 'I think Father Constantine is expecting you, my Lord,' he added as if to hurry me.

It was true that the good Father was indeed expecting us, so we were ushered into a lobby where we removed our weapons and were told to wait until summoned.

After some time, I alone was shown through to the main Hall which, given its supposed humility of purpose, was much grander than it needed to be, having walls bedecked with numerous icons of the Holy saints and fine tapestries depicting scenes from the Bible. A large and elaborate chair had been placed at one end, which had a cushioned footstool and a canopy of fine yellow silk. I recalled that it was there that Father Constantine liked to sit in order to receive people, particularly those he wanted to impress. I clearly didn't warrant such treatment as he entered the Hall from an arched doorway to the side and came directly to greet me.

I knelt at the abbot's feet and kissed his ring in order for him to bless me. 'Father abbot, I have come to...'

'I know full well why you've come,' he said, graciously allowing me to stand. 'Lord Alfred in his wisdom has sent word of what he intends and has asked that you be allowed to renounce your vows free from penance. Given that he's truly such a great benefactor of the Holy Church, I'm minded to accede to his request but first we must pray together for guidance on such an important matter.' So saying, he led me towards an alcove which housed a simple wooden cross and the Abbey's most precious relic, a small jewelled reliquary which contained a rag said to have been dipped in the blood of St Paul.

I knew from experience what praying together would involve. The goodly abbot thought nothing of praying for a full hour at a time and sometimes more. As a novice, I'd learned how to deal with this by lying prostrate on the floor, something which Father Constantine took as a sign of humility and devotion. In reality it was simply a way for we novice monks to avoid the pain of having to kneel for so long on the cold, hard tiles.

When at last he'd finished, he bade me rise and went across to sit on his magnificent chair whilst I stood before him with my head bowed in reverence.

'So Brother Matthew, what are we to do in this matter?'

'Father abbot I must confess that I've strayed since I left this hallowed place but have always strived to keep my faith in God.' I omitted to mention all the doubts I'd been having about my faith and the many sins I'd committed.

'I've followed your exploits with interest,' said Father Constantine. 'Word has reached us even here of some of the things which have befallen you. I cannot say that I approve of all I've heard but am glad that you've retained your faith despite your many trials and temptations.'

I wondered what he'd actually heard and hoped that he wouldn't press me to make confession, fearing that if he did I'd be there for a week! 'Father, my heart has readily confessed my many sins but I now feel God has shown me the path he wants me to follow.' I then told him about the monks we'd come across during the retreat from Chippenham and of the church they intended to restore based on the Holy Splinter, a relic which they believed had been part of the cross on which Christ had been crucified. 'They showed me that it's better to play a small part of something that's good rather than a large part of something that's not. Thus I recognise that it's my Christian duty to serve Lord Alfred, though I know it may well cost me my life on this earth if I do.'

'Matthew, that's all to the good but I fear that some of the sins you refer to include the shedding of much blood and also consorting with pagans. Do you truly repent those sins?'

'Father, all is not as you fear. I didn't willingly consort with Ingar but trusted her to heal a dreadful wound which I suffered whilst in the service of Lord Alfred. It's true that she took advantage of me but it was not of my accord. As for the men I've slain, it was never without good cause. Many Holy men have done as much for the glory of God and for the protection of the Holy Church.'

He nodded wisely as though accepting all I'd said. I noted that he seemed not to know about Emelda and our unborn child and I deemed it better not to enlighten him lest that gave him further cause for concern.

'This is not the time for confession, rather it's an opportunity to review and set right your standing within this Holy community. To that end, if this severance is what Lord Alfred and you both truly desire, it's a relatively simple process given that you didn't progress beyond the station of being a novice. I have here letters of renunciation of your vows which shall suffice and which I shall send to Lord Alfred and to the Bishop. However, I'm bound to raise the matter of the contribution made by your father when first he sought for you to join our order.'

Knowing that the Church had a keen eye when it came to receiving and keeping donations, I struggled to resist a smile. In my case, my father had gifted lands in perpetuity to procure my position there and I realised that Father Constantine was worried I might require him to give them back. 'My father was a pious man,' I said. 'I'm sure he'd wish that his generosity will ensure that the order continues to thrive. I would therefore endorse his gifts and ask only that you offer prayers for his soul and for that of my dear departed mother.'

The abbot looked much relieved. 'That's very generous,' he acknowledged. With that he insisted we pray some more.

When at last we were done, I mentioned the other issue which Alfred had asked me to raise. 'Whilst here, my friend, a man named Aelred, would like to make confession,' I said, knowing that would provide me with the time I needed for some quiet thought and contemplation on my own. 'He's travelled with me for that very purpose. Although not of noble birth he, like me, is assigned to undertake a dangerous mission on the King's behalf for which he'll be pardoned for all his crimes in this world, but Lord Alfred would have him cleanse his soul as well in readiness for the next.'

Father Constantine seemed to be expecting me to ask this. 'Then have him come forth and I will hear his confession in person,' he said. 'And after that no doubt you'll both stay to share our meagre supper?'

I couldn't resist another smile knowing that the abbot always set a fine table, laden with the bounty which the Abbey's very fertile precincts provided.

As Aelred made his confession, I went to a small chapel and there sat in silence, allowing my mind to think back through all that which had befallen me. Whatever conclusions I reached, there could be no going back on what I'd promised to do on Alfred's behalf. My life belonged to him and there could be no returning to the Church, but I was still troubled by the prospect of leaving Emelda unaware that I was still alive as Alfred had suggested, for that seemed to be a betrayal of all that which had passed between us. And of course, there was now Ingar who, if what she'd told me was true, also carried my unborn child in her womb. As always I found more questions than answers but, before I could dwell any more on those matters, it seemed Aelred had made his confession and had come to tell me that we were expected at the refectory.

We supped well that evening on roasted meats, fish and all manner of honeyed pastries, all washed down with a strong mead. When we'd eaten our fill, Father Constantine offered us the chance to stay the night. However, we were both anxious to return to Alfred's Vill and besides, we knew full well that if we stayed at the Abbey we'd be roused long before dawn for yet more prayers. We therefore made our excuses and left.

*****

It was dark as we made our way back to Winchester, but the road was one which I knew well. As we went, I was aware that Aelred seemed not overly impressed by the prospect of the pardon Alfred had promised him. For my part, I expected to feel relieved that the burden of my vows had been lifted but, strange to say, all I felt at that time was an emptiness – as if something which had so long guided me in life had been taken from me.

'So, did you confess all your sins?' I asked.

Aelred hesitated. 'Well, obviously not all of them,' he admitted. 'Only the ones I thought the abbot wouldn't find too worrying.'

'You were supposed to unburden yourself completely!' I said, scolding him for not having done so.

'Unburden myself of what?' he argued. 'So far as I'm concerned what I've done, I've done. And I don't see how telling some priest all about it will change anything.'

'It's about cleansing your soul,' I explained. 'Something we all of us need to do if…' At that I realised that Aelred was not a man who worried unduly about such things.

'I'll wait until I've committed a few sins worth confessing,' he promised. 'Then I'll go to see him again if that pleases you. But will Alfred really absolve me of all my crimes without even knowing what I've done?'

‘That was the plan,’ I told him.

‘So what if I’d killed my wife? Would I still be pardoned for that?’

I nodded.

‘Then I wish I’d known that a few months ago.’

‘Why?’ I asked.

‘Because then I could have killed the nagging bitch and her poisonous mother and got away with it!’

‘Alfred’s pardon won’t absolve your soul,’ I reminded him. ‘That was why you were supposed to confess your sins to the abbot and thereby to God.’

He shrugged as though it didn’t much matter to him one way or the other. ‘So when do we leave for Leatherhead?’

‘In a week or so,’ I said. ‘I have first to go with Alfred for a meeting with Guthrum and after that I want to visit the grave where my brother is buried.’

‘Do you want me to come with you?’

‘Only if you’ve a mind to. After that we have to be on our way as I’m anxious to get things started at Leatherhead, though God only knows how we can fulfil our orders. Hopefully all will become clear once we get there. I recall you said that you once served in the fyrd?’

‘I did, though I managed to avoid it whenever I could. Not that I minded battle training you understand; it’s just that it was always a good time to go poaching when everyone else was busy elsewhere.’

‘How on earth did you get away with that? Surely everyone who’s fit and able is obliged to take their turn?’

‘Ah, well, you see the Reeve who took the roll was always partial to the odd hare or two…’

I laughed as only Aelred could have got away with that.

'Don't worry, I know how to stand in the shield wall well enough and as you've seen, I know which end of the spear goes where. I won't let you down if we run into any trouble; you can depend on that.'

* * * * *

Once back at Winchester I was told that Alfred wanted to see me even though the hour was late.

'Matthew, how was your journey?' he asked as I was shown through to the small chamber which adjoined the Great Hall where he was supping mead with Lord Ethelnorth, the much-respected warrior who had played such an important part in the battle at Edington. I was offered a beaker but declined to join them as it was late and I was already tired.

'It passed well enough, Sire, and was not overly arduous.'

'Good. And did you renounce your vows?'

'I did, Sire. I also had Aelred make confession as you asked, though I doubt he admitted all his sins as he was meant to.'

Alfred seemed to take that news better than I expected. 'Well,' he reasoned. 'Not all men take their faith as seriously as you and I.'

'But you'll still grant him a full pardon?'

'I will. In fact, I have.' With that he passed me a small vellum scroll which recorded the fact. 'And what have you decided about your name? Are we to continue to call you "Matthew" or will you revert to your given name?'

I hadn't thought about that since discussing it with Aelred. 'My Lord, I feel I'm known to all as "Matthew" so have decided to keep that name, though I hope I don't imply any disrespect to my father by doing so.'

'I think that's wise and am sure he'd approve. Your reputation is well known and respected, so to change your name now would serve no purpose.'

I thanked him and made as though to leave.

'Matthew, will your friend Aelred come with us to meet with Guthrum?' asked Lord Ethelnorth.

It hadn't occurred to me that he wouldn't. 'If he and I are to deal with Hakon's horde then it would be as well if he did,' I ventured.

Both men nodded their agreement.

'Good,' said Alfred. 'Your mission at Leatherhead will be like entering a den of lions and if we're to keep you safe he'll need to fully understand the implications of all that's going on there, both military and political.'

'Never mind all that,' added Ethelnorth. 'Just make sure he's there to watch your back.'

Chapter Two

Having rested and restored myself, I had Aelred join me as we went with Alfred and Lord Ethelnorth for the prearranged meeting with Guthrum, accompanied by Alfred's personal guard which was led by my old friend Osric. That he remained as head of Alfred's personal guard was testimony to how well Osric had fulfilled that role through the difficult times at Athelney and, for the journey to meet with Guthrum, he commanded a force of no less than twenty well-armed warriors, all personally chosen by him for their loyalty and their weapon skills. The party also included many servants, a line of pack horses laden with supplies, a priest who kept himself very much to himself and several monks who would take turns to act as scribes in order to record all that was agreed. Such large processions were not unusual in less troubled times as Kings often travelled throughout their realm, staying at one of their Royal Vills or seeking lodgings for the entire party with an Ealdorman or, failing that, at an Abbey.

Even from the outset I sensed that Osric was uneasy about Aelred's presence. Whilst I could determine no cause for that, I saw little reason to worry given that Aelred would play no part in the proceedings we were about to witness and was just one member of such a large party.

'You should attend your master more closely,' Osric told Aelred soon after we'd set off.

Aelred, who was busy talking to one of the women servants at the time, didn't take well to the suggestion. 'He's not my master,' he replied curtly. 'He's my friend and I serve him as a matter of choice.'

This seemed to shock Osric. 'We all of us have a master of one kind or another,' he pointed out.

'If that's so, then you serve who you will,' replied Aelred. 'But I'm a free man and have Lord Alfred's blessing to regard myself as such. I'm therefore obligated to no one, save the King.'

Osric left it at that but I felt uneasy about what he'd said and wondered whether I should have intervened and explained matters. In the end, I reminded myself that although I still knew very little about Aelred, I had good cause to trust him. As for Osric, whilst he was a man I much respected and admired as a warrior, I remembered that he'd been slow to recognise the treachery of Cedric whilst at Athelney, so much so that at the time many suspected that he was the traitor in our midst, not the giant from Northumbria. Thus I dismissed any concerns he had about Aelred and concentrated instead on all that lay ahead of us.

I had never before attended a meeting of such importance, except perhaps when Alfred accepted Guthrum's surrender. From what I'd been told, the meeting we were to attend was just one of many which would be needed to negotiate the terms of the peace treaty given that both sides had cause not to fully trust the other. All the meetings were to be conducted in relative secrecy in a hunting lodge at a place called Wedmore, not far from Athelney, with just a few trusted men in attendance from each party to avoid the possibility of matters being disrupted because of old scores which needed to be settled. All the other warriors would wait outside, though no doubt held ready in case they were needed.

Travelling slowly, we reached Wedmore within three days and, as soon as we arrived, Osric ordered Alfred's personal guard to check the lodge for any signs of an ambush or a possible attempt on the King's life. That done, they then secured it to ensure that once safely ensconced, the parties would not be disturbed. It was a wise and necessary precaution given that there was still much unrest within the realm, despite Alfred's great victory at Edington.

The lodge was a humble building for such an important meeting, being thatched and crudely built, intended to provide some measure of shelter for a hunting party if the weather turned against them. We had enough provisions to stay there for several days and nights if needed, though Guthrum was not expected to remain that long.

The powerful Viking leader arrived early the next day. He brought just two senior jarls as he felt his presence in Wessex might draw unwelcome attention to the proceedings. That said, his personal retinue of warriors, servants and slaves was large enough to worry Osric lest it implied the possibility of a trap – so much so that the camps were set completely apart. They were also guarded so as to ensure there were no quarrels, particularly that first night given that there was much drinking, feasting and revelry in both camps.

Come morning, those of us who were to attend the meeting itself were ushered into the lodge and took our places on benches either side of a long table. Once settled, Alfred and Guthrum entered, both accompanied by their armed guards and both dressed in their finest robes. Alfred was wearing a dark blue tunic with a scarlet cloak trimmed with ermine whereas Guthrum was wreathed in furs. They acknowledged each other and exchanged gifts before each taking a seat at opposite ends of the table. With the formalities out of the way, all the guards and servants from both parties withdrew from the lodge, but leaving Osric present to guard Alfred's person, something which seemed to be accepted by the Vikings.

Guthrum was just as I remembered him from when I'd seen him the night I went to spy on his camp and also when he'd surrendered after the battle at Edington - a huge bear of a man with a vast yellow beard. I'd like to think that he also remembered me. In fact, he did acknowledge my presence with a nod and a smile but otherwise said nothing. What surprised me was that these two very powerful men who had once fought each other so fiercely seemed almost to be friends. Less than six months had passed since Guthrum had boasted how he would cut out Alfred's heart and eat it, yet neither seemed to hold any form of grudge.

The priest led us all in prayers and, as he did so, I noticed that all the Vikings bowed their heads, thereby acknowledging their new-found faith even though that had been foisted upon them as a condition of their surrender following the battle at Edington. Before leaving the lodge, the priest blessed our endeavours, but one of the monks remained with us to record whatever was agreed.

Having welcomed the Vikings, Alfred had a large but rather crude map unrolled and laid out on the table for all to see. It depicted a rough outline of the whole country on which had been drawn several lines dividing the land beyond

Wessex virtually from one side to the other, although it had clearly been revised many times as you could see where the vellum had been scratched away to note the changes. As we all stared at it, Alfred insisted on speaking first.

'I would begin by first raising an issue which is of concern to me,' he said.

This was translated for Guthrum who nodded his agreement.

'I've received word of a large force of men gathering on the southern banks of the river at London,' he said bluntly. 'Do these men answer to you?'

Guthrum smiled and said something to the translator.

'My Lord Guthrum says these men are simply waiting for their ships to be repaired which will then carry them abroad.'

'To raid or to trade?' asked Alfred pointedly.

Guthrum shrugged when he heard this, seeming to think that it mattered not one way or the other.

'You say the ships are being repaired. Is that so, or are they being constructed there?'

The translator consulted Guthrum who seemed in no doubt as to the position.

'My Lord says that the ships were used by some of Jarl Hakon's men to cross from our homelands. During the journey the vessels fared badly from a storm and are now undergoing extensive repairs.'

Both Alfred and Ethelnorth looked at me as if expecting me to confirm this. 'Sire, I can report only that which I saw from the river. It looked to me that they were being built but I cannot say for certain.'

Alfred seemed to accept that. 'Whether being repaired or constructed, they are assembled very close to the borders of my realm,' he added. 'As such they could present a threat to all we're discussing here.'

Again the translator spoke to Guthrum then repeated what he said. 'Whilst Jarl Hakon is an ambitious man he, like others, now knows better than to cause any concern to the Kingdom of Wessex.'

Alfred nodded. 'Very well, then do I have Lord Guthrum's word on this?'

If Guthrum was surprised to get off so lightly he didn't show it. Instead, he simply shrugged then nodded. 'London is a wilful place,' said the translator, though at that point he seemed to be speaking of his own accord, not for Lord Guthrum. 'There both Saxons and Vikings seem to tolerate each other, though it is hard to say who governs them. I have been there twice and both times have been glad to leave for it is not a settled place and is one where I fear violence is the norm. Daily they drag bodies from both sides of the river. Also, both settlements stink and the water which flows between them is foul.'

For a moment no one spoke as we all considered what had been said.

'Are you saying that Lord Guthrum has no control over the settlement?' asked Ethelnorth.

The translator shook his head. 'I say only that where no man rules, Lord Guthrum can hardly be held responsible for what transpires.'

'But Jarl Hakon is his to command, is he not?' said Alfred. 'Young Matthew here recalls that Hakon sat beside your Lord at Chippenham and was there subservient to him in every way. Is that not so?'

Guthrum smiled, clearly then recalling the night I'd visited his camp at Chippenham where I sang and danced for food as I tried to ascertain the number of men there. He leaned across and spoke to the interpreter.

'Lord Guthrum says that Hakon is a warlord, not a servant. He commands those who follow him but has no cause to try the authority of Lord Guthrum who, having given you his word, assures you that he will do all he may to ensure that you have nothing to fear from the forces there. To that end, he will personally send word to Jarl Hakon and persuade him of the wisdom of becoming a Christian. Will that not set your mind at rest?'

Alfred seemed pleased but was not ready to let the matter drop. 'That's to the good, but Lord Guthrum still doesn't use the name he was given at the font. Does that mean that he's not yet fully convinced of the relevance of the one true God?'

The translator smiled. 'My Lord is secure in his new faith. He will take and use his new name when the time is right.'

We had no option but to accept that; however, it was clear that Ethelnorth was far from convinced. He leaned across and whispered his concerns to both Alfred and myself. 'Sire, I suspect Hakon has been stationed there to intimidate us. His presence is like the heavy sword of Damocles hung above our heads.'

Alfred nodded his agreement, then tried a different tack. 'What about the raids which continue to harry the settlements throughout my realm? Will Lord Guthrum put a stop to those as well?'

The translator spoke to Guthrum again. 'My Lord cannot be expected to command all the bands of robbers and warriors who now seek to profit on their own account. But he will discourage them and offer land to entice them away from your realm and thereby ensure that Wessex is left in peace.'

'Then we shall require terms that prohibit men who have left our realm from re-entering it without my consent. Is that agreed?'

Guthrum seemed not to like that provision when it was explained to him but chose not to contest it.

With that we all settled down to look at the map. In particular, Alfred and Guthrum tried to settle upon the position of the line which would basically cede control of all the lands to the north and east of it to Guthrum. Once the boundary was agreed, a full written description would be worded with reference to known trackways and rivers and such like, as that was always felt to be more reliable than marks made on a map. There was then much discussion about Alfred's rights as overlord in certain areas which Guthrum contested but as these were not part of Wessex, it seemed not to be a significant issue. It was then left for each man to think further on the implications of that.

Satisfied that they'd made some progress, Guthrum then left. It had been a short but amicable meeting but the doubts about the Vikings' sincerity remained. So much so that I wondered whether there could ever truly be peace between the two peoples, as was King Alfred's dream.

*****

Lord Ethelnorth took the opportunity to return direct to his Vill in Exeter from there, taking just a small escort with him, whilst Alfred and the main party were intent on returning to Winchester. I'd already planned to attend my brother Edwin's grave so, taking a single pack horse with us to carry the supplies we'd need for the journey, Aelred and I made our way towards Chippenham. From there we would go to Edington and to the site of the great battle itself.

The journey was a relatively simple one, but we noticed how the leaves were already beginning to turn. Then, when we arrived at the site of the battle, we were both aware of a distinct chill in the air, though I suspect that had little to do with the weather.

'It's eerily quiet here,' observed Aelred as we stood at the top of the ridge from where Alfred had commanded his loyal supporters. Perhaps he sensed an echo of all the terrible slaughter which had taken place during the battle or perhaps, like me, he couldn't dispel the thought of all the ghosts that tarried in that dreadful place. 'So tell me, how was the battle actually fought?' he asked.

I explained how Alfred had taken up a position on the ridge and how Lord Ethelnorth had goaded the Vikings into attacking before they were fully ready. 'He was magnificent as he rode in front of their lines carrying baskets in which he'd stowed the heads of all the men we'd slain at Combwich. He then upended the baskets so that the heads rolled down the slope towards the Viking ranks. That done, he hurled Ubba's head towards them as well.'

'Hah! Yes, that would rile the bastards!' agreed Aelred, clearly enjoying the thought of the Vikings being thus incensed.

'Even so, it was a bloody contest,' I said, recalling all the dead and wounded I'd seen strewn across the battlefield. 'We were formed into three ranks,' I continued. 'My brother led the first, Lord Ethelnorth the second and I commanded the third but under Alfred's direction. We advanced down the slope in that formation and forced the Vikings back. In the end they fled and holed up within Alfred's Vill at Chippenham where we kept them besieged until they deigned to surrender.'

'Did you actually see your brother fall?' he asked softly.

'No, I knew nothing of it until after the battle. He was sorely wounded by a blow to the head with no hope of life so we had no choice but to set his spirit free.'

Aelred needed no elaboration on what that entailed. 'I've heard that he was truly a great warrior. No doubt that's where you learned your battle skills.'

I nodded as if to acknowledge the point then rode down in silence towards the cross which had been erected at the foot of the slope to mark where much of the fiercest fighting had taken place. As I drew closer, I dismounted as a mark of respect to all who were buried there alongside my brother and approached the cross on foot. Aelred tactfully didn't follow me, realising that it was something I needed to do alone.

Edwin had been buried to one side of the cross with Dudwine, who had fought so bravely to seize the Vikings' raven banner, on the other. I felt uneasy about stepping on ground below which so many brave men had been buried but was obliged to do so in order to reach the cross. Once there, I knelt in silent homage and recalled my brother, regretting that we'd shared so little that wasn't tainted with pain and loss. I was tempted to tell him of all that which had happened to me since then: of my being so cruelly wounded, taken by the slavers, captured by Torstein and then appointed to serve Lord Alfred himself. I knew the latter would have made him proud though was not sure how he would have viewed all the ordeals I'd endured or the fact that I'd possibly sired children with two women – one of them a whore who he'd so strongly disapproved of and the other a Celt.

I must have stayed at the graveside for some time for I was suddenly aware how cold it had become. Wrapping my cloak around me, I managed a few short prayers before rising and, with tears in my eyes, returned to my horse. Aelred was waiting patiently on the ridge for me to return and no sooner had I reached him than we rode off together without another word being said between us.

* * * * *

Having returned to Winchester, I knew Alfred expected me to attend him and therefore went straight to the Great Hall where I was shown through to his private chamber.

He was already there, construing various documents. As I entered he gave me the letters I would need to underpin my authority once I reached Leatherhead. 'I won't have these refuted,' he said firmly. 'If any question them you are to refer them to me direct.'

I decided to read them later, anxious not to take up too much of the King's time given that there were still so many people who were anxious to see him.

'So, what did you make of all that Guthrum had to say?' he asked indicating that I was expected to take a seat. 'Are you now satisfied about Jarl Hakon's intent?'

'Sire, my only concern is why so many travelled so far and yet discussed so little.'

'That is the way of these things,' explained Alfred. 'You'll find that such delicate discussions need time for due consideration and, quite often, consultation with others. Like me, Guthrum must be certain that his senior men are all agreed otherwise the treaty will be worthless.'

'But they were there so had their chance to speak,' I reasoned.

Alfred smiled. 'Some of them were there, but by no means all. And remember, what they say in private between themselves is not always what they wish to say in front of us. Besides, if Guthrum does accept what's offered, he'll need to think carefully about how he'll then divide the land he's to govern between his Jarls. Already they will each be vying for more than their entitled share!'

'Does he not rule most of it already?' I queried.

'In name perhaps. But others have claimed lands and the boundaries between the settlements have evolved by chance or through raids and such like. Indeed, many were taken by force. Therefore he must settle whatever claims and disputes remain. Hence these discussions will take time and cannot be implemented as quickly as we might wish.'

'Then, Sire, do you believe that Guthrum has taken his baptism seriously?' I asked.

'I do,' said Alfred. 'And I believe he will one day take on his new Christian name and allow himself to be known as Aethelstan.'

'Then what of the others who were baptised at Bath alongside him?'

Alfred's hesitation in replying showed that even he had doubts on that score. 'I can't speak for them all,' he acknowledged. 'A dozen Jarls of senior rank were baptised with Guthrum but it wasn't at Bath. As feelings were still running so high at that time, I felt the risk of reprisals there was too great so they took instruction at Aller instead.'

I could well see the sense of that. 'Then Sire, do you believe them all to be secure in their faith, or was it just a ruse to ensure their lives were spared?'

'No, I believe they were in earnest. These Vikings seem to be very much in awe of our Christian ways though they struggle to understand how we manage with just one God.'

'The nailed God,' I muttered, recalling how curious Torstein had been about why we'd nailed the son of our God to a cross.

Alfred smiled. 'Yes, you can almost believe that they'll one day convert of their own free will. If they do then all we've done here may well be vindicated.'

'Then Sire, I pray that will be the case,' I assured him. 'But until then, are you minded to believe what they've said about Hakon's intent?'

'I don't have much choice,' said Alfred. 'As we've already discussed, I have no army to send to London, for all are committed elsewhere and, frankly, I wouldn't send one if I had. I can't afford to tie up so many men just to deter an upstart like Jarl Hakon. Besides, as I've said, Guthrum will feel slighted if it appears as though I don't trust him and that in turn would prejudice the debate for the peace we strive to achieve. Hopefully, Matthew, you will be able to resolve the situation for me once you reach Leatherhead, but you must take care. If at any time you feel threatened you must withdraw and then report to me. Is that clear?'

I nodded my agreement.

'Have you yet formed your plan?'

'No Sire, I'll be better placed to determine that once I get there. As I see it, there's little I can do to stop Hakon if he attacks before the fyrd are ready, particularly if the fortifications are not complete. I'll therefore concentrate on that first but as you've said, he's not likely to attack until his ships are ready and the weather allows. That will give me a chance to get matters underway. I recall you have spies watching the Viking camp in London. It would help if they could come first to warn me if Hakon starts to move, then come to you so that you can send the reinforcements. At least that way I'd have time to form whatever defence I can muster, whatever stage the defences have reached.'

Alfred acknowledged the sense of that. 'And what of the raids and the questions we have about all that's happening within the Shire?'

I thought for a moment. 'I may have to ignore the raids at first. I'm hoping they'll be less frequent as winter approaches but as you've advised, I won't take the raiders on until I can be sure of defeating them.'

'Good. And you'll try to ascertain whether Oeric, Ealdorman Werhard's stepson, does indeed have a hand in them?'

'I will Sire. Though I may need to be wary as I gather Lord Werhard has appointed him as his thane to manage the settlement.'

'That is Lord Werhard's privilege, but even so, as a thane his stepson must have due regard for those beneath him.'

'Then if guilty I'll deal with him as he deserves, my Lord.'

Alfred seemed pleased with all I'd said. 'So how will you fortify the settlement?' he asked.

'Sire, I'll need to survey it before I decide how best to secure it, but I don't think I'll have the resources to render it into one of your fortified burghs. After all, it's not a major settlement and couldn't muster enough men to sustain a permanent guard, even with those who live there serving in rotation.'

'All you can do is your best, Matthew. No one can ask more of you than that. And remember, you have only to ensure that the defences will suffice to delay Hakon if and when he makes his move. You'll not have the means to do more than that.'

Chapter Three

Before leaving for Leatherhead, Aelred and I needed to equip ourselves properly for all that lay ahead. I'd already made Aelred a present of a fine tunic which I felt befitted his new station. 'You'll be travelling as my companion so must look the part,' I told him.

Of more concern was the question of arms, given that neither he nor I had much in the way of war gear. True, I had my sword and I was able to borrow a mail vest which, although not a good fit, was the best I could find. Even so, it was too heavy and cumbersome to be worn whilst travelling, so, with Alfred's permission, I took Aelred to the armoury, there to properly equip us both. Aelred selected a new spear whilst I arranged for us to have shields, helmets and leather jerkins. The latter would be much more practical than mail but, whilst offering protection enough if worn with a fleece undershirt, I doubted they'd suffice if it came to a full battle. There was not time enough to procure anything further so I decided all that would have to serve unless we could obtain anything more suitable once we arrived at the settlement itself.

Alfred generously allowed us each to select a good horse from his personal stable plus a sturdier animal which was to serve as a pack horse for all our belongings. To that end, baskets were strapped to a leather harness draped across its back which were then loaded with all we thought we might need both for the journey to Leatherhead and for the duration of our stay.

I planned for us to follow a route which would take us along the Harroway – an ancient tin-mining track which ran all the way from Canterbury to Winchester and beyond. Because it was so well used, it was as safe a route as could be devised.

Sure enough, once we joined it we made good time and hoped to reach Leatherhead in just two days, although that allowed us no time to venture into any of the settlements we'd pass along the way in order to seek lodgings. Instead, we planned to make our camp overnight using whatever shelter we could find.

We pushed on as hard as we could before coming to a small clearing just off the main trackway. We decided that was as far as we could manage that first day so whilst I unsaddled the horses then took them to drink at a small spring, Aelred quickly built a fire and prepared some hot food for our supper. I worried lest the fire should draw unwelcome attention to our being there but Aelred reckoned we'd be safe enough.

Still wary, I agreed on condition that we take turns to keep watch through the night, pointing out that our three horses alone would be a tempting target for thieves.

As we ate our supper Aelred mused that it seemed strange to be travelling without the company of dear Brother Benedict.

'He was a good man,' I acknowledged. 'His devotion to his calling did him great credit.'

'Aye, though I count him a fool to have thrown his life away for no good cause,' said Aelred. 'Did he really think the Vikings would turn back just because he, unarmed and unworldly, stood in their path?'

'I think he sacrificed himself to salve his conscience,' I said. 'It was almost as though he welcomed the chance to prove his faith by offering his life for others.'

Aelred seemed not to agree. 'Perhaps,' he said. 'But I'll warrant that he didn't expect to die as he did. To be strung up to a tree and then flayed alive is no way to meet your maker. No man in his right mind would perish thus if he had a choice.'

'Is there a good way?' I asked, recalling the many times I'd so narrowly escaped death myself.

'Well,' said Aelred grinning broadly, 'if I was forced to choose I'd ask to be taken whilst abed with some comely wench. That'd be as good a way as any!' I think he was about to say something more, but we were both suddenly aware of an old man wending his way towards us along the Harroway. It was getting dark by then and he seemed to keep stumbling as he tried to find the path then, as he drew close enough, he called out and asked if he might share our fire for a few moments in order to warm his old bones. As he was alone and carried nothing more than a sack slung across his shoulder, he seemed to pose no threat. Besides, with his back bent and rounded he looked to be so frail that my conscience wouldn't allow me to deny him what comfort we could offer. As he gratefully settled down beside us he seemed amiable enough, though was clearly not of noble birth.

'I am called Godwine, my Lord,' he said after we'd introduced ourselves. As befitted his age, his weathered face had a toothless grin and his long grey hair and beard were much tangled and matted. He seemed surprised to be allowed to sit with us given my station but made no comment as, with the nights turning colder, he was grateful for the privilege.

'So Godwine, where are you headed?' asked Aelred as he passed the old man some food which was gratefully accepted.

'I travel west to stay with my son for the winter,' he explained.

'Is that wise?' I asked. 'To travel alone and at night?'

'My Lord, I've nothing worth stealing,' he reasoned.

Aelred didn't look convinced. 'Even so, thieves have been known to strike first then search your baggage afterwards.'

'You're right, friend, but if that's our fate then surely we can do no more than accept it?'

'Aye,' said Aelred. 'That's true enough, albeit those of us who stand closest to the grave should perhaps take more care than others.'

Godwine seemed perturbed by that. 'If you allude to my age, friend, then all I can say is that I've seen more young men die than old, and often for no good cause.'

'What do mean by that?' pressed Aelred.

'Only what I said. That in these perilous times many men die before their time.'

As according to Ingar I could expect to die at any time, what he said troubled me. 'It's not how long you live, but how well you live that matters,' I ventured.

'Ah, that's easy for you to say,' quipped Aelred. 'Living well is the birthright of noble folk but denied to the likes of us. Perhaps that's why men like me and Godwine here don't fear death, for we've a lot less to lose than you have.'

The old man looked at us strangely. 'It's true enough that I've no fear of dying,' he said. 'After all, many have gone before us and as yet I've never heard tell of any who are wont to return. Therefore it follows that they've gone to a better world than this one.'

Aelred glanced at me, perhaps wondering whether I would mention that I was the exception given that I'd supposedly died once already, but it was not something I wanted to discuss with a stranger, particularly the likes of Godwine.

Perhaps sensing there was something I wasn't saying, the old man continued. 'Anyway, death will come to us all soon enough. For my part, I'd as soon meet it here beside this fire, warm and well fed, than live in pain or hunger. But then none of us can know what life has in store for us. Is that not so?'

'If we did I doubt we'd ever leave our homes,' I mused thinking of how my own life had seldom followed the path I expected or intended. 'All we can do is look to God and pray that when our time comes we can meet it bravely. That and for him to then receive our souls.'

'Amen to that,' said Aelred.

Godwine laughed. 'Amen indeed, for which of us can say for certain what will come in the night to harm us or waits beyond the next turn in the road?'

There was something about that last comment which seemed to worry Aelred as much as it did me, perhaps reminding us both of the many times we'd been forced to confront the unexpected. In a way I was beginning to regret having invited Godwine to join us but decided that the Christian thing to do was to let the old man stay the night. He thanked me and offered to stand the first watch. With that, Aelred and I checked the horses and then unfolded our blankets leaving Godwine to remain beside the fire as we settled down for the night a little way off with our saddles and baggage beside us.

For my part, sleep eluded me, so much so that I drew my sword and laid it alongside me beneath the blanket where I could retrieve it quickly if it were needed. I then lay there resting with my eyes closed, though remained awake.

It seemed my concerns were justified. After about an hour or so the old man was joined by two rogues, both of them younger than he but equally as wretched. I could barely see them except by the light of the fire but I could hear them whispering to each other. I looked across at Aelred but found him to be sleeping soundly and could see no way of rousing him without revealing that I was still awake. I therefore prepared myself, watching the newcomers through my half-closed eyes and thinking that rather than simply confront them, it would be better to take them by surprise if they made any move towards me or our horses.

'The boy has a sword which should be worth a goodly sum,' I heard the old man whisper as one of the two went to untether the horses. With that his companion came towards me with his knife drawn. As he leaned over me intending to lay the blade across my throat, I opened my eyes.

'If you so much as move your hand one of us will die,' I warned him. So saying, I raised the sword beneath the blanket and prodded his belly with the tip of the blade.

He stared at me, hardly daring to breathe.

'So, what's it to be?' I demanded. 'Shall I open your belly or will you back away?' With that I pressed a little harder with the sword. 'Or perhaps you've never watched a man die from a wound to the gut?'

He shook his head.

'Well, I have,' I said, recalling the time I'd tended the dying man at the ruined farmstead where Edwin and I first learned of the planned attack on Chippenham. 'It can take a long time to die and I'm told it causes terrible pains. So, if I were you I'd lower your blade and step away from me.'

He didn't hesitate. As he took a few steps back his two friends both looked surprised, but I was on my feet in an instant. 'Leave the horses!' I demanded loud enough to wake Aelred. He at once scrambled to his feet, seizing his spear as he did so.

'Now what are we to do with you?' I asked, circling around them with my sword raised. 'It seems that having sampled our hospitality, this ungrateful wretch would sell us short to the likes of you – two thieves who haven't the wit to do more than steal from men who are sleeping.'

'No, my Lord, that's not the way of it,' said one of the younger men who it seemed was inclined to speak for them all.

'Then explain yourselves. And don't think to try my hand or we'll leave all three of you to bleed out where you fall.' I then looked at the old man. 'And you my friend who has no fear of dying shall be the first to feel the edge of my sword.'

'My Lord, we're hungry and have not eaten for several days,' said the rogue.

'So to fill your bellies you'd rob and murder innocent travellers? Is that to be the way of it?'

For a moment he was silent. 'We're not strangers, my Lord, and it was not our intent to harm anyone,' he pleaded. 'Particularly you, for we know full well who you are.'

I looked at him, trying to recognise him.

'We stood with you at Edington, my Lord, if you recall. Stood firm against the heathen horde as they swarmed towards us up the slope.'

I then looked at them each in turn but still couldn't place them. 'Not in my rank you didn't,' I said firmly.

'No, not in your rank, my Lord, it's true. We had the honour to stand with your brother. But we were there right enough. Now because of wounds we suffered that day we can no longer ply our trade so have taken to seeking food and shelter wherever we can find it.'

I confess that I was surprised and therefore determined to question them further. 'So how came you to this end? Every man who served in that battle left with a goodly share of the spoil.'

'You can't eat silver,' he explained. 'Besides, my Lord, that was many months ago and what we earned that day was quickly spent, for the price of silver was not as it was when so many had so much of it to sell.'

'Besides, my Lord,' said old Godwine. 'My sons both suffered grievously in that battle. My youngest there is now mute and has not uttered a word since that day except to call out in the night when the fearful dreams which remind him of it all come to haunt him. My eldest son lost his hand in the fray so can no longer ply his trade.'

With that his son held up the stump as if to prove the point. I knew that many men had paid a fearful price for Alfred's victory and been reduced to begging and thieving as a result and was therefore minded to be merciful. 'What was your trade?' I asked.

'My Lord, I was a carpenter so, deprived as I am, I can no longer earn enough to keep us all except by…'

'Except by robbing innocent travellers.' At that I lowered my sword. 'Then tell me, if you stood with my brother that day, did you see him fall?'

He looked at his father before speaking. 'I did, my Lord. I was fighting only a little way off but could do nothing to help him.'

'Then how did he fall?' I asked having heard so little about what actually happened.

The man smiled. 'You know what your brother was like,' he said. 'Never content unless in the thickest part of the fray. He was hacking with his sword, spinning round this way and that, felling as many men with the edge of his shield as he did with his blade. When he was struck by an axe from behind I thought his helmet might spare him, but he fell and didn't rise again. I knew he was harmed but couldn't reach him. I swear he was a man blessed with so much courage that he was bound to fall sooner or later.'

I stood for a moment recalling the day and knew that what he'd said was true, for it matched the reports I'd been given at the time. 'If you truly did serve Lord Alfred you deserve better than to die here like thieves. Nor should you live with an empty belly. Take enough food from our provisions to last a few days then be gone from here. I'll not kill men who were brave enough to serve their King when needed. But be warned, my compassion won't stand to be tested twice so find a better way to feed yourselves and don't let me catch you thieving again.'

With that they went to fetch some of the food, though were careful not to take too much.

'My Lord, is your good Lady well?' asked the eldest son.

'My Lady?' I queried.

'Aye, the fair Emelda. I recall she joined you soon after the battle. I gather she'd been with you at Athelney.'

I hesitated, wondering how much he knew of what Emelda had been whilst sheltering with Alfred in the marshes. 'Is that any concern of yours?' I asked unkindly, for I could tell from the look on his face that his comment was intended to make it clear that he knew she'd been a whore, information no doubt gained from speaking with others even if he'd not been there in person. Given my intentions towards Emelda and that she now carried my unborn child, I had no wish for him to share that information as it would tarnish her reputation and thereby mine. I therefore raised my sword again and casually studied the blade. 'The fair Emelda is indeed well, though if I thought that any man was inclined to speak falsely about all that happened at Athelney, I would be minded to secure his silence. Particularly one who wasn't there.'

The man looked at me. 'My Lord, I meant only...'

'I think I know well enough what you meant,' I warned. 'And all I would advise is that if you desire to keep your tongue in your head, first learn how to keep it still.'

*****

The next morning we pressed on towards Leatherhead, leaving at first light and hoping to complete the journey before dark. Aelred seemed much affected by the incident with the robbers and was surprised that I'd been so lenient.

'So, what was all that about Emelda?' he asked.

'Nothing!' I snapped. 'Just private business.' I realised then that I'd told Aelred very little about all that which had transpired whilst we sheltered at Athelney, but I saw no cause to enlighten him further, at least, not then.

He seemed to accept that. 'Well, those rogues should count themselves lucky. Not many men would have let them off so lightly.'

'Yes, but I'm not sure that his intent was to kill me. He just wanted my sword and some food.'

Aelred shook his head. 'He held a knife to your throat!' he reasoned. 'Anyone else would have given him the sword – straight between his ribs.'

'Perhaps. But they were once good men who've since fallen on hard times through no fault of their own,' I explained.

'Aye, that's true enough,' he said. 'They should not have been forced to live as they do. Living rough can be hard in these difficult times and not everyone gets the justice they deserve.'

The comment made me think about the task ahead of us and how I was expected to mete out justice to Lord Werhard's wayward stepson – and in particular whether what Alfred had in mind in that respect was indeed 'fair and just'. But as Aelred had said, not everyone gets what they deserve whilst others always seem to evade punishment altogether.

We said no more on the matter but as we approached Leatherhead Aelred was no doubt wondering what he'd got himself into, perhaps with good cause given that I'd yet to form my plan.

'I suppose we'll first visit this Ealdorman you're so concerned about,' he ventured.

'Lord Werhard's not the problem,' I reminded him. 'It's his stepson, Oeric, we're worried about. It seems he's been appointed as a thane but actually governs in his father's stead and abuses that privilege. I'm hoping he may reveal his true demeanour if I offend him in order to incur his wrath. Thus we'll leave it until tomorrow before I call on him and thereby not show him the courtesy I might normally allow a man of his rank.'

Aelred shook his head. 'What, even though we're bearing arms? I think you might at least try to get them both on side. After all, we'll have enemies enough once you tell all the good people of Leatherhead what's expected of them.'

'What do you mean?' I asked, not sure what he was implying.

'As soon as you mention more training and building fortifications you'll have everyone set against you, particularly at this time of the year when they'll want to spend their time building up their stores for the winter.'

'But surely they'll realise that it's all for their own good? Poorly trained and without fortifications they'll be wide open to even more raids than they're suffering now, not to mention the threat posed by Hakon's horde.'

'Mark my words, Matthew, they won't thank you for taking them away from what they need to do to survive the coming winter. You'll make enemies of them all if you're not careful – and with near two hundred Viking warriors armed and ready to attack at any time, you don't need any more of those.'

By early evening we were close to Leatherhead. Aelred seemed curious to know more about the settlement, having never been there before.

'It's set at the head of a gap in these hills through which runs the river Emele,' I told him. 'It's a wide but slow river that flows from the south towards London. There's no bridge at Leatherhead but there is a ford which is shallow enough to cross even on foot.'

'So, do the people live beside the river?' he asked.

'No, there's a watermill close to the ford but most people have made their homes on higher ground away from the river.

Lord Werhard's Vill is also sited there, though it's poorly defended and not well guarded.'

Aelred shook his head. 'With the Vikings at London barely a full day's ride from there you'd have thought he'd be more worried about being attacked.'

'Exactly. And as I've said, we have reports of many raids at farmsteads and such like, but even they seem to go unchallenged. Any man worth his salt would do what he could to deter any raiders if only to protect himself.'

'So how many households live in the settlement itself?'

'Probably about thirty in all. There might be a few others nearby but I didn't have time to look more closely whilst I was there as I needed to get back to Alfred to warn him about Jarl Hakon and his longships.'

It was getting dark by the time we reached Leatherhead and crossed the river at the ford. The crossing itself was made easier by a series of large flat stones which had been placed in the river so that travellers on foot could simply walk across by using the slabs as stepping stones even when the river was in spate. We stopped long enough to look at the watermill, the wheel of which was set in a channel formed between the riverbank and the edge of a large island, of which there were several in that part of the river. A forge had been set up beside the mill and there were also several stores, but the main settlement itself was on the higher ground to the north-east side of the valley. To reach it, we continued up a steep road until we came to an untidy group of buildings clustered around a crossroads. They were mainly simple dwellings formed from timber and thatch, some with adjoining workshops or stores and most having a small fenced yard to the side or rear. As I'd told Aelred earlier, the settlement comprised perhaps thirty households, all looking to sell their wares and services to travellers who were seeking to access the Harroway from there or to use the ford.

As we rode through, I could feel the eyes of the people who lived there fixed upon us but I doubted whether any recognised or even remembered me given that unlike before, I was now dressed as befitted my station. That said, they were all respectful enough, averting their eyes and in many cases bowing their heads as we passed. From there, we ignored Lord Werhard's Vill which we could see just beyond the settlement and instead continued northwards in search of a small Monastery where I planned to stay until such time as I could establish more fitting lodgings.

*****

To reach the Monastery we continued roughly northwards before turning westwards through what were mainly open fields and woodlands. On the way we stopped at a small farmstead on the pretext of seeking directions. The old man who lived there was a bluff, red-faced fellow who kept several swine in a pen set close to his house and a few goats and geese in a field beside it.

'We're travelling to the Monastery,' I explained after I'd introduced myself. 'There to seek lodgings for the night.'

He bowed respectfully and told me that his name was Wilfrid and that his wife was called Aleesa. He then pointed to the track which continued towards a hill ridge which was heavily wooded. 'Continue as you've come, my Lord. The Monastery is atop that hill yonder, though offers little more than a good view of all the land around these parts.'

'Is it far?' I asked.

He thought for a moment. 'On foot it would take the better part of several hours but much less on horseback if your mounts are not too tired. As it's now late, can I offer you refreshment, my Lord? It isn't much but you're welcome to what little we have.'

I thanked him and, even though we had ample supplies of our own, accepted his offer of hospitality knowing that he'd expect payment. My hope was that we might learn much from this simple fellow, so allowed him to show us through into what was little more than a hovel, but which he assured us was more comfortable than it looked. 'My good woman there will see you right, my Lord,' he said as he went to water our horses.

The man's wife poured us mead from a pitcher and I had to admit that it was good, though very strong to my taste. Aelred drank his in a single gulp then wiped his mouth with the back of his hand and held out his beaker for more.

'So you've business in Leatherhead, my Lord?' said the man as he returned from tending our horses.

'Aye. I'm to train the fyrd there,' I said thinking we might prompt him to tell us more about the way of things in those parts.

'Then God bless you, my Lord,' he said. 'For goodness knows we need whatever help we can find in that respect.'

'What do you mean?' I asked.

He seemed reluctant to say more at first and instead glanced at his wife as if afraid to speak. 'It's just that they're never around when you need them,' he managed.

'Who are never around when you need them?' I pressed.

'Why the fyrd, my Lord. More noted for their absence than for anything else.'

'Tell me, does Lord Werhard's stepson not command them?'

Once again the poor man seemed unwilling to speak.

'Well does he or not?' I insisted.

'In truth he does, my Lord. Though I warrant he's much else to do within the Shire as well.'

'Then why are the fyrd not here when you need them?'

'It's not for me to speak of my betters, my Lord.'

'Nor is it fitting for you not to answer when spoken to,' I chided. 'Now speak up, whatever you say here will go no further, on that you have my word.'

He thought for a moment. 'Let me just say that the members of the fyrd are not overly troubled by too much training. Nor are they summoned if some parts of the Shire come under threat.'

'What do you mean by that?' I insisted.

'Just that, my Lord. Nothing more.'

Aelred touched my arm. 'Let him be, the poor soul is clearly terrified and fears he's already said too much.'

I could see he was right but there was more I needed to know. 'And you hold this farmstead from Lord Werhard's stepson?' I asked.

'I do, my Lord. I work three days each week for him in lieu of my dues and three days more to repay what I owe to him. What I can earn on the seventh day from this modest farmstead is all we have to keep us.'

'You owe him so much?'

'I do, my Lord, and more. He owns all except my soul and there are days I'd willingly trade that for enough to feed myself and my poor wife in our dotage.'

I was horrified, for it went against our creed for a free man to be thus encumbered. I said nothing more but instead gave the man a coin in payment for his hospitality and let the matter rest.

'So there you have it,' said Aelred as we continued on our way. 'No wonder you were told that all is not well in this place. Those poor folks back there have been reduced to being little more than slaves. If that's to be the way of things here we'll need to take care, for I sense you'll not be welcome at the Vill if you mean to set such matters to right.'

'Aye,' I agreed. 'And doubtless word of our coming will reach Lord Werhard and his stepson even before we do.'

*****

'You don't mean we're staying here!' complained Aelred as we rode up the steep track which led to the Monastery. It was a narrow path, just wide enough for a small cart to bring in supplies, though deeply rutted and poorly maintained. Despite this, it was easy enough for the horses to follow even in the dark provided they picked their way with care.

When we reached the top we found a large single-storey thatched building with several stores, shelters and a dovecote, all centred on a small square chapel built from brick and flint. Although considerably reduced in height, the chapel looked to have been formed from what remained of a Roman watchtower, no doubt placed there on the hill from where most of the surrounding land could be seen, including the gap through the hills at Leatherhead.

It was usual for an Abbey or even a small Monastery to offer hospitality to noble men and women who were travelling and the monks at that particular enclave were no exception. They were followers of St Columba, a much-revered saint and, as such, they adhered to a very strict calling, praying often and owning nothing beyond that which was essential for their day-to-day existence. To that end, the members of their order worked tirelessly, worshipping devoutly between their labours.

As we approached, one of the good brothers came forth to take our horses and, once we'd dismounted and removed the bags attached to the saddles, led them off to a small fenced compound with an open-fronted hut which was clearly all that could be offered in the form of stabling.

The abbot came out to greet us in person and introduced himself as Father Gregory. We found him to be a kindly soul, thin and frail and having a tonsure but with silver hair that hung down at the back and sides like a fringe. He seemed genuinely pleased to welcome us and, having introduced myself and Aelred, we were ushered into the main building and there offered refreshment.

Inside, the building was dark and smoky, with a large table to one side and an open fire in the centre. Most of the far end had been partitioned with wicker panels to form a dormitory for the monks and a separate cell for Father Gregory, thereby affording him a degree of privacy and a place in which to work.

'Father, I'm here at the behest of Lord Alfred,' I explained. 'My companion and I require lodgings for several nights at least if that will not trouble you unduly.'

'We shall be honoured, my Lord. It's a condition of our calling that we offer hospitality to strangers so you'll be most welcome. However, I fear we can offer no chamber such as might befit your station. This is a very small order and we have only what you see.'

'No matter,' I assured him. 'My companion and I are well used to living on the road so a roof above our heads will be comfort enough. Can you provide us with supper as well, or do we need to look elsewhere for that?'

'We partake of only very simple fare, my Lord, but all are welcome at our table. If you'll come with me I'll show you to my own cell which you are most welcome to use whilst you're here.'

'I'd not have you moved from your bed on my account,' I protested. 'Aelred and I will take whatever else you can offer and be glad of it.'

'But my Lord…'

I insisted that he show me what other lodgings he had to offer. It turned out to be one of the shelters we'd seen outside, roughly thatched and sparsely furnished with just two cots and a table. The floor was strewn with damp straw and there was a basin set in one corner at which we could wash plus a bucket we could use to relieve ourselves.

'We're not used to such important guests,' explained Father Gregory, looking embarrassed.

'It will suffice,' I assured him. 'For we shall be about our business for most of the day. And you must not let our presence deter you and the good brothers from your devotions. I'm well used to life in an Abbey and therefore know how important it is for the routine to be observed.'

The abbot seemed pleased at that. 'Then, my Lord, you'll know that prayer is at the heart of all we do. You're most welcome to join us in our devotions if you are so minded. We have in the chapel a relic which is said to be a finger taken from the body of St Columba himself and which we believe brings his blessings on all who reside here and…'

'Thank you, Father. Our own work may well mean we'll be pleased for any support we can get from the Holy Saint. But for now we must rest, for our journey has been both long and tiring.'

With that he promised to have clean straw provided for the floor and blankets for the cots, together with fresh water and a brazier, then turned to leave.

'Father,' I said. 'What's the way of things here?'

He hesitated. 'What do you mean, my Lord?'

'Only that I sense all is not well within this Shire. Those I've met seem little more than slaves and I'm told that the fyrd are barely troubled to stop the raids.'

He was slow to answer, as if considering his words with care. 'The people here support a Lord who has costly tastes and habits,' he said simply. 'That makes the burden they carry ever harder.'

'But he can only demand what's due,' I said.

Again he hesitated. 'What's due depends on what's owed and to whom. Those are matters which trouble me as much as anyone, but I can do little more than to offer prayers for their burden to be eased. It's not for me to meddle in whatever contracts they've forged with their betters.'

Chapter Four

'I'm beginning to wish you'd accepted Father Gregory's offer to let us use his cell,' said Aelred as we made our way back towards the settlement at Leatherhead the next morning. He was scratching himself as he spoke having, like me, been bitten many times by fleas during the night. 'I reckon we'd have fared better if we'd slept with the horses!'

'I don't doubt it,' I acknowledged. 'But we mustn't give offence by complaining. These monks are very devout men who eschew worldly comforts and just endure whatever hardship God sends. They see such trials as a test of their fortitude and devotion. Anyway, I doubt his cell would have been much better.'

Aelred seemed to accept that. 'I assume that we're now going to see Ealdorman Werhard where we can expect an even more uncomfortable welcome?'

'Don't worry, he'll be pleased enough to see us. As I've said, I've met him before and take him to be a good man. It's his treacherous stepson we need to be wary of.'

Aelred said nothing for a moment. 'So, what exactly is it that you think he's done?'

I hesitated, not sure how best to answer. 'From what we saw yesterday I suspect he's treating his stepfather's people unfairly, but it may go deeper than that.'

'In what way?'

'We think he's somehow profiting from all the raids, but it's not yet clear exactly how – or indeed whether both crimes are related.'

'So what will you do?'

'That depends on what we find. Hopefully we'll need only to show him the error of his ways.'

'And if not, I take it you'll drag him back to Winchester to answer for his crimes?'

Until then I'd avoided saying more about what Alfred and I had discussed as that aspect of his plan still worried me. 'I'll do what's needed,' I managed. 'Suffice to say that Alfred has much to do within the realm and shouldn't be troubled by minor matters such as a tyrant who needs taking down a peg or two.'

As ever, Aelred was quick to grasp the meaning of what I was saying. 'By that do you mean there won't be any need for a trial?' he pressed.

I looked at him, at first not sure how best to answer. 'If we find proof of his abuse or of his involvement in the raids, then a trial may not be in anyone's best interests,' I explained. 'Given his rank, he'd have the right to be tried by his equals, some of whom may be as guilty as he is and might thereby help him to avoid justice.'

'So Alfred would have you deal with the bastard without a trial. Is that the way of it?'

Put like that, I felt even more uneasy about what was expected of me so didn't answer.

'And those are the orders of our King? That we train the fyrd, deter the raiders then fortify the settlement against an attack from a horde of Viking warriors. And whilst we're about it, we're to find out whether or not the Ealdorman's greedy stepson is abusing his position and, if he is, you've to deal with him as you see fit?'

'In essence, yes. Those are Lord Alfred's orders,' I admitted.

'Phew! That's a lot to ask of any man, particularly if what you find warrants his execution. For if so, there's a flaw in your plan.'

'What's that?' I asked.

'Matthew, I'd match you against any man if it comes to a fight, but you're not a cold-blooded killer, not like Torstein or those slavers we fell foul of. Oh, you'll kill in self-defence or in combat readily enough. You'll even kill for a cause you believe in, but you're not an executioner and, if it comes to it, I can't see you putting a man to death without a trial.'

I acknowledged his point. 'I will if I have to, but it'll greatly trouble my conscience so will first do all I can to ensure that justice is served. Even if that can't be achieved, I'll still do what's needed, for I'm committed to this duty whether I like it or not. And, in a way, so are you. If that troubles you then take comfort from the fact that from all I've learned whilst serving Lord Alfred, he has good cause for everything he decrees. What's more, he's usually right.'

*****

It had occurred to me when we first arrived at Leatherhead that the watermill beside the ford might be the ideal place to make a stand against Hakon if and when he did attack. Not only could it control access to the crossing, but having the river to its rear meant that it could be attacked only from the front, so if a stout stockade was erected there it would be easy enough to defend, at least for a time. Most important of all, the island which lay directly behind it would also make a good area to retreat to and regroup if we were overrun.

'Why not just use the Vill?' asked Aelred when I suggested this. 'Presumably that's fortified already?'

'Not really. And as you'll see, it's sited up beyond the main settlement so Hakon could simply march right past it. We need to control the pass and in particular the ford if we're to stop him.'

'Stop him or delay him?' queried Aelred.

'Delay him,' I admitted. 'We won't have the resources to do more than that.'

'So we're expected to hold off this horde for a week with nothing more than an old converted watermill and a fence. Is that about the strength of it?'

'More likely it'll be for just a few days, but yes, it might be a week at worst. It all depends on how long it takes Alfred to raise enough men to relieve us.'

'This is all beginning to sound more like a siege to me – and I don't like sieges,' he said. 'Have you ever been holed up in a place where the Vikings throw everything they can at you or try to starve you out?'

I shook my head, though it occurred to me that the situation at Athelney was not unlike a siege, except that we were pretty much free to come and go as we pleased using the causeway and other secret paths through the marshes. 'We'll stockpile provisions and weapons within the fortifications,' I suggested, taking his point. 'And whilst we control the ford others can use the island to bring in anything else we need from across the river.'

He seemed happier with that so we resolved to inspect the mill more closely but went first to see Lord Werhard.

His Vill was centred on a magnificent thatched Hall with elaborately painted fascias and two carved pillars which framed the entrance. There were also numerous outbuildings, which included several separate lodges where guests could stay, some fine stables and many stores and sheds, all arranged around a sort of courtyard and enclosed with a timber fence, albeit that seemed woefully inadequate for such an important Vill.

Aelred and I were not challenged as we rode through the gates. It was only as we dismounted that the very same man who had been so unwelcoming when last I visited there came rushing over, still chewing on the remnants of a leg of poultry.

'What's your business here?' he ordered gruffly, tossing the half-eaten leg aside. He clearly didn't recognise me, perhaps because, unlike before, I was dressed as befitted my station.

'Don't you remember me, you insolent oaf!' I challenged.

Still he seemed not to know me.

'I'm Matthew,' I said. 'And I've come to see Lord Werhard.' I omitted to mention my heritage and didn't trouble to explain that I had orders from his King as I wanted to see how he behaved.

'Lord Werhard is resting and my orders are that he's not to be disturbed.'

Both Aelred and I went over to look this knave in the eye. I'll warrant he was more afraid of Aelred than he was of me, for being stout and so heavily built, Aelred was never a man to be taken lightly.

'We'll decide whether Lord Werhard is to be disturbed or not,' said Aelred. 'Not scum like you. And unless you've a liking for the feel of my foot up your arse, you'll send word to tell him we're here.'

The guard looked shocked, particularly when Aelred moved in closer so that they stood toe to toe, then stared hard into his eyes. The guard looked away and tried to step back, but Aelred simply shadowed him.

'You must state your business,' he said, looking and sounding much less sure of himself. He then made as though to give Aelred's shoulder a somewhat half-hearted push intending to ward him off, but Aelred had the measure of him at once. He caught him by the arm, twisted it, then turned it up behind his back, forcing the guard to bend almost double. Leaning forward so that he could speak directly into his ear, Aelred reminded the guard of his station. 'If Lord Werhard is resting, then I suggest that you go to fetch his stepson. If he's reluctant to greet us, then haul him off whatever whore he's tupping and drag him back here by force if necessary. If he protests just tell him that Matthew, son of Lord Edwulf, is here and that he carries orders from Lord Alfred himself. Do I make myself plain?' With that he shoved the guard off so hard that the man stumbled and nearly fell before scurrying off to do as Aelred had instructed.

It was sometime before Oeric appeared, his bloated body lumbering towards us with the guard running beside him and three others following behind, two of whom I recognised as having been among those who'd accompanied me back to Winchester after my last visit. 'My Lord, I was not given word of your arrival,' he said, then stopped in his tracks when he realised who it was.

'And there was me thinking that in these troubled times most good men hold themselves ready for the unexpected.'

He ignored the jibe and made some excuse about 'entertaining' or some such nonsense. It was clear that Aelred's comments about him being with a whore might not have been so far from the mark, for he was hastily refastening his belt around his bulging belly and looked to be dishevelled. 'So my Lord, may I offer you refreshment whilst you tell me what brings you back to my Vill?'

'Your Vill?' I queried. 'I'm advised by Lord Alfred that so far as he's aware Lord Werhard is still Ealdorman here. Unless perhaps word of your having been appointed in his place has somehow been overlooked given all that's going on within the realm.'

Oeric looked uneasy. 'My father has appointed me as his thane and charged me to manage matters in his stead,' he said, then clearly expected us to follow him as he led the way towards the main Hall, leaving the guards to attend to our horses. As we entered the outer lobby I refused to hand over my sword as was expected. 'There can be no need for you to hold it as I'm known and trusted here, am I not?' I said firmly, fearing that we were far from safe, though I instructed Aelred to let them hold his spear. We were then shown through to the main Hall itself, a large open chamber with a fine stone chair at the far end which was mounted on a dais. To one side there was an open fire which burned brightly and, to the other, a large table around which were set several benches. We were taken to the table and offered seats. There, over a veritable feast of smoked fish, fruits and such like, I explained that I'd been sent by Lord Alfred himself to train the fyrd and told him that others would be doing the same at all the major settlements as part of a plan to improve the defences of the realm. I didn't mention that we had special cause to do so in the case of Leatherhead.

'Surely you can see that the defences here are in good stead,' he insisted.

I leaned back in my chair and smiled. 'So good that we were challenged by just one man and he so easily overcome that I had not even to draw my sword to do it. He then left his post with your gates wide open and all your household at risk.'

Oeric said nothing.

'Where are the rest of your men?' I asked.

He looked flustered at first. 'I need only keep a small contingent here, for we're well protected as you can see. Our fortifications are well founded and the gates could be quickly closed against any attack.'

It was an almost laughable explanation as he had many servants yet only eight permanent guards. Only a man who was sure he would not be attacked would dare to structure his household thus, and there were few in the realm who could be certain of that. 'So what about the fyrd,' I asked. 'When were they last summoned for training?'

'There's little need at present. They're busy gathering supplies at this time of year, for we must all eat come winter, is that not so?'

With that Lord Werhard arrived in person and, as Aelred and I rose to our feet as a mark of respect, he welcomed us both to his Hall. Oeric didn't trouble to rise even as the Ealdorman joined us and he made no attempt to greet his stepfather, something which I thought both arrogant and discourteous.

As Lord Werhard settled himself I noted that he seemed even older than I remembered, his long white hair and beard looking unkempt and untended.

‘So Matthew, what brings you back so soon?’ he asked. He was no doubt surprised that Aelred, who he took to be my servant, should be seated at the table as well, but said nothing.

I took the letters I’d been given by Alfred to confirm my orders and passed them across to him. ‘I’m charged by Lord Alfred to take over running the fyrd here and to fortify this settlement,’ I said formally as he examined the letters. ‘Lord Alfred is concerned at the number of Vikings gathered in London under Jarl Hakon and fears an attack may be imminent. The Vikings are building or repairing many ships which they may sail around the coast then use them to supply and reinforce Hakon’s army. If so, he’ll march south to meet them. That means they’ll likely pass through here and, if they do, must be stopped at all costs.’

Lord Werhard examined the letters briefly then placed them on the table beside him, clearly intending to study them more closely later or perhaps accepting them as read. ‘We had word that someone would be coming but were not told it would be you,’ he said. ‘What is it you would have us do?’

‘First my friend Aelred and I will get to know the settlement here.’ Both Oeric and Lord Werhard looked surprised that Aelred was referred to as ‘my friend’ but neither said as much. ‘I would have you summon all the thanes who reside within the Shire to attend me here the day after tomorrow so that I may review the position.’

‘All of them?’ queried Oeric sounding surprised.

‘Yes, all of them. How many are they in number?’

‘Twelve who reside within a day’s march from here,’ said Lord Werhard. ‘Others would take much longer to reach us…’

'No, that will suffice. If they would take longer than a day to reach us they're too far away to assist, even if needed.'

'Then I will have my Reeve prepare a list of their names and then send word to summon them,' said Lord Werhard.

'Good. Now, where do you have the people assemble?'

'At the Common Field which lies just beyond this Vill,' said the Ealdorman. 'Although not ideal, it is the usual meeting place in these parts.'

'Why do you ask about the Common Field?' queried Oeric. 'The thanes should meet here, at the Vill, as befits their station. Or do you mean to have me call a Moot as well when there is yet so much work which needs to be done before winter?'

'No, not you. As a thane you'll simply be required to attend. When I'm ready I'll ask Lord Werhard to summon all the men and women of this settlement to assemble, as is his right.'

Lord Werhard seemed to accept that but I could see that Oeric was about to object, which is why I'd saved the best until last. 'All the cost of our endeavours to protect this settlement and improve the fortifications will be drawn from your own purse. I trust you'll pay up willingly enough. Remember my friends, these are uncertain times and, as I've explained, you may one day have good cause to thank us for the work we do to strengthen your defences.'

Oeric hauled his huge bloated body from the chair and stared at me, his face reddened with rage. 'I command here!' he stormed, almost spitting the words. 'Who are you to tell us how to spend our coin?' he challenged.

I rose to my feet in order to respond. 'I'm the one appointed by the King of this realm to attend to matters here, that's who. And you may huff and puff all you like,' I added. 'But from what I've seen thus far you'd best be careful not to offend me, for this is the first Vill I've ever seen which I could take single handed. That my friend, is not something you would wish me to report to Lord Alfred, for he abhors any such neglect of duty.'

*****

Having taken offence, Oeric muttered his excuses and left, but Aelred and I stayed to speak further with Lord Werhard.

'Matthew, I'm pleased to see you again and grateful that you saw fit to heed my warning when last you were here.'

'My Lord, as you might expect, Alfred was much concerned by all you told me,' I said, avoiding mention of any suspected treachery. 'But as I said, the real reason for my being here is to prepare for the possibility of an attack from Jarl Hakon.'

'This is to the good,' he said simply. 'And not before time. I will of course render what support I can.'

'Thank you, my Lord. I fear your stepson did not see things quite as clearly as you have.'

Lord Werhard made no attempt to defend Oeric. 'My stepson is a wilful but able man,' is all he said. 'I apologise if he's given offence.'

'It's of no matter,' I told him. 'But tell me, the raids which you mentioned when I was last here, do they continue?'

'They do, though may become less frequent now that the winter will soon be upon us. No doubt they'll prefer to warm their arses by their hearth rather than venture too far afield once the weather turns.'

'And where was the last one?'

Lord Werhard led us to a small table on which there was a crude vellum map depicting an outline of the Shire and noting the position of all the settlements and farmsteads within it. 'The last one was here,' he said pointing to a position to the north of Leatherhead. 'It was the home of a forester named Godric who is an honest cove. His home was burned and all but destroyed just a few days ago.'

'But he was not harmed?'

'Nor any of his family, thanks be to God, though they'll suffer through the winter now that all they have has been taken or destroyed.'

'But you'll no doubt offer him support?'

'My stepson assures me that he's already done so, but that Godric refused our help saying that he'll rebuild his homestead for himself and see out the cold months as best he may. How he'll do that and still meet his dues I've no idea.'

Aelred spoke at that point, voicing something I was also curious about. 'What about other recent raids? Where have they taken place, my Lord?'

Lord Werhard showed us various locations and explained what had transpired at each. All seemed to have been a surprise attack resulting in the destruction of property and the theft of livestock and provisions, but few casualties.

'My Lord, is it not strange that in all the raids in the area around Leatherhead none were killed or taken?' asked Aelred. 'After all, elsewhere within the realm raids are almost always accompanied by rape and butchery. And as Matthew and I can both testify, they're usually not coy about dragging off a few people to be sold as slaves as well.'

Lord Werhard shrugged. 'Such seems to be the way of it. The raiders who come here steal or destroy all they can, but seem to have no appetite for slaughter.'

'And is that always the case?'

'Not always, but mostly so.'

'What is the cause for that, do you think?' I asked.

He hesitated before answering. 'I don't know,' he admitted. 'Perhaps they come here from London to thieve supplies, but fear reprisals if they harm anyone. They have an uneasy alliance with those at the Saxon settlement across the river and would not wish to disrupt that, for it benefits all.'

That did make sense. And if so, it also meant that it was the men who served Jarl Hakon who were the most likely culprits. 'So in what numbers do they come?'

He shrugged. 'Perhaps ten or so at a time. Sometimes more.' Lord Werhard then changed the subject. 'Matthew, shall I have my household prepare chambers for you and your friend?'

'Thank you, my Lord, but we've arranged to stay at the Monastery where we shall be comfortable enough.'

'Ha! You'd be more comfortable sleeping in one of my stables!'

'Father Gregory has made us most welcome and even offered his own bed, though of course we declined.'

'I don't blame you!' said Lord Werhard laughing. 'I have it on good authority that the abbot sleeps on a bed of thorns in order that he doesn't dream of the things most men do!'

I ignored the quip.

'And at least there's no risk there of us being murdered in our beds,' whispered Aelred under his breath.

At first I wasn't sure what Aelred implied by that, but then realised he was worried about the prospect of someone quietly being rid of us once we set about making things right within the Shire. I recalled that both Lord Ethelnorth and Lord Alfred had voiced similar fears.

Before taking our leave, Lord Werhard summoned the Reeve he'd mentioned, a man named Leonfrith. He was a little man with long silver hair but bald on top. Having joined us he respectfully remained standing as we took our seats at the table once more.

'These men are here as my guests and at the direction of Lord Alfred himself. You will assist them in any way you can,' instructed Lord Werhard.

Leonfrith bowed his head to acknowledge the orders.

'They require a list of all the thanes within the Shire who reside within a day's march from here. Once compiled, you will send word to them all to assemble here the day after tomorrow. If any need to stay overnight they may lodge here as my guests.'

'Very good, my Lord, but that leaves little time for them to be summoned.'

'We don't have much time!' I said firmly. 'All our lives may depend on how quickly we can muster our defences. How many men can each of the thanes call to arms at any one time?' I asked.

I was impressed when Leonfrith was able to answer without first consulting his records. 'Between eight and ten men each if they are to leave enough to continue working in the fields, more once the last of the harvest has finally been gathered in and the supplies and provisions have been set in place for the winter. Thus, including those from this settlement, we can normally rely on a muster of at least a hundred men who are eligible and able to fight at any one time,' he said.

That was indeed welcome news.

'My Lords, I should remind you that the fyrd is mostly comprised of ordinary men such as farmers or those with skills or trades; they are not well trained in matters of combat. Nor are they fully armed.'

It was a good point and I knew I would have to improve on those matters. 'Thank you Leonfrith. I fear there is yet much I need to achieve, but must first take stock of how things are. How many men can be mustered to serve with the fyrd from the settlement here in Leatherhead alone?'

'Just ten, my Lord. But they also lack training or weapons.'

'That's as I expected. Now, with Lord Werhard's consent, I shall need you to arrange a Moot for all the people here in Leatherhead so that I can tell them what's needed. The thanes can also attend that as well, but I shall address them afterwards. Seeing their betters summoned will help to ensure that the good people here take what I have to say in earnest, though I doubt they'll like it. Can you arrange that?'

'I can, my Lord.'

'Good, then we must get to work without further delay.'

'My Lord, would you have the thanes meet here, at the Vill?'

'Yes, they should assemble here first then come with us to the Common Field to attend the Moot. There I shall make my plans known to all as there must be no doubting my authority here.'

With that we prepared to take our leave, promising to return before the Moot and the meeting with the thanes so we could first inform Lord Werhard of all that which we had in mind before announcing it to the others, as was his due. Leonfrith walked with us to where our horses were tethered.

'So you're Lord Werhard's Reeve?' I asked.

'I am, my Lord, and I serve him as best I may as indeed I shall serve you.'

'Then you shall be rewarded for your service,' I promised.

'My Lord, I require nothing more than that which I receive from Lord Werhard already,' he said, much to my surprise. 'What you have in mind is much needed for the benefit of all who reside within this Shire and I shall do my best to assist you where I can.'

I thanked him, but was curious to know his own feelings on the matter. 'Will you serve me with your heart or because your Lord commands it?' I asked.

'Both,' he said simply. 'All know that things are not as they should be here and I pray that you can set them right. That said, it will not be an easy task, my Lord, but I suspect you know as much already.'

*****

We left the Vill having enjoyed what had been our first full meal in several days – a feast compared with the frugal food the monks would have provided. We decided to visit the homestead Lord Werhard had mentioned and, along the way, see a little more of the Shire. Thus we made our way north to the area where most of the Viking raids had taken place. The terrain there was very mixed, with hills and cleared pastures as well as large areas of woodland. We passed a number of small farmsteads, none of which seemed to have suffered unduly or, if they had been attacked, the buildings had been quickly restored.

In fact, all seemed as it should until we passed through a large forest which was clearly being actively managed. To that end, there was a small clearing beside the road containing what remained of someone's home, most of which had been burned to the ground so that virtually nothing remained standing. I assumed it had once been the home of the forester Lord Werhard had mentioned. If so, he had since formed a crude hovel, hastily put together using timbers which were leaned against each other and loosely thatched with ferns and leaves. We dismounted and walked towards it through the blackened ruins, examining the debris though learning very little. The surprising thing was that we found no graves, which seemed to confirm all Lord Werhard had told us about the nature of the raids. It was then that I noticed an old woman who was watching us from a short way off. I called out to her, but she pretended not to hear and instead busied herself preparing a woodpile to make charcoal.

'Woman, I would speak with you,' I said again, walking towards her. She made no attempt to run away and, in any event, looked to be so old that I doubt she'd have got very far if she had.

'My name is Matthew, son of Lord Edwulf and...'

'She knows who you be, my Lord,' bellowed a voice from somewhere over to one side of the ruins. When I looked I saw a forester carrying a large axe on his shoulder. 'Word reached us of your coming. You're here to train the fyrd, or so they say.'

I waited until he joined us. 'Not before time by the looks of these ruins,' I said. 'You, I take it, are Godric, the forester here?'

'Aye, my Lord. And I'm beholden to Lord Werhard's stepson for my living here. In fact, even more so now that my home has been destroyed.'

'What do you mean?' I asked.

'I mean, my Lord, that he has offered support, but I dare not incur the cost of that. I could never repay such a debt even if I worked eight days in every week, let alone six.'

'So where was the fyrd when this place was attacked?'

The man roared with laughter. 'The members of the fyrd were where they always are, toiling in their fields to ensure they've enough to meet their own dues and obligations.'

'To Lord Werhard?' I asked.

'I wish it were, my Lord. In his day he would have had his Reeve collect what's due but always allowed time for payment when things were hard, but now it's not him who holds out his hand for settlement; it's his stepson, a man who makes free with all within the Shire.'

'You say that as though he demands too much?'

'They all demand too much, my Lord, but him more so than most.'

'Fool,' screeched the old woman. 'You'll keep a still tongue in your head if you've a grain of sense. Else mark my words, you'll end up with your feet dancing beneath the branches of a tree!'

He looked at me, clearly wondering whether he had indeed said too much.

'Have no fear, I'm not here to punish honest Saxon folk, only to learn what's going on in these parts.'

It was the woman who spoke again. 'Pah! Tell that to the poor fools who've been punished already just for speaking their mind! Tell it to those who, like us, no longer have a roof over their heads or have lost lands which their forefathers have worked for years beyond knowing!'

I acknowledged the point. 'Anything you say to me is for my ears alone,' I assured them.

The old woman tilted her head to one side as she looked at me. 'So what are you really come here for?' she asked.

'We're here to set things right.'

She nodded. 'We'll see about that,' she said. 'Though Lord knows it's high time someone did.'

'Well, let's start with what happened here,' I suggested. 'I assume it was a Viking raid?'

Godric shrugged. 'Most likely, my Lord, but who can say? They struck whilst we were away cutting timber. When we returned we found our home as you see it now and all we owned taken and our stores gone.'

'And you lived here?'

'I did and I still do,' he said, solemnly pointing to the shelter he'd erected. 'I and my family built a good home here with our own hands, cleared the trees and put everything we had into it. Now all of that is gone.'

It was Aelred who then spoke. 'Well, if that hovel is all you have by way of shelter, you'll be lucky to survive the winter.'

'I have no other. Friends have offered to help us where they can, though I doubt many of them will have enough to share. Besides, I'm not a man who readily relies on charity. I'll therefore try to rebuild my home but, as I must still meet my dues, it'll take time and, as you so rightly say, the coming winter will be hard.'

'Were any of your family killed or taken?'

The man shook his head. 'Like I said, we were not here at the time so our lives were spared but all we owned was taken or destroyed.'

'Was there much which can't be replaced or rebuilt?' I asked.

'There was a pin, my Lord. Not gold or silver, but pretty enough. It was a gift to my wife from Lord Werhard's wife.

She nursed and cared for the old lady when she was sick and was given the pin for her trouble. Like I said, it wasn't worth much, but my wife valued it for what it was and is troubled to have lost it.'

'Would you recognise it again?' I asked.

The forester looked at me long and hard. 'I would, my Lord. For when you've little enough to your name, everything you own is precious, whether it be valuable or not.'

'Then we'll see what can be done,' I said simply, not sure how that would help.

The old woman stepped closer and fixed me with her stare. 'What can be done will never be enough,' she warned. 'All I can see is fire and bloodshed in this place. And that will come sooner than you think.'

The forester looked embarrassed. 'My mother has the way of seeing what may befall us,' he explained. 'Though what she says she sees is not always what you think it is.'

'That's a gift many would love to share,' I said simply.

'A gift you say?' she exclaimed, spitting the words out like pips from a sour apple. 'Pah! It's not a gift for those that have to bear it. It's a curse!'

Both Aelred and I were not sure what to say.

Sensing our disbelief she spoke again. ''Tis true that I have eyes that see more than God intended,' she said, then turned to her son. 'Terrible things no mother ought to see concerning her son for, as I've warned you many times before, you must beware the flames which may one day embrace you. These things will come to pass, you mark my words.' Then she turned and pointed her long bony finger at me. 'You also have cause for much concern, for I see in you a man living beyond his years and searching for his grave,' she said. 'You have more to fear from what I've seen than anyone.'

*****

As we rode away Aelred was strangely quiet.

'You look worried,' I said. 'Was it what the old woman said?'

'I've found that such women sometimes seem to know of things which are not obvious to us lesser mortals,' he explained.

'Well, that doesn't amount to much if all she predicts is fire and death – God knows there's been enough of that in this realm and given what we know about Jarl Hakon, there's bound to be yet more. Even I could predict as much!'

Aelred still seemed ill at ease.

'What would Brother Benedict have said about it?' I asked.

He gave a wry smile. 'I think she and he would have had much to debate,' he said. 'And also Ingar. What worries me is that she seems to know about your wound.'

'It seems to me that everyone knows about my wound! My reputation is founded on it and seems to precede me everywhere I go.'

'But not everyone knows about what Ingar told you.'

That certainly touched a nerve. 'You mean about the given years?' I asked.

'Aye, the given years. Did that old hag back there not say the same? *A man living beyond his years and searching for his grave*. Doesn't that trouble you?'

I shrugged. 'Of course, but there's nothing I can do to change it.'

'You're a brave man to accept your fate so readily when so many seem to be foretelling your death. And all of them people who might well know about such things.'

'So what would you do if you were me?'

He thought for a moment then realised that there was actually not very much that could be done. 'I reckon I'd find a tidy whore and spend whatever days I have tupping her until my heart gives out and I die in her arms,' he said, then looked at me and laughed. 'Or I might do what you seem intent on doing.'

'What's that?' I asked.

'Getting yourself killed as quickly as you can and thereby getting it over with.'

Chapter Five

'These monks are strange folk,' complained Aelred once we'd retired to our lodgings after a sparse and very plain supper.

'Why do you say that?' I asked.

'Well, it's all very well if they want to live like this but they shouldn't expect others to pay for board and lodging which is wanting in almost every respect.'

'Ah, but that's not the way of it. We're not expected to pay for our keep. In fact, they'd take offence if I offered to do so.'

'You mean you take advantage of their hospitality even though they scarce have two coins between them?'

'It's not as simple as that. All they ask is that we respect their ways whilst we're here. When we leave, we can make a donation to their calling. That's all they'll require of us, though there are some orders which would refuse even that.'

'Where's the sense in that?' he asked, clearly puzzled.

'Remember what I told you about how these good brothers are followers of St Columba?' I explained. 'Their creed requires them to follow his example and live a simple life of prayer and contemplation whilst showing hospitality to strangers.'

'It sounds like the sort of thing of which Brother Benedict would have approved. I know I'm going to regret asking, but who was this St Columba?'

'He was a very pious abbot who was always looking for ways to simplify his life. One day he saw a woman collecting nettles to make a soup which was the only food she had. He thought that if she could live on nettle soup alone then so should he and therefore instructed the monk who prepared his food to serve only that from then on. The monk was anxious for Columba's health so secretly mixed milk into the soup as well. Of course Columba thrived on that diet and so urged others of his order to do the same. So keen were the goodly brothers to follow his lead that the monk who prepared the food soon found that their meagre supply of milk was quickly gone. In the end he had no choice but to confess what he'd done. Far from being angry, Columba declared that God had taught him a lesson in humility, reminding him that it was only from pride that he'd boasted to others of his simple diet. He was therefore grateful to God for showing him the error of his ways.'

'So what's the point of the tale?' asked Aelred.

'It teaches us the need for humility,' I said, though I suspect the moral was lost on Aelred as were most of the things Brother Benedict had tried to explain to him.

The fact remained that the followers of St Columba at the Monastery where we were staying were indeed true to their vows. They numbered no more than eight monks, plus two boys who were intent on becoming novices and a single lay member who provided much-needed help with practical matters, just as Seth had done for my old order. As such their enclave was much too small to be considered as an Abbey, but, nonetheless, the monks there greatly impressed me, as they did even Aelred, despite all his complaints.

'So will you ever return to the Church?' he asked.

It was a difficult question for me to answer. 'Perhaps I will one day, though the course of my life may not now allow it.'

'You mean because you count the King and important Lords as your friends and move in high circles now that you're restored to being a noble and a very wealthy man?'

'That's all true,' I admitted. 'But my faith is always there and I wouldn't wish to lose or betray it in any way, for I still much respect the calling. Indeed, I've met other men who walk that path, men I regard very highly indeed.' I was thinking again not just of poor Brother Benedict but also of the monks I'd met whilst on the way to Athelney after the battle at Chippenham. As I'd explained to my old abbot, despite having been attacked by raiders and seen many of their order slain, they remained intent upon restoring their ruined church which they intended to dedicate to the Holy Splinter.

'Theirs is a hard road right enough,' he mused. 'With scant regard for the comforts of life, though I reckon you could say the same about us. By rights you at least should be tucked up warm and abed with that woman of yours, though as I recall you didn't even trouble to see her when we were back at Winchester.'

At first I didn't answer.

'What, were you no longer wont to lay with her?'

'Things were not as I expected,' I said.

'Ha! You mean someone else had been warming her bed whilst you were away!'

'No, not that,' I assured him. 'But things have changed and I must bide my time. Besides, I was ordered by Alfred to undertake this mission so could hardly refuse.'

'Surely he'd have allowed you a few nights with her after being away so long?'

I shrugged. 'It was just not to be, so let's leave it at that.'

As always, Aelred had the final word on the matter. 'Well, faced with the choice of laying with my woman or going on a pointless mission that may well get me killed, I know which I'd have chosen.'

*****

As we rode through the Shire the next day we looked for signs of other farmsteads that had been raided. There was certainly some evidence of that and when we enquired further it was clear that whilst many had been robbed, had their homes ransacked or, in some cases, burned to the ground like poor Godric, we heard of very few people who'd been harmed. As we went, I asked Aelred whether he had ever been the victim of a raid.

'No, and I thank God for that small mercy, for life was hard enough for me as it was.'

'In what way?' I asked.

'When I was a boy I watched my father labour in the fields till his hands were raw. Seven days a week he'd work, using every hour of daylight God gave him.'

'So what happened?'

'What happened was that he wasted his life as he struggled just to put food in our bellies. If he ever managed to earn more than he needed, something would happen to snatch it away from him. He was like a man struggling to stand against a strong wind so that whenever he managed to get up, the wind would knock him down again.'

'What did he do?'

Aelred shrugged. 'What could he do? He had mouths to feed so he kept working and eventually died a broken man.

Not from the work itself, you understand. He always said that hard work harmed no one. It was the relentless grind of it all which killed him.'

'So what became of you and the rest of his family?'

'Mercifully, my mother followed him to the grave within a matter of weeks. My sister took a wealthy husband who promised her a better life but gave her nowt. She bore him two fine sons, but all she got from him was a regular beating whenever he was in drink, which it seemed to me was pretty much always. I took myself off to the coast. I'd no idea what to expect there, but reckoned it had to be better than a life like that which my poor father had endured.'

'Surely your Lord would not have allowed you to leave? He'd have kept you indentured to the land your father worked?'

Aelred shrugged. 'I didn't stop to ask him. Besides, he had others more able to screw enough from the land to pay his dues than I could. There was no one else there who owed me a living so I went off in search of work, thinking that perhaps I could set myself to a trade. As you know, I made my way to the coast and there I found a girl whose widowed mother scratched a living from her dead husband's holdings. It seemed too good a chance to miss so, in order to improve my lot, I settled for that instead and married the girl. We lived with her mother and I bent my back to the plough and blistered my hands just to feed the three of us, but it was never enough. It seemed that I'd got myself a shrew of a wife and a mother-in-law who had a tongue as sharp as flint. I realised soon enough that I was doing just like my poor father had done and that as like as not would end my days the very same way that he did. So, when I saw my chance to leave, I took it.'

'That's when you took to living rough?'

'Aye. Like I told you, I served in the fyrd as a spear man, though avoided the training as, whenever the Reeve could be persuaded to look the other way, I went poaching instead. It seemed not to matter at the time for we weren't much troubled by the Vikings as we had a sort of arrangement with them whereby they let us be in return for safe moorings and fresh water after having been so long at sea. But other settlements nearby had no such arrangement so we were set to help them fight off a raid and I had no choice but to join them. In the skirmish which followed I was knocked down and left for dead. When I came to I saw my chance for freedom so joined others in the forest who'd also grown tired of working for the benefit of their so-called betters. They dirtied their hands, robbing and thieving anything they could.'

'But not you?'

'No, not me. That was never my way, but I earned my keep by providing food for their bellies, using those skills I'd learned as a poacher.'

'So what happened?'

'One day the fools killed a man who refused to hand over his coin. I was not there you understand, but I knew I'd hang just like the rest if ever we were caught. The rest of it you know. I left in haste and, on my way, met with that bastard Ljot. I thought to trade with him just as I'd done when I lived at the coast, but all I got for my trouble was to be taken for a slave instead.'

'You say you regretted having been involved with those who killed a man? Yet you've never shown any reluctance to bloody your hands when it comes to slaying a few Vikings.'

He grinned as if to acknowledge the point. 'That's true enough,' he said. 'I reckon I'm as good with a spear as any man, and a damn sight better than most.'

'And that's now your weapon of choice?' I asked, knowing that his battle skills could well be needed on a mission such as the one we were undertaking. 'Or would it serve you better if I got you a sword or perhaps a battle-axe?'

He laughed. 'Ha! Bless you for thinking of it, but I'd not know how to wield a sword even if I had one – and the axe is such a brutal weapon that I'd not relish doing what's needed if I was to use one, even in battle. I reckon either would quickly be the death of me. The spear is, as you say, my weapon of choice – and don't worry, whilst I didn't relish killing a man for no purpose, I've no scruples about skewering a few Vikings or even robbers. Killing doesn't trouble me. It's getting hung for it afterwards that I'm keen to avoid.'

* * * * *

Once we reached Leatherhead we went first to inspect the mill again to see what else would be needed if it was to suit our purpose. Strategically it was, as I'd already determined, ideally placed to defend the ford, but it was nowhere near big enough to provide a refuge for all who lived within the settlement itself. Yet even so, I decided it was indeed the ideal place for us to build our fortifications and from which to make our stand.

'We should have warning enough of Hakon's coming in time to get the people across the ford to safety,' I said, looking at the extensive pastures on the other side of the river.

'To what purpose?' asked Aelred.

'So they can't be taken as hostages by Hakon and then ransomed to persuade us to let his army pass.'

Aelred seemed to see the sense of that so between us we began to look at the watermill more closely. Although in very poor repair, it hardly seemed to matter for, with the river and the island to its rear, it would be easy enough to defend. All we would need to do would be to erect a stout fence to the front, extending it to the side almost as far as the ford itself. It could also be extended at the other end to enclose the forge and all the stores. The largest store looked to be big enough to provide temporary accommodation for ourselves so that we'd be on hand in the event of an attack and one of the others could be used as a dry store for weapons and supplies. All the rest could remain for use by the mill, though I fully expected the miller to complain bitterly at being thus deprived.

Curious to see what we were about, the miller ventured over to speak with us. 'May I be of service, my Lord?' he asked meekly, clearly worried by what was going on.

I introduced myself and Aelred, though he already seemed to know who we were and why we were there. 'So are you the owner of this mill?' I asked.

He seemed to find that amusing. 'Bless you my Lord, but that's a dream that'll never be realised. At least, not by the likes of me.'

'So who is your master?'

He shrugged. 'Well, he who controls everything around these parts of course.'

'Mind your tongue when speaking to your betters!' warned Aelred, sensing the man had not been sufficiently reverent.

The miller hesitated for a moment. 'I beg your pardon, my Lord, I meant no disrespect. Lord Werhard is master here, though his stepson governs in his stead.'

'And is he not a fair master?' I asked.

The miller didn't answer and I decided not to press him further.

'I'll need your mill to form a stronghold here,' I said simply. 'I'll speak with Lord Werhard, but would first hear your view on the matter.'

'My Lord, I struggle to earn a living as it is,' he pleaded. 'The river is slow and lazy so it takes time to grind corn and at this time of year I'm always busy with the last of the harvest as folks make ready for the winter.'

'We can leave the mill as it is but would need two stores, one to serve as a place for us to lodge, the other to secure weapons and provisions.'

He looked at the buildings in question, but said nothing.

'We'll need to erect a fence to the front of the mill but can provide gates so that you may continue to trade as you do now.'

He still looked less than happy with the proposal so I produced a few coins and handed them to him. 'This should compensate for whatever business you lose. You'll also be compensated for the buildings which are taken, though they look to me to have been much neglected.'

He suddenly seemed more at ease with the position as he took the coins and bit them one by one as if to test them, probably more out of habit than anything else. 'And I can carry on as I do now?' he asked.

'You may.'

'Thank you, my Lord, you'll receive no complaint from me. But I fear there's much to be done if you're to render that store ready for a man as noble as yourself.'

Aelred laughed. 'I assure you,' he said, 'noble or not, my Lord here has slept in worse. And I can surely testify to that, for we both have the flea bites to prove it.'

*****

'He seemed amiable enough,' said Aelred once the miller had gone.

'And so he should. What I gave him would take him many weeks to earn by grinding corn.'

'Then why so generous?' he asked.

'These people have been deprived enough. We need them to see us as helping them, not taking yet more from their diminished lives.'

'So you'll buy their support?'

'Not buy it. But I will need it. And remember, if we are attacked there won't be much left of that mill by the time the Vikings are done with it so that poor wretch who depends upon it for his livelihood will then have much to complain about. Hakon won't offer him compensation if we're beaten, of that you can be certain!'

'And presumably it's Lord Werhard's purse which you're distributing so freely?' he said.

'That's true enough. I wonder whether he'll hold with being so generous?'

'I suspect it'll not trouble him unduly as judging by his Hall, he must be a very wealthy man,' suggested Aelred. 'But I somehow think his stepson Oeric will take it as a slight. I doubt he has a generous bone in his body.'

*****

'What happens if Hakon comes by river?' asked Aelred.

Even as he said it I realised it was not something I'd even considered. Yet he was right to raise it. The river Emele flowed all the way north until it joined the river at London so would be easy enough for Hakon to access. 'Surely it's too narrow for his longships?' I suggested, not sure that I was right.

'Do we know that for certain?' pressed Aelred.

I shook my head. 'No, but I hope that is the case.'

'Well, it's wide enough here so is probably even wider once it reaches London,' he suggested.

'They'd have to row all the way upstream,' I observed. 'And once here there's scarce room for two longships to be rowed side by side.' My mind was already thinking back to the battle at Combwich where we'd used such constraints to our advantage, though whether we could do so again was far from certain. Then I had an idea. 'Chains,' I said, almost relieved at having thought of it. 'We need to draw chains across the river just downstream from here, but within bow range of the island. They can lie below the surface of the river and be raised if we're attacked. That should slow them up long enough for us to fill their boats with arrows.'

Aelred seemed impressed. 'We could also drive some stakes into the riverbed. That should keep them busy and make them easy targets as they try to get past them.'

It all seemed logical enough, but would mean even more work for us to do in anticipation of their coming. With that I noticed that the miller was still watching us so called him over and asked him more about the river.

'They couldn't easily come by river, my Lord,' he assured me. 'At least, not using craft big enough to carry more than half a dozen men at a time.'

'Why is that?' I asked.

'I've tried taking things downriver by boat several times myself. Mind, never as far as where the river meets the one at

London, but there are parts where they'd need to carry their boats.'

'You're sure of that?'

'Aye, my Lord. I'm certain of it.'

Reassured as I was by that, I knew that it was not beyond the Vikings to manhandle their boats across shallows and any other obstacles they encountered. I therefore resolved that if time allowed we would still draw the chains across just in case, but there was much which needed to be done before that; matters which were indeed more pressing.

*****

The realisation that I'd overlooked the possibility of Hakon coming by river caused me to look again at everything I'd planned.

'So...' I said, speaking aloud once Aelred and I were alone once more. 'Assuming they'll come from the north, there is but one road from London.' In truth that was not quite the case, for there were other tracks and trails which led to some of the farmsteads and to the Monastery, but they were all too narrow for so many men to use with ease. They could of course come directly across open fields or through the woods and forests, but it would make no sense to do so when they had a good road which would lead them straight to their objective. Then, once they arrived at Leatherhead, they could follow that same road past the Vill and down through the settlement to the river.

'Aye,' said Aelred when I explained all that. 'Which is why you're right to think in terms of getting everyone out of their homes and across the ford to safety.'

'Exactly. But what about the Vill itself? Should we leave a few men there to attack the Vikings from behind?'

It was a difficult question given the size of the force we were up against.

'Well, if you do, I wouldn't want to be one of them,' said Aelred. 'As like as not they'll all be slaughtered. Besides, what good would a few men do against so many even if they take them by surprise?'

It was a good point. 'Then best not to divide our force. We'll struggle to hold the Vikings back as it is with the numbers we'll have.'

With that the matter seemed to have been decided. All that remained was to put whatever plan I could come up with into effect, though whether that would suffice rested solely in the hands of God.

Chapter Six

'I'm already getting weary of all this riding back and forth,' said Aelred as we started out yet again for Leatherhead the following day.

'I'll have Leonfrith start work on preparing that store at the mill for us to use,' I suggested. 'I don't want to distract him from other works, but the sooner we can stay there the better, as we'll then be on hand to oversee matters and be better placed if and when the attack comes. Even so, converting both stores could well take at least a week.'

'We could stay at the Vill,' suggested Aelred. 'I'll wager that might be a sight more comfortable than some rat-infested grain store.'

'Yes, but then as you surmised, we might wake one morning to find an assassin's knife pressed against our throats.'

'Ah,' said Aelred. 'There is that. So what have we to achieve today?'

'First we go to see Lord Werhard, then we meet with the thanes and explain to them what's needed. After that they'll come with us to attend the Moot where all the good people of Leatherhead will have gathered.'

'And what exactly will you tell these noble thanes?'

'I'll tell them they must prepare their men to help defend the Shire when called upon to do so. That's their sworn responsibility anyway, but I fear they may have become somewhat lax given the example set by Lord Werhard's son.'

'Then you'll break the news to all the common folk about the extra work they'll be expected to do,' said Aelred. 'All I can say is that we're not going to be the most popular people in this Shire when you do.'

'We weren't sent here to make new friends,' I said. 'But as like as not they'll thank us when they realise what's about to descend upon them.'

*****

When we reached the Vill we went first to speak with Lord Werhard to outline my plans, as always carefully avoiding any reference to our thoughts about his treacherous stepson. Leonfrith then joined us and gave me the list of thanes I'd asked for. As I examined it, I noted that he had a good script so that his writing was both neat and clear. He'd also been extremely thorough and included a note of their respective holdings.

'My Lord, I've marked with a cross those who cannot attend today,' he explained.

'Are they to be excused?' I queried.

'Two of them are unwell, my Lord, and one is even now at Winchester where he was summoned to speak with Lord Alfred regarding lands he holds elsewhere.'

I acknowledged the point. 'These holdings are extensive,' I said as I looked at the list, but Leonfrith was ahead of me on that.

'As I said, my Lord, all told they could levy a hundred men whilst still keeping in reserve those needed for essential work elsewhere.'

I thanked him and asked him to attend the meeting with the thanes and the Moot to act as scribe to record what was said. 'When done, I would have you make a copy to send to Lord Alfred so that he knows how things progress here,' I added. 'Also, send a copy to all the thanes who are here and the three who can't attend. I want there to be no doubt about what's expected of them.'

With that, Aelred, Leonfrith and I went with Lord Werhard to the main Hall where the thanes waited, seated on benches around the table. Most had brought one or two servants or slaves with them, though some of those looked to be more like bodyguards than domestic staff. As Lord Werhard entered, all the thanes stood respectfully, including Oeric who had taken pride of place at the other end of the table, opposite where his father would sit.

As I looked around the Hall I could see that four of the Vill guards had been stationed there as well, two at the doorway and two to stand behind their Lord, all armed and dressed as if ready for battle. It seemed an unnecessary precaution given that we were supposedly among friends but then I remembered that after the meeting we would be attending the Moot, which might warrant at least a token show of strength if only to deter any would be dissenters.

I stood beside Lord Werhard with Aelred behind me. The Ealdorman looked around the room as if noting who was there and who wasn't, then took his seat. As he did so, the thanes were all seated as well, though some of them had to shuffle along so that I could sit next to Lord Werhard, as was his wish.

Having greeted them all and offered prayers, Lord Werhard began at once. 'As most of you know, I've received word from Lord Alfred that he fears an attack from Jarl Hakon who has the makings of an army gathered on the southern banks of the river at London. He has sent Matthew here to ensure we can withstand that assault when the time comes, so I've asked him to explain to you what's needed. When he's done so, we shall go together to the Common Field to attend a Moot at which all will be explained to the people of this settlement. You are charged to attend that meeting as well so that all there can see that Matthew has authority from me and the support of you all. Afterwards you must each pass the information to all those within your charge.'

'Then are we to take orders from this boy?' asked one of the men.

'Matthew is no "boy". He's a warrior who has earned the respect and trust of our King. You must answer to him as you would to me, just as I must answer to him as I would to Lord Alfred himself.'

With those rather stark remarks I stood to speak. 'My name is Matthew, christened Edward. I'm the third born son of Lord Edwulf and my brother was the warrior Edwin. Hence I've been appointed to this role.'

I stopped there for a moment, anxious to ensure that my credibility had been fully established before continuing.

'I'll outline all that's needed when we address the Moot, but for now understand that my purpose here is crucial to the safety not only of this Shire, but to the whole realm of Wessex. Hakon gathers forces as a dog gathers fleas. He has yet but two hundred men, but his numbers may well increase. Already he's building or repairing ships which we fear will sail around the coast and, when they do, he'll then march south to meet them and use them to supply and reinforce his army. To do that he must first pass through here. My mission is to ensure that he cannot do so and, for that, I need the full support of you all.'

'Two hundred warriors you say?' said one of the thanes. 'Between us, those mustered here could barely raise a force of half that size, yet you mean to stop him?'

'I do. As I say, I'll outline my plan at the Moot and then have you remain afterwards so that we can then discuss it in more detail as befits your station. All I will say is that we face huge danger and the task ahead of us is not one to be undertaken lightly. Do I make myself clear?'

None seemed inclined to object so, led by Lord Werhard, we rose from the table and followed him from the Vill. From there we made the short walk to the Common Field which lay almost directly beyond the Vill and where virtually every man, woman and child who lived in Leatherhead had assembled.

*****

The Common Field was a large open area which also served as a meeting place for a Moot – a gathering that would determine important local matters and at which all freemen could speak if they had a mind to do so, regardless of their station. When not used as a place of assembly, it was set aside as an open pasture where the people of the settlement could graze their stock without charge. At that time there were some swine and a few goats there, plus two sturdy farm horses which remained tethered by a long leash. The area for meetings was denoted by a few fallen trees which were to be used as benches and were set around a small standing stone which had been hauled there to serve as a rostrum.

I went to stand beside Lord Werhard with Aelred to one side of me and the four Vill guards arranged in a line behind us. The other guards had remained at the Vill as a precaution, though it seemed unlikely they'd be needed there. Leonfrith sat at a small table set to one side from where he could observe and hear all in order to make a record of what was discussed.

The thanes followed us, filing through the crowd and seating themselves on the fallen trees, as did Oeric, leaving the ordinary people to stand behind them.

As Aelred had predicted, it was apparent that no one was pleased to be there. I could almost sense their hostility even as Lord Werhard was, with my assistance, seated at a fine chair which had been carried there for his comfort and convenience.

The old man spoke in a surprisingly loud voice for one so frail. 'As your Ealdorman and Lord I now demand silence so that these proceedings may commence,' he said, then paused before asking a priest to lead us all in prayers and bless our endeavours. Once done, Lord Werhard continued. 'I think all here will know by now why you've been summoned but I shall leave our guest to explain more fully. He is welcome in this Shire and I would have you all remember that in whatever dealings you have with him.'

With that it was my turn to speak. 'My name is Matthew, christened Edward, and I'm the third born son of Lord Edwulf. I serve Lord Alfred and am charged by him in person to secure the settlement here at Leatherhead and also to ensure the safety of all who live here. For that I would take charge of the fyrd and assume responsibility for all matters pertinent to the security of this place. To that end I propose to fortify it and thereby hold the pass through those hills yonder which might otherwise be used by forces intending to encroach upon the realm of Wessex. I have letters of authority from Lord Alfred which Lord Werhard has seen and verified to be valid. If any here have cause to doubt my authority let him now speak.' I paused here long enough for Lord Werhard to confirm that he had indeed seen the letters and also for anyone to raise an objection if they doubted what I'd said. There were the usual mumblings and complaints, but none were prepared to question that authority, at least not openly. I therefore continued.

'I know full well that what I propose will be hard for many, particularly those who have already more work to do than time in which to do it. But hear me in this. The settlement at Leatherhead is much at risk and with it, the realm of Wessex itself. I intend to put a stop to the raids which have harried the people here for far too long, but my job is more important even than that. I have seen for myself that which you face, a threat so potent that it cannot be ignored.'

'Perhaps you should explain what it is that should so concern us,' suggested one of the thanes. I couldn't recognise the man who spoke, but it was a fair point and a timely one.

Again I paused long enough for the throng to quieten down. 'There are at least two hundred armed Viking warriors assembled at a camp to the south of the settlement at London,' I said pointedly.

'They've been there for months, why should we worry about them now?' asked another man.

'Because like the rumblings of a distant thunder, they herald a storm,' I said. 'They now have ships or at least they will have when the repairs are complete. Those ships could well sail around the coast to support an invasion of Wessex itself. If they do, Jarl Hakon, who commands them, will march south to meet them and you are all that stand in his path. Your lands will be ravaged and your families butchered like sheep. Is that not reason enough to heed what I say?'

'Who says he'll attack Wessex?' It was the same man asking yet another question and I wished I knew who he was.

'No one says he will, but he's a Viking and I've fought enough of them to know their ways. I've already visited their encampment and met Jarl Hakon in person. Whatever his intent I can assure you it's unlikely to be peaceful.'

'So what have you in mind,' demanded Oeric, looking at the others as though to cajole them.

I was beginning to tire of the interruptions. The thanes were all entitled to speak as was anyone who was present, but, given their seniority, I expected them to support what were, after all, orders from their King. 'I will address those of noble rank after this Moot for they have duties common to them all. But every man and woman here must do their share of the work needed to fortify this place and those who serve in the fyrd will be required to hone their skills with additional training. This is for the benefit of all and Leonfrith will organise rotas accordingly. Anyone who fails to do their share shall answer to me. Is that clear?'

No one seemed surprised as presumably the rumours had been rife. Nor were any tempted to question what had been said as the people of Leatherhead knew their place well enough. I already suspected that convincing the thanes would be the hardest part, therefore I signalled to Lord Werhard to close the Moot, then waited for the crowd to disperse. When they'd gone I addressed the thanes once more.

They remained seated, though some of them had their servants bring refreshments. Slaves and servants were permitted to stay with their masters, though could take no part in the proceedings.

'Thank you for remaining,' I said trying to sound appeasing. 'I know full well that you each have duties and business to attend to. You've all heard what was said earlier and I'm obliged to say that it applies to all, yourselves included.'

There was a murmur of dissent, but no one spoke out, so I continued. 'Each of you must look hard at those within your charge and ensure that the fyrd is fully trained and, more importantly, properly armed. Lord Alfred intends that the latter will soon become the duty of all thanes, but given the severity of the situation here, you must undertake it now.'

'What? Are we to pay for weapons and such like to arm our men from our own coffers?' called out one man.

'Your Ealdorman will defray the cost of all that's needed, but the training remains your responsibility. You are charged to ensure that all members of the fyrd know how to stand in the shield wall and how to fight.'

'We can't possibly spare people now! All are still busy finishing the harvest and gathering their provisions for the winter. Or would you see us all starve or freeze to death? Wait a month or perhaps a few weeks. After that all can be accomplished.'

'We cannot wait even a day, never mind a week. Your lives and those of all within the Shire depend upon it,' I insisted. 'Not to mention the whole of Wessex and the life of your King.'

'What if we can't spare the time?' asked one of the men.

'Then make your excuse to Lord Alfred. Though I doubt he'll be best pleased to hear from you in that respect.'

There was silence as all there considered that. Even though what I'd said went beyond that which most expected, it would have been foolhardy for anyone to even think of shirking their duty or seeking to be excused from it without very good cause for doing so.

'Why is it so important for us to train our men still further? Already they serve well enough when needed.'

'Because if Hakon moves to attack, the few men who make up the fyrd here at Leatherhead will not suffice to stop him. Your task will be to join us and stand with us to delay the Vikings long enough for Lord Alfred to arrive with an army. Even then I have no doubt that you and all your men will be needed to fight beside him as well.'

'How will we know when these Vikings are coming?' asked one man.

'You already have beacons to signal the presence of a raid. From now on you're required to build another to stand beside them, set close together. If one is lit it will signal a raid, just as it does at present. If both are lit it will be the signal for you to come here with all possible haste, armed and ready for battle. The lives of the men here and the security of all Wessex depend upon it, so don't tarry hoping to avoid the fray.'

'Then who are you to arrange that defence? I mean no disrespect for Lord Werhard has told us of your experience in matters of war, but others here are also proven in battle, yet Lord Alfred entrusts the defence of this Shire to a stranger.'

'Lord Alfred has entrusted me with this duty because he knows I'll see it done without fear or favour. As for my experience, I've faced battle and death more times than you can count. I stood shoulder to shoulder with our King at Edington and was even trusted to command part of the army there, thus sharing in that great victory.'

For a moment there was silence as all considered what I'd said.

'There are others here who were at Edington as well,' ventured one man.

'I know it and they will no doubt remember me,' I replied knowing that I needed their full support, but could sense that not all of them were convinced of my right to command. 'Those who were there will also attest to my competence to lead in these matters, but, for those of you who weren't, this should tell you who I am.' With that I stripped off my cloak and opened my tunic to bare my chest.

A gasp went up from within the group as they saw and recognised my scar.

'Are you saying that you're the…'

'The warrior with the pierced heart? Yes, I'm he. No doubt you've heard of me and know that it's said that I can't be slain. I don't know if that's true but all I would say is that many have tried my hand and few have lived long enough to tell of it.'

There were a few mumbles and whispers, but none seemed to question my authority after that, nor my right to command.

*****

As the thanes filed away none of them seemed overly happy with all I'd said, but I was not prepared to say more, at least, not at that point. Instead, Aelred and I met with Leonfrith again whilst the thanes went back to the Vill with Lord Werhard.

'I need all the members of the fyrd who live in this settlement to assemble here the day after tomorrow,' I told Leonfrith. 'They should come with whatever weapons they have.'

'That won't amount to much, my Lord,' Leonfrith warned me.

'Then we shall need to furnish more. What have you in the armoury at the Vill?'

He shrugged. 'Just what the guards use plus perhaps a few spears and bows.'

'Well the guards can attend the training as well. Order them to bring all you have with them. Tomorrow I would have you meet with Aelred and myself at the mill to agree what works are needed there.'

'You mean the watermill by the river, my Lord?'

'I do. I propose to make our stand there as it's the one place from where we can best control the ford. It will need a fence to be built to the front which, with the river to the rear, should then be a viable stronghold. Two of the buildings there are also to be repaired, one for Aelred and I to lodge in so we are permanently on hand and the other to be a store for weapons and supplies.'

Leonfrith looked doubtful. 'We'll need stakes and timbers, plus nails and such like to build the stockade,' he said. 'With your permission, the stakes can be cut from the forests and then dragged here, but we'll need to borrow ropes and a pulley from the blacksmith for that.'

'Very well, then see it's done. I assume the forester Godric can help with cutting and transporting the timber and his labour can be set against his dues. That should also serve to ease his troubles. Also, you'll need to set the extra beacons into place so that we can send word of any attack to all the other settlements.'

'Of course, my Lord.'

'That should be a priority, for they may be needed sooner than we think.'

He nodded. 'Very well, my Lord. I'll also prepare a full inventory of all that will be required.'

'Good. Let me have that as soon as you can and I'll speak with the blacksmith myself.'

*****

'Can you trust the thanes to properly train their men?' asked Aelred.

'Why? Don't you?' I asked.

'In my view they're all too full of their own self-importance. Sitting there with chests puffed up and their servants quivering in attendance. A bit of hard graft or a spell in the shield wall wouldn't do any of them any harm.'

I laughed, knowing that it was an opinion shared by many ordinary men and women. 'It doesn't matter much what they do so long as they bring their men when needed.'

'But will they? Or will they dally hoping to avoid becoming involved in what they'll think of as an impossible fight?'

'They'll come,' I assured him. 'I suspect they're already worried about the raids but are afraid to speak out for fear of offending Oeric and thereby their Ealdorman, Lord Werhard.'

'And that's all we have to work with?' mused Aelred. 'A hundred reluctant men pressed into defending an old mill.'

'I'd rather be defending an old mill than fighting a full-scale battle,' I said. 'Particularly commanding men who are untried and not fully trained.'

'But they may still have to fight the Vikings hand to hand,' warned Aelred. 'Particularly if the defences fail.'

'Not if the spies in London bring us word in time. With a hundred men we should at least be able to hold Hakon back long enough for Alfred to reach us. But we have to first train them as fully as we can and will then test them by dealing with the raids.'

'But you're not convinced these raids are the handiwork of Vikings, are you?' asked Aelred.

'You mean because of what the forester said?'

'Aye. For I know you well enough by now to know what you're thinking. Raids without bloodshed doesn't sound much like the Vikings, does it? At least, not from all we've seen and know of it. It could just as easily be a band of robbers hoping the Vikings will be blamed, which might explain why they're loath to kill anyone. Thieving and destroying property is one thing, murder is something else altogether.'

'If caught the outcome for them would be the same, as they'd be hung for such treachery whether they've killed anyone or not,' I pointed out. In fact, he was right, it had occurred to me that it might be the work of thieves or robbers rather than Vikings and, whether true or not, I was pleased to note that Aelred was being every bit as vigilant as I was. 'Besides, ten or more men would be a large number for a band of robbers,' I noted.

He considered that for a moment. 'It would,' he agreed. 'Though large groups of such men are not unheard of.'

'Yes, but it's more likely the work of Vikings. What I can't understand is how Lord Werhard or his stepson could benefit from the raids. As you found to your cost, bargaining with Vikings is like dealing with the devil himself, and there can be little profit in that.'

Aelred laughed. 'I think you're missing the point. Like all our so-called "betters", you know nothing of the way of things for us ordinary folk.'

'What do you mean?'

'I mean that dead men don't pay dues. And remember, we're not just talking about coin or payment in kind – some folk owe labour or service to their Lord, all of which he depends on for his comfort, prosperity and his security. Therefore it might well suit Oeric's purpose to let the Vikings steal and pillage at will, provided they don't kill the people who are obliged to serve and support him.'

'So where's the profit in that? And why would destroying their homes suit his purpose? As their Lord he'd be obliged to help them to rebuild what's lost.'

'And what happens when the poor farmers can't repay what's owed for that support or can no longer meet their obligations?' he asked.

'Then they become indentured to him until they can,' I said.

'Exactly, so in that way he reduces them to penury and thereby turns freemen into little more than slaves trapped in bondage from which they can never hope to free themselves, for they'll never earn enough to pay back what's owed whether in coin or in kind.'

I was shocked, for it was against our Saxon creed to treat freemen thus. 'Alfred will skin him alive if that's true!'

'Yes, but Alfred isn't here,' said Aelred. 'But you heard what that farmer said and also the forester. They work six days a week for Oeric's benefit, leaving just one to earn enough to feed themselves and their families. In the end they'll starve or he'll throw them out and replace them with others able to screw more from the land than they did.'

I could see he had a point.

'What's more,' he continued. 'If Oeric is collecting dues under the guise of being a thane, he'll be paying a share of that over to Lord Werhard as Ealdorman and keeping the rest for himself. Thus it'll all be added to the family coffers one way or another, so it's little wonder that Lord Werhard and his stepson live so well and can afford to keep such a grand Hall.'

I was ashamed at having not seen all that for myself.

'Mind, it still doesn't explain how he could deal with the heathens, especially if he can't speak their language,' continued Aelred. 'It would be a very dangerous game for him to play given how treacherous they can be.'

'Except that Oeric's half Viking himself,' I said. 'When I was last here Lord Werhard told me that his wife had been raped during a Viking raid. Is it therefore not possible that Oeric could have kin among the raiders?'

'Of course it's possible,' said Aelred. 'But surely that wouldn't count for much given that he's therefore a bastard?'

'Perhaps, but Torstein assured me that Vikings are none too fussy about such things. To them blood is blood, particularly among those who spend so much of their time raiding and pillaging abroad.'

'Phew! Then that puts a different colour on things. So where do we start if we're to unravel all that?'

'We'll start by going back to the Vill to collect our horses,' I suggested. 'We then return to the Monastery to eat, sleep and prepare ourselves for tomorrow.'

'You mean for the meeting with Leonfrith at the mill? He's the only one I've met so far that I feel we can trust.'

'I agree. Leonfrith seems a competent and trustworthy soul. The hard part will be meeting with Oeric later.'

'To what end?' asked Aelred.

'To incur his wrath,' I said teasingly. 'I mean to provoke him hard enough to rouse his ire. It'll be like prodding a sleeping bear insomuch as only when you wake it can you count its teeth and hear how loud it roars.'

'Why the hell would you want to wake a sleeping bear?' asked Aelred.

'To snare it of course,' I explained. 'When it rears up you can more easily slip a rope around its neck. Then, once secure, you can bait it and teach it how to behave.'

'Or rile it and make it even more angry,' suggested Aelred.

'There is that risk,' I agreed. 'But that's what I want from Oeric. I want him to rear up and roar so that I have cause to challenge him, face to face.'

'And then what?' asked Aelred.

'Then I'll take him down a peg or two. Or better still force him to confess and repent his crimes and thereby save us all a great deal of trouble.'

Chapter Seven

Aelred and I met with Leonfrith the next day to finalise our plans. As we stood just outside the watermill, I tried to visualise all that which would be needed. 'The posts for the stockade must be at least head high even when inserted into the ground,' I instructed. 'Ideally higher so as to provide as much cover as possible.'

'I've already spoken with Godric,' advised Leonfrith. 'He's selecting timber from the forest which can be cut and I've offered to let him use the team of horses from the Vill to drag it all here.'

'Good. He'll need men to help him as well. Have you yet considered how many?'

'That depends on how many I'll have at my disposal,' said Leonfrith.

'Every man, woman and child over the age of twelve years will be required to assist with the works. You'll need to organise them by rota so that they each serve say, one day in three. That should not impinge too heavily on their lives.'

Aelred looked doubtful. 'That's easy for you to say. For most of these folk the loss of several days labour in every week could well mean that their families go hungry through the winter.'

It was a fair point. 'Hopefully they won't be needed for more than a few weeks and during that time I'll ask Lord

Werhard to offset the time they spend here against their dues and obligations.'

'That won't help them much. They need to lay down stores and provisions and it'll be too late for that once the weather turns,' chided Aelred. 'Can we not organise things better than that?'

'In what way?' I asked.

'Well, we could divide the work so that some are tasked with building the fortifications and whatever else is needed whilst others continue to work the land and gather stores and provisions for all. Those supplies can then be held by Leonfrith at the Vill and be shared throughout the winter according to need.'

Leonfrith seemed to agree that could work, provided the winter was not too long or too harsh and the Vill wasn't plundered by the Vikings when they attacked the settlement. 'My Lord, there are barns beyond the river where it could all be stored more safely,' he advised.

'Good, and what about the rotas?' I asked.

'We should be able to count on seventy or eighty people who can be rostered,' suggested Leonfrith. 'I shall divide them into three groups and allocate the tasks according to their skills and ability. One group to help Godric cut and collect the timber and one to continue to work in the fields and gather stores as Aelred has suggested.'

'And the third?'

'The third will comprise the women, children and older men who'll undertake lighter tasks such as rendering the main shed habitable for you both and making the other one watertight to form an armoury and a store. I'll also set them to building a second beacon alongside each of the existing ones, as you ordered yesterday. After that they can make arrows and gather stones which can be used as sling shot.'

He had clearly thought it through and I was much impressed. 'What about the mill itself?' I asked, turning to survey it more closely. Although two storeys high in parts, it was in very poor condition. Even the water wheel was in need of repair, being covered in weed and slime.

'With respect, my Lord, that's not our concern,' said Leonfrith. 'In the event of a siege we could position men with bows on the higher floor, but only for a while, as being formed of thatch and timber it's likely the attackers will quickly set it ablaze. We therefore shouldn't waste too much time on it.'

That also seemed sensible so I returned my attention to the stockade. 'The posts will need to be placed in a semicircle in front of the mill and be set up tight against each other – fill any gaps with daub, but leave slits through which our men can shoot their arrows.'

'Big enough to accommodate how many men, my Lord?'

That was a good question. Too big and the stockade would be hard to defend, too small and half our forces might be left outside where they'd be easy targets and little use in holding off the attack. Once again it was Aelred who provided the answer.

'Make it big enough to house fifty men,' he advised. 'That should be about half our force. The others can wait across the river either to provide reinforcements if needed or to form a second line of defence on the far bank. The people from the settlement can then wait safely behind that line or seek shelter in the hills.'

'You mean form a shield wall on the far bank?' I asked.

'Exactly. You could also place some wicker panels on the island and position bowmen behind them. From there they could harry any Vikings trying to use the ford to attack the shield wall, picking the bastards off like flies.'

'That makes sense,' I agreed. 'I was thinking we could use the island to escape to if the stockade is overrun, but you're right, it could form part of our defences as well.'

Leonfrith seemed similarly impressed. He began to step out the logical position for the posts which would form the stockade, scratching a rough line in the dirt with his staff. 'I'll calculate how many stakes we'll need,' he offered. 'Presumably it should extend across the full width of the mill and as far as the ford itself?'

'Exactly,' I said, pleased with all that had been agreed. 'Ideally you'll need to sharpen the top of the stakes and include some which are tilted towards the attackers to prevent them getting too close. We have to make things as difficult as we can for them.'

'And a few in the river,' suggested Aelred. 'As a temporary arrangement we could also remove the stepping stones to make the water as deep as possible, which will slow down those Vikings trying to cross and make them easier targets – and don't forget the chains.'

'Ah yes, we're going to need at least three which are long enough to cross from one side of the river to the other. They must be draped so as to rest on the riverbed but then raised to hang just below the surface if Hakon should decide to come here by boat.'

Leonfrith looked pensive. 'I doubt he'll try that, my Lord. There are many parts of the river between here and London which are much too shallow to allow it.'

'Yes, the miller said the same,' I acknowledged. 'But Viking longships have a shallow draught and can be hauled or even dragged if needs be. I saw for myself how easily they managed that at Combwich. That being so, we'll put the chains into position just in case. Can you provide what's needed?'

'We'd have to forge them,' he said, looking doubtful. 'Especially if they need to be strong enough to hold back boats. And the blacksmith will be hard pressed to make all the weapons and other equipment we're going to need as it is.'

'We only have to stop them long enough to set their boats ablaze,' suggested Aelred. 'Surely rope will suffice for that?'

'That might work,' I said. 'Presumably ropes will be easier to come by, though I've no doubt they'll cut through them quickly enough.'

Aelred was ahead of me on that. 'They'll try,' he agreed. 'But as I suggested, if we set them just downstream from here but still within bow range of the island, that should give the bastards something to worry about. Let's see how well they manage to free themselves whilst being showered with arrows!'

Leonfrith nodded. 'We can join lengths of rope together which should then suffice,' he agreed. 'We'll need to weight them and also stiffen them with pitch so as to render them harder to cut.'

It all began to make sense, but the question remained as to how feasible it all was and, more importantly, how long it would take to put everything into place.

Leonfrith raised his eyebrows when I put this to him, as though not sure of the answer. 'Perhaps three weeks,' he estimated. 'Longer if the weather impedes us. Also, we're going to need nails and lifting gear and I don't know how long it will take the blacksmith to forge all that.'

'You're right, he's going to be kept busy enough forging spear points and arrow heads.'

'So which would you have him do first?' asked Leonfrith.

'The men levied by the thanes will hopefully come fully armed. Send word to remind them how important that is and order them to bring their own supplies of arrows and sling shot with them. That way the blacksmith only has to worry about arming the men from this settlement, which probably means just twenty spears and as many arrows as he can manage. That shouldn't take him more than a week if we leave the women to affix the arrowheads to the shafts and fletch them.'

Leonfrith had been making some hurried calculations. 'Which should work out well for it will take several weeks to cut and haul the stakes here. Therefore once he's made the weapons the blacksmith can start work on the nails and any brackets or fixings we'll need.'

'Then let's hope that Jarl Hakon doesn't deign to make his move before we're ready,' said Aelred.

Leonfrith gave a little laugh then looked down at his feet. 'I can see the danger in that,' he admitted. 'But few of the people here will regard it as a matter of great concern if he does.'

'How so?' I asked.

'Because only Lord Alfred has cause to fear the consequence of a Viking invasion. The ordinary people will first hide themselves and their belongings then, once all is determined, they'll rebuild their homes and learn how to live under Viking rule as best they can, as have those in Mercia and Northumbria. It wouldn't be an easy yoke for them to wear, but at least they'd still have a neck on which to rest it.'

*****

'This should be interesting,' said Aelred as we walked back towards the Vill leading our horses by the reins. When we got there a stable lad took the mounts aside and I told him to feed and water them, then rub them down well as their care had been much neglected at the Monastery. As he led them away the guards said nothing, but I guessed from their sullen demeanour that Leonfrith had, by then, told them they were all required to attend the training of the fyrd. I knew none of them would like it but only one of them – the one who had always proved so surly – actually objected. He gave me an awkward glance then muttered something and shook his head before scurrying off towards the Hall.

'What was that all about?' asked Aelred.

'We'll find out soon enough,' I said.

We didn't have to wait long before Oeric appeared with a look on his face as black as thunder. 'What's the meaning of this!' he stormed as he strode towards me.

'The meaning of what?' I asked calmly.

'I'm told that you've now commandeered my personal guard to serve in the fyrd as well!'

'Not all of them,' I said. 'Just those who I think may be up to the task.' I then pointed to the awkward sod who had gone to fetch him. 'You can keep that arrogant oaf for a start, for I've no use for the likes of him. Whilst training he can keep watch on your Vill, though precious little good will it do you for he's about as much use as a broken shield. Fortunately for you we'll only be over there in the Common Field to do our training, therefore close enough to reach you if needed. Will that suffice to ensure you sleep soundly – or whatever else it is you do in your bed?'

He stared at me, hatred and defiance oozing from every pore. 'What right have you to do anything here without my consent?'

I laughed. 'More right than you have to stop me, that's for sure!'

'I command here!' he shouted. 'It's not your place to meddle in my affairs.'

I drew my seax and stepped close enough to press the tip of the blade against his throat. 'This is my right,' I said. 'This and the letters I carry from Lord Alfred. But feel free to argue with either or both if you've a mind to.'

Oeric swallowed hard against the pressure of the blade, the look on his face having turned to one of fear.

'Now listen to me you arrogant fool,' I continued. 'You'll not deign to cross me nor will you question any order given by me to anyone, the Vill guards included. Is that clear?'

He didn't answer so I pressed a little harder with the seax. 'I said is that clear?' The seax made a very small cut to the side of his neck and a trace of blood dripped down on to his tunic.

He nodded his head, though was careful lest in doing so he cut his own throat on the blade.

'Good. Now hear me in this. I mean to have weapons and equipment made for the fyrd to use and you, acting in your father's stead as it seems you're wont to do, have kindly volunteered to donate the cost of that from your own coffers.'

'B-but…'

'There are no "buts". From now on it's your responsibility to provide arms and you'll do so willingly or you and I will need to speak further. What's more, you'll ensure that the blacksmith is paid promptly and well for his work. Do I make myself clear on that as well?' I held the seax at his throat just a little longer then sheathed it and turned away. Even as I did so I heard the sound of his sword being drawn as the blade rasped against the scabbard. Instinctively, I spun round to confront him and, as I did so, my hand streaked towards my own sword, but I stopped short of actually drawing it. For a moment he looked like a startled hare, hardly daring to move so much as a muscle. 'Go on,' I challenged him. 'Just try it! I'll warrant you'll need both hands just to keep your head on your shoulders if you do!'

He smiled weakly and muttered something as he sheathed his sword, then turned and sloped away like a dog with its tail between its legs.

Aelred came to stand beside me. 'Well, I think that about serves your purpose. You've certainly taken him down a peg or two, though I somehow doubt you've heard the last of it.'

'In a way I hope you're right. I wish now he'd fully drawn his sword as I would then have had the right to take him on.'

'Then it's as well he wasn't fool enough to try it,' he said.

Before I could answer I noticed that Lord Werhard had been standing behind us and had therefore witnessed all. I went across to speak with him and started with an apology as to draw any weapon in anger within the confines of his Vill was a matter of disrespect. He waved aside my apology.

'You did only what I should have done many years ago,' he said. 'For that I'm grateful.'

'My Lord, I must also apologise for having assumed your support in certain matters as well,' I offered.

'You mean recruiting men from my guard to join the fyrd? In my view that's to be expected. After all, it's their job to protect me and what's mine, and that must surely include this settlement.'

'Yes, but I've also made free with your purse to pay for weapons for the fyrd.'

He nodded and smiled good naturedly. 'You have the authority for that from Lord Alfred himself,' he said. 'All was set out in those documents you brought with you. As such you may assume that you have my consent for anything more you need. Though as a matter of courtesy, I would have you ask me first.'

*****

The blacksmith worked at the small forge which was set alongside the watermill, presumably so he could access the river for water needed to ply his trade. It was a simple structure, mainly formed from woven panels with an awning stretched across them to keep out the worst of the weather, but otherwise left open to the elements.

Despite this, as I entered I could scarce believe the overpowering smell of the burning charcoal and red-hot iron. Although smaller than many forges I'd seen before, it seemed well equipped with a proper hearth, bellows and an anvil. There were also several benches plus a rack from which hung an array of tools and hammers. The blacksmith himself was certainly not a man to be taken lightly as, like many of his kind, he had hands that looked almost too big for his arms with shoulders to match. He also had a vast black beard which glistened with sweat as he hammered away at the metal he was working on. Neither he nor the boy who aided him stopped working or even looked up at us as we entered, something which Aelred regarded as a slight. He wanted to rebuke the man, but I stopped him, knowing that the blacksmith dared not stop beating the iron lest it cooled and his work was thereby spoiled.

'What's your name?' I asked when, still using the tongs, he held up the metal, as if to inspect it, then quenched it in a pail of cold water.

'I'm known as Eagbert, my Lord,' said the smith. 'The boy here's my son.'

'Then Eagbert I've work for you,' I said simply. 'I need weapons – spear points and arrowheads. I shall also need many nails together with brackets and hinges and such like.'

'I was at the Moot so know well enough what you'll need,' he said, his voice deep and measured.

'Is that work you can undertake?'

'I can forge anything, my Lord, but will still require payment whether it's for my betters or not.'

'You'll be paid. It'll be charged to Lord Werhard's account.'

'Then I have to ask whether I shall be paid at all,' he said.

'What do you mean by that?'

'Much of the work I've done for Lord Werhard's stepson remains unpaid. Why would this be any different?' With that he took another piece of glowing metal from the coals and began hammering it into shape on the anvil.

'Because if your account is not settled promptly, Oeric will answer to me.'

Having finished with the metal he quenched that as well then looked up at me and, holding my gaze for just a moment, nodded his head. 'I judge men by what I see, not what they tell me,' he said.

'And what do you see when you look at me?' I asked.

He laughed. 'I see a boy, but I also see one who has iron in his soul. I like iron, for it's the one thing I can trust and be sure of.'

It was my turn to smile. 'And I like men who are not afraid to speak plainly. I can see that you and I will get along well enough. Do you serve in the fyrd?' I pressed, thinking he was just the sort of man we needed.

'I do, my Lord, though my son here is not yet of age.'

As I looked the boy over it seemed to me that he was certainly old enough, but then decided he was better employed helping his father given how much work we needed him to do.

'Then we shall meet again. Leonfrith will tell you all that's required but fear not for your purse. I shall ensure that whatever's due is paid promptly – and in full.'

*****

As we returned to the Monastery, Aelred seemed amused. 'That fool at the Vill didn't put up much of a fight,' he said. 'I judge him to be a coward as he didn't have the guts to stand his ground, even when accosted in his own home!'

'And I've not done with him yet. It's Lord Werhard I feel sorry for. I don't think he was all that happy about me going ahead without consulting him.'

'He didn't seem overly concerned.'

'No, but I must show him due respect and not take his assent for granted just because he's old. Tell me, that rogue among his guard, the one I've taken against. Do you yet know his name?'

'He's called Otto,' he said. 'And you're not the only one who dislikes him.'

'Why do you say that?'

'The other guards think he enjoys too many favours for their liking. He sups ale with Oeric and they're often found together, almost like friends. Though what they have in common is hard to say.'

'That's interesting.'

'Why so?' asked Aelred.

'Let's just say that to my mind they make a natural pair. Both insolent and both so devious that I'm not sure which of them I distrust the most.' With that I noticed that Aelred's attention was focused on something in the trees to one side of us. 'What is it?' I asked.

'I thought I saw someone,' he said, his gaze still checking for any sign of movement.

'Where and how many?' I asked.

'Over yonder in those trees. I think it was just the one man, but he's now gone.'

'Probably a poacher then,' I suggested. 'No doubt anxious not to be seen.'

'Unlikely,' said Aelred. 'He'd have waited till it was dark before setting about taking game that doesn't belong to him.'

'Then we'd best be wary for I seem to have made a few enemies here already.'

'And you think someone might set about trying to harm us? That's a risk which has worried me all along, but I've not yet seen anyone man enough to try!'

'Maybe not in person. But they could have others do their dirty work for them.'

Aelred looked worried at that. 'You mean a paid assassin? I'd thought that might be a problem if we stayed at the Vill, but you're right, on these narrow tracks any skulking coward with a bow could take us down without even showing himself!'

'Exactly. So the sooner we can lodge at the mill the better,' I said. 'In the meantime, you watch to the right of the trail and I'll watch to the left. From now on we'll wear the leather jerkins when we ride out, just in case.'

We arrived back at the Monastery safely, but were greeted by one of the good brothers who it seemed had waited anxiously for our return. He rushed forward to greet us and hardly gave us a chance to dismount. 'My Lord, there's someone to see you,' he said taking the reins to both horses. 'A lady.'

My thoughts went immediately to Emelda, though I couldn't imagine how it could be her given that Alfred had sent her to a nunnery and wouldn't even tell me where. I asked the brother if he knew the name of this lady, but he just shook his head and looked flustered. 'A very beautiful lady,' was all he could manage before leading the horses away.

Aelred followed me into the Monastery where Father Gregory was also waiting. 'The lady has asked to see you as soon as you return, my Lord,' he said. 'I've shown her to my cell that she may rest there for a while for I gather she's travelled far even though she is with child.'

I went alone to the abbot's chamber and knocked on the door, then waited for an answer. As soon as I heard a voice entreating me to enter I knew it wasn't Emelda.

'What on earth are you doing here?' I asked as Ingar struggled to get up from the cot where she'd been resting. On seeing her, my first thought was that her beauty had faded and that she looked very tired, her features being drawn and overly wan. Certainly she was not as I remembered, even her flame red hair looked tangled and spoiled.

She struggled to her feet and although obviously pregnant, she wore a long shift which covered the swell to her belly.

'Matthew, I must speak with you,' she said, without even bothering with anything resembling a greeting.

I realised she meant alone so closed the door behind me. Then I bade her to sit once more on the cot. 'On what matter?' I asked.

'As I told you when last we met it was given that I would bear the children of two men at the same time. So it has come to pass.'

'Are you sure?'

'Of course I'm sure. But hear me in this. Both have the blood of their fathers in their veins. One Saxon and the other Viking. As I warned you, they will be as different as night and day and already they fight within my womb. When the time comes for their birth I fear they'll contest as to which of them will be the first to be born. The pains I suffer now will then be much worse and I know already that both will need to be cut from my womb.'

'But surely you can't…'

'Trust me, Matthew, that is the way of it. I shall not survive their birth so I must look to you to help me as once you said you would. I'm asking you to ease my pain when the time comes so they can both be freed. Their survival is more important than mine.'

'What, are you saying that you want me to…?'

'That's exactly what I'm asking. You must kill me then cut them from my womb. My life is of no consequence in this and you must therefore ensure their safety and protection, not only from all the ills in this world, but also from each other. And if you're no longer alive when the time comes, have Aelred promise to do it for you.'

'You can't ask this of me or of him!' I said, horrified at the prospect.

'Matthew, I will die in great pain if you don't and both babies will be lost. All I ask is that you, as a friend, help to ease my path from this world so that I can die in peace. As a warrior you'll know how and where to cut to cause as little pain as possible, but you must then act swiftly, for the babies cannot live long in my womb once I'm gone.'

I stared at her, hardly able to believe what she was saying.

'When it's done bury me in the forest, for I shall rest there more easily, but I want no marker for my grave. I desire simply to become a part of the earth.'

'You can't know all this for certain and may yet survive giving birth. Few are better placed to endure it than you with all your skills of healing.'

'It's my skills which tell me how it will be,' she said. 'I've tended enough women who are with child to know the signs, so trust me in this. What I'm saying is for the benefit of your child as much as it is for Ljot's.'

'I'm not sure that I can do what you ask,' I said. 'Are there no roots or potions you can take which will ease your pain?'

'None that would not harm the babies. You must therefore find the courage, for believe me, there's no other way.'

'And what then? Would you have me raise the bastard son of the slaver Ljot! Is that what you want me to do?'

She shook her head. 'No,' she assured me. 'Matthew, you look well enough but we both know that you're likely to die from your wound, perhaps even before these babies are born, so their welfare must be entrusted to others. They must also be separated at birth or one will surely kill the other,' she explained.

I must have looked stunned by all she'd said and could barely find the words I needed.

'Go now and speak with Father Gregory for he seems a goodly soul. He knows only that I fear I shall not survive giving birth, so therefore say nothing of what I've asked of you, for his creed would not countenance such a thing. But he is best placed to ensure the protection of both babies by finding two women who will love and cherish them. But remember, they must each go to a different home, they must not be reared together. In the meantime, could you find somewhere for me to rest during my confinement?'

Mystified and troubled, I turned to leave, intending to speak with Father Gregory as she'd asked.

'Matthew?' said Ingar. 'How is your wound?'

I hesitated before speaking. 'It fares well enough and barely troubles me,' I assured her.

'Just remember what I told you. You have the given years, nothing more. I hope for your sake they are many and fruitful, but, if so, don't take that as a sign of your body having healed. When the time comes it's likely to be without warning and for no obvious cause, so you must take care.'

I turned to face her again. 'I feel well enough,' I managed. 'But tell me, how did you find me here?'

She laughed. 'That was easy enough. It seems everyone has heard of the great warrior with the pierced heart. Your reputation led me here as surely as any trail.'

I acknowledged her point and then went to find Father Gregory. He was anxiously waiting with Aelred and rose to his feet as soon as I approached. 'Father this woman is known to me and, given that she is with child, I need to find somewhere she might rest.'

He looked at me sternly. 'She can't stay here, my Lord,' he said simply.

'Surely you can find a room for her?'

He looked at me suspiciously. 'Tell me, what is she to you?' he asked.

'She once saved my life when others would have deemed it lost,' I explained.

'Saved your life, my Lord? Using what, her pagan spells and incantations?'

'She has no spells or incantations, she's a Celt and as such her ways are those of the earth. She's a great healer and you could learn much from her.'

'Good God!' exclaimed Aelred, suddenly realising who we were talking about. Like me, he'd initially assumed it would be Emelda. 'You mean it's Ingar?' He quickly checked himself. 'She's surely a good woman despite her ways,' he managed.

'Even so, she can't stay here.'

'Why not?' I insisted. 'She offers no threat to you or to any of the brethren. As I said, there's much she could teach you. Besides, is it not your way to offer hospitality to all?'

'Even so, my Lord, she can't stay here,' he insisted even more firmly. 'And it's not because of her beliefs that I deny her.'

'Why then?' I pressed, trying not to sound angry.

'Because, my Lord, she's a woman – and one of great beauty. I cannot allow that she will distract the brothers from their devotions.'

'So what's to be done?' I asked him. 'As I said, she'll need care and shelter.'

'My Lord, are you the father of the child she bears?' he asked pointedly.

I nodded. 'It is possible,' I admitted. I decided to make no mention of Ljot, knowing that it would all be far beyond his understanding.

'Then there's one who could help, though her home is not fit for a lady who bears the child of one who is of noble birth…'

'Who do you have in mind?' I asked.

'You've met the good woman and her husband. His name is Wilfrid and she is called Aleesa. They are old and poor, but she's borne and raised four children of her own, thus knows the way of such things.'

I remembered the hovel in which they lived, but saw at once that it did make sense. Given that Ingar had been living in a cavern when I first met her I didn't think she'd mind sharing such humble accommodation, so nodded my agreement. 'I will insist on paying for her keep,' I said simply. 'For I know they're both in much need.'

With that settled, I decided to say no more about the fact that she was bearing twins, for I was sure Ingar would speak of that to Aleesa when the time came. As to what she required when the babies were born, that remained a matter for Aelred and I to determine and I saw no cause to inform anyone else.

*****

I went back to tell Ingar of all that had been agreed. 'Nearer the time I'll find two families who will each take one child, just as you've asked,' I assured her. 'For now, say nothing more on that subject.'

She seemed happy enough with that, but I wondered whether she would object to the babies being given to Christian families. When I asked her she said that it would make no difference so long as they were kept apart. 'All this is a part of the Earth Mother's great plan,' she said, looking relieved. 'She'll ensure that all is resolved according to her wont.'

'Not quite,' I said. 'You once told me that you'd conceived a daughter from our union, one who would assume your role as a healer, following in your mother's path and that of her mother before that.'

'That's true,' she said.

'Yet now you say that the infants fight within the womb. Surely that means that both the babies you carry must be boys?'

'Why do you assume as much? Do you not yet realise that some women have a strength well beyond what you might expect from their sex?'

'Strong enough to fight with the bastard son of a Viking?' I asked.

She smiled and I saw in that something of the Ingar I'd known at the cavern in the forest. 'The question is whether he will hold his own against a woman who has the strength of her father,' she said.

*****

Once alone, I told Aelred of what Ingar had said. 'She believes she cannot survive giving birth,' I explained. 'She's asked me to attend and if all transpires as she thinks it will, has charged me with cutting both babies from her womb. For that she says we'll need to kill her first.'

Aelred looked stunned. 'But you can't do that!'

'Well, you had better hope I can, for if I'm unable to the task then falls to you.'

'That would amount to murder!' he said.

'It would,' I agreed. 'Though I doubt if anyone would see it as such. After all, many women die in childbirth and she's asked to be buried in the forest with no marker for her grave so no one will be any the wiser.'

'Surely with her skills of healing it won't come to that?'

'Perhaps, but she seems convinced it will and what concerns me is that she's usually right on such matters.'

Chapter Eight

The following morning, Aelred and I escorted Ingar to the small farmstead where old Wilfrid and his wife lived, allowing her to ride in a cart which we'd borrowed from the Monastery. Because the road from there was steep and rutted, I feared she'd find even travelling like that hard, but she endured any discomfort without complaint.

When we arrived, Wilfrid and Aleesa seemed concerned to see us. 'My Lord, you are of course most welcome here, but I wonder what it is that brings you to our door?'

I dismounted and went across to speak him. 'I need a man I can trust on a matter of great importance to me,' I told him.

'My Lord…?' he asked, clearly concerned about what it was I intended to ask of him.

'This lady is with child and in need of care,' I explained. 'She's known to me and Father Gregory has suggested that you and your wife might be the ones who could tend to her needs. I will of course pay for her keep and for your trouble.'

Without hesitation, Aleesa went directly to the cart and helped Ingar down, then led her into their hovel where she began to prepare a cot on which Ingar could rest.

As Wilfrid still looked worried I thought it best to explain further. 'She's a healer who once saved my life,' I said. 'She also once helped both Aelred and myself to escape from slavers, so we've reason enough to see her well.'

'A healer you say, yet she cannot tend herself?'

'She'll know what needs to be done, but may lack the strength to do it,' I explained. 'All you and your wife need do is help her as best you can.' With that, and whilst Ingar wasn't looking, I gave him a few coins. More than satisfied with that, he promised to give Ingar whatever care she needed.

'Thank you. I'm anxious not to draw attention to her presence here, but will call by from time to time to see how she fares. If you need to get word to me, contact Father Gregory and he'll know how best to reach me.'

'Is it to be a secret then?' he asked, seemingly curious as to why that should be so.

I hesitated before replying. 'Not a secret as such, but there are those who may seek her out as her skills are in much demand and I would not have her troubled when she needs to rest.'

He looked at me in such a way as to imply that he knew that was not the truth of the matter, though stopped short of actually saying so. 'She's a very striking woman, my Lord,' he observed. 'Is she something more to you than a friend?'

I could see that he suspected that the child she carried was mine, but I could ill afford to admit as much to him. In any event, to speak to me thus on such a personal matter was greatly overstepping his position but, before I could rebuke him, he explained that he had good cause to ask.

'My Lord, I don't mean to pry, it's just that I need to know if there are those who might have cause to harm her.'

'Whatever she is to me is of no concern to anyone,' I said. 'But you were right to ask, for with all I'm charged to do in this Shire there are bound to be those who would rather see me gone. There could therefore be some cause for concern as to her safety so I would have you watch out for her on that account.'

With that Aelred and I bid farewell to Ingar, then thanked Wilfrid and his wife for their help, reminding them to contact me through Father Gregory if anything was needed. That done, we took the cart back to the Monastery and once again joined the brethren for a sparse meal of broth and dry bread.

Once we'd eaten and refreshed ourselves, we started out towards Leatherhead once more, both wearing our jerkins as proof against any would-be assassin. As we had time to spare, we followed a different route which we thought might give us a chance to assess yet more of the Shire, something I needed to do so that I got to know it better. The track we followed was as straight as the shaft of a spear, only occasionally veering to one side or the other to avoid a large tree or a hollow. At one point it passed through a forest of oak and alder whilst following the line of a muddy ditch. We were not paying much mind to the problems we faced at Leatherhead as meeting Ingar again had set us both to reminiscing about the time we'd spent together as captives of Ljot and his band of slavers. As such we failed to notice a hooded figure in the trees who, unbeknown to either Aelred or I, had been following us, probably since leaving the Monastery that afternoon.

At first he kept his distance, tracking us whilst using whatever cover he could find. Once we had both seen him, we kept a close watch on his movements but he suddenly ducked into the undergrowth and disappeared from view. Fearing the worst, we stopped and scanned the trees for any sign of him. Then, without warning, he stepped boldly into the open, raised his bow and loosed an arrow that sped direct towards us. Instinctively, both Aelred and I ducked as the arrow embedded itself in a tree, barely missing my shoulder.

Aelred leaped from his horse and used it as cover. I, on the other hand, was anxious to remain in the saddle so that I could better surmise whether there were others with him who might also be intent on harming us.

'Over there!' said Aelred, pointing to a figure who seemed to lope between the trees. I couldn't see clearly beyond the fact that the man was wearing a dark hooded cloak and was still carrying a bow.

Aelred immediately started to give chase, but I called him back lest the assassin turn on him to shoot again, fearing that a second arrow might prove more deadly than the first.

As he came to stand beside me again I reached out and pulled the arrow from the tree, then examined it.

'You were lucky,' said Aelred as I handed it to him to look at. 'It would seem that somebody does indeed want you killed.'

'Well, whoever he was, he was working alone. We should be grateful for that.'

Aelred remarked that the arrow seemed well made and noted that it had a metal head, which suggested that the man's intent was indeed to kill.

'I doubt that,' I said as I took it and examined it again before putting it into one of the bags attached to my saddle. 'More likely it was a warning.'

'A warning!' queried Aelred. 'Pah! He couldn't have come closer to killing you if he'd tried!'

'Exactly,' I said. 'The arrow was made by a man who knows his craft. As such if he'd meant me killed he wouldn't have missed, not at that range at least.'

'A warning from whom?' he asked.

'Well, I can think of at least one man who would rather I wasn't here.'

'You mean that fat oaf Oeric? Then we'd best have a few more words with him.'

'All in good timc,' I said. 'But I'll wager that if he set this rogue on to us he'll have a dozen men or more who'll swear he was with them at this time. If we're to accuse him then we need first to gather proof, but, in the meantime, we must mind our backs even more closely.'

*****

It was mid-afternoon by the time we reached Leatherhead. With yet a few hours before it was fully dark we went straight to the Common Field where the members of the fyrd were already waiting. As Leonfrith had said, there were nine of them, all looking reasonably strong and able. The tenth man would have been Eagbert, the blacksmith, but he'd been excused duty on the grounds that he had so much work to do in forging the weapons and the ironmongery needed for building the stronghold. Leonfrith confirmed he'd taken down the names of all those who were present and sent word for the guards at the Vill to join us.

I gave the list of names to Aelred and asked him to call them out so we could identify each of the men in turn. He seemed to struggle with the list until I realised for the first time that he couldn't read. To save him embarrassment, I hastily took it back and asked Leonfrith to read it aloud instead whilst Aelred inspected each of the men as they stepped forward in answer to their name.

As they were all freemen, they were entitled to be treated with due respect, but were a mixed band and all I hoped was that they would at least have some idea of how to fight. Their number included the forester, Godric, and two brothers, Aethelred and Aethelbert. The elder of the two seemed to speak for them both whilst the younger one, who seemed slow and shy, barely said a word except to answer his name when called. There was also a thatcher and a man who I was told was a tanner. The rest were all farmers who had smallholdings just outside the settlement and included a father and his son.

No sooner had we read the names than all eight guards from the Vill arrived, marching in an untidy gang rather than as an ordered troop. They were each wearing a rather basic mail tabard and a helmet but were armed with only a spear, a seax and a shield.

Aelred glanced at me then ordered them to line up alongside the members of the fyrd.

'Where are the other weapons for the fyrd to use?' I asked Otto.

'They each bring their own,' he sneered.

'Not any more they don't! It's your Lord's duty to see them properly armed,' I said harshly. 'Like everything else around here such responsibility seems to have been much neglected.'

'There are some bows plus a few more spears and shields at the Vill, but otherwise this is all we have,' explained Leonfrith.

I turned to Otto and barked my orders. 'Then fetch them here and be quick about it!'

Otto seemed to think that it was beneath him so turned to order one of the more junior guards to oblige.

'No, you useless fool,' I bellowed. 'You couldn't be trusted to sharpen the weapons, never mind wield one in battle! You've no place here so fetch the spears yourself. After that your job is to man the Vill whilst the real warriors are training.'

As we watched him stalk off, Aelred was grinning. 'I think you've frightened the poor wretch half to death,' he said.

'I'll do more than frighten him. And that's nothing compared to what a Viking warband will do if they catch him or any of these men so ill prepared.'

I asked the guard nearest me his name and he said he was called Osmund. I recognised him as one of those who'd accompanied me back to Winchester after my first visit to Leatherhead and of whom I'd formed a good impression at the time.

'My Lord, I need to know that Lord Oeric is aware that we're here,' he said.

'I don't know, but Lord Werhard does and it's him you answer to, is it not?'

He acknowledged the point, though still looked concerned.

'Don't worry, we're close enough to the Vill to be on hand if needed. Now, in Otto's absence I need to appoint someone to command the fyrd. Are you the man for that?'

He looked pleased at the prospect. 'I will strive to do my best, my Lord,' he offered.

'I ask no more than that of any man. Have you any skill with that spear?'

He glanced at the men on either side of him. 'My Lord I've trained as much as any man here,' he said sheepishly. 'And have practised more than most.'

'I somehow don't think that amounts to very much. Have you ever been in a battle and stood in the shield wall?'

'Only once, my Lord.'

'And have you ever faced a man in armed combat?'

He grinned. 'I have, my Lord. Apart from the battle, it was once left to me to apprehend a villain who'd been stealing cattle. He wasn't overly anxious to be taken knowing that the noose awaited him.'

'Did you kill him?'

He looked at me. 'I was ready to, my Lord, but was able to avoid it. I put him down and, with others here, dragged him back for trial.'

It was a good answer. I wanted men who were not afraid to fight but didn't kill for the sake of it. 'Good, then I think your best efforts will suffice. You shall answer to me and to Aelred in these matters, none other. But now we must see which of these rogues can be relied upon to serve alongside you.'

As Osmund started to form them into a rank, Leonfrith asked my permission to leave and go to the mill where he wanted to check his measurements for the stockade, which of course I agreed to at once. Aelred then came across to discuss what I had in mind. 'First let's see what they can do,' I suggested. 'Though we can't afford to be choosy for they're all we have to work with.'

'And the guards from the Vill?' he asked.

'As I told Oeric, we can use them all except that fool Otto. He's too disrespectful and we don't have the time to teach him the error of his ways. Besides, he'll mislead the others and cause dissent if we let him, which is why I've set him to guard the Vill. He can call us back if needed, though if Hakon was to arrive in force I reckon we'd all know about it long before he troubled to stir himself.'

'He didn't seem overly pleased at being left out,' noted Aelred.

'I don't mean to please him or anyone else for that matter. Pleasing them won't stand for much once the Vikings descend upon us. What I mean to do is form a small squad of warriors I can rely on if it comes to a battle. For that they'll need discipline as well as an ability to handle their weapons. I doubt our friend Otto has either. The question now is do any of the others?'

Apart from the members of the Vill guard, only about half of those assembled had anything which could be described as war gear. Some had helmets or leather caps which had been scavenged from what had been left on some previous battlefield and several had some sort of seax, though most of those looked to be old and tarnished. Two men, including Godric, carried axes which had probably been taken from the byre or more likely the woodpile and were thus barely fit for use as a weapon. The rest carried nothing more than a staff.

'It's just as well they haven't managed to find the Vikings,' said Aelred loud enough for them all to hear. 'They'd have been slaughtered if they had.'

'Who here as ever been in a battle?' I demanded.

Needless to say, apart from the guards from the Vill, only three men raised their hands.

'Who then has any skill with a weapon, be it spear, staff, axe or bow?'

To a man, the guards all said they had and several of the others said they knew how to use a bow, probably more as a tool for hunting than as a weapon. Most claimed some skill with a staff.

I walked along the line looking at each man in turn. 'Know this,' I shouted. 'My name is Matthew, christened Edward,' I told them, repeating what I'd said at the Moot in case there were some there who hadn't attended. 'I'm the third born son of Lord Edwulf. I'm also a warrior and I commanded part of Lord Alfred's army at Edington where we scored a famous victory over the Vikings. I learned my craft at the hand of my brother, Lord Edwin, who perished there but was one of the finest warriors in all Wessex. I am come here to train you on orders from Lord Alfred himself, for it has come to his attention that your battle skills are woefully lacking whilst raiders in these parts make free wherever they chose to strike.'

I paused there, waiting for any sort of response, meaning to take anyone who spoke out of turn to task, but all were silent. I'd deliberately not mentioned that I was also known as the warrior with the pierced heart, though Aelred later told me that rumours of that had been rife given that all the thanes knew following my meeting with them.

With that Otto arrived carrying the weapons which he left in a pile, then, without another word, returned to his duties at the Vill.

Once he'd gone, I continued to address those assembled. 'This man is Aelred who will train you in the art of combat, aided by Osmund. I advise you to listen to all they say, for your lives may well depend on it.'

'My Lord, who is he that he might train us how to fight?' asked Cedric, a strong man who was also a member of the guard and looked able to give a good account of himself.

I glanced at Aelred who knew at once what I was thinking. He nodded his agreement so I called Cedric over, telling him to bring his shield and spear with him. 'I order you try Aelred's hand,' I said. 'He will then show you what you can learn from him.'

'But my Lord, he's unarmed,' said Cedric.

With that Aelred stepped forward. Instinctively, Cedric moved back and raised his spear, jabbing with it as though he meant to hold Aelred at bay. But they were weak, half-hearted strokes, intended more as a warning than anything else and certainly defensive. With lightning speed, Aelred seized the shaft of the spear and used it to pull his man sharply towards him. He then twisted the spear and deftly snatched it away from the guard. Barely had poor Cedric realised what had happened than Aelred struck him with the shaft so hard in the belly that he was winded. A second blow upended him and sent him sprawling to the ground. He dropped his shield in the process and almost at once Aelred was on to him with the spear point pressed against his throat.

'Now fool, would you have me skewer you and thereby finish the lesson, or have you learned enough from me for now?'

Cedric got up, collected his weapon and his shield then sloped back to the line.

'That was done so easily because it's hard to wield a spear with any force whilst holding a shield, but it's something you must all learn,' I told them. 'Right, now stand up tall and straight, not crouching with your shoulders hunched and rounded like puny boys. Be firm, be strong and be proud, for you are all Saxons, are you not?'

I waited whilst they all did as I'd ordered. 'From now on you will train every evening for the next two weeks, by which time you'll know how to fight.'

'But, my Lord, we have fields to tend and…'

'Unless you learn how to defend what's yours you won't have your fields for very much longer, will you? Do I make myself clear?'

There was a murmur of assent.

'I said do I make myself clear!'

This time they all spoke louder and none complained. 'Tomorrow when you come here you're to form your line like this. Stout and firm. You're to bring your weapons with you and I expect them to be fit for purpose – spears and knives sharpened, shields mended and anything else properly honed or strengthened. From then on you bring what weapons you have every time you're summoned. Any man who fails to do so will warrant three lashes. The penalty for failing to bring them to a battle may be worse, for that may well cost you your life.'

*****

We shared a meagre supper with the monks that night, washed down with a stronger mead than was served during the day, but one which we learned they'd also brewed for themselves.

'We've had worse fare,' said Aelred as we walked together after supper. He was no doubt thinking of the time we'd spent as captives of the slavers.

'We've also had better,' I remarked, though regretted it for it seemed churlish to be ungrateful for hospitality which was so freely given. 'What do you think about the man who shot that arrow at us earlier?' I asked. 'Do you think he also followed us to old Wilfrid's farmstead when we took Ingar there?'

'You mean does he know she's there?' he asked.

'Exactly,' I said. 'I'd prefer that as few people as possible know of her presence. After all, I've made few friends here and some powerful enemies.'

'Yes, you've done well on that account,' teased Aelred. 'So far you've upset the local thanes, one of the guards at the Vill and most of the fyrd. You've also offended an Ealdorman and held your seax to the throat of an Ealdorman's son.'

I laughed. 'Yes, that's about the way of it,' I admitted. 'Now all we have to do is learn which of them was responsible for some wretch shooting an arrow at us in the forest.'

'Then let's hope they make their next move soon and choose somewhere we can deal with them as we should,' he said. 'Mind, it won't be as simple as that. It never is where you're involved. You seem to thrive on danger and live your whole life under a threat of one kind or another.'

'There speaks the man who follows my every step of his own accord,' I replied. 'It seems you've a nose for danger almost as keen as my own.'

'So, if asked, what do we say to explain Ingar's presence at the farmstead?' asked Aelred.

'We'll say simply that she faces a difficult confinement and is being cared for by a kind woman who knows the way of such matters. None will find that strange.'

With that Father Gregory came to join us, seemingly glad of the chance for some conversation which didn't revolve around the administration of the Monastery.

'Father, I hope that Ingar's coming here didn't prove too much of a distraction. I much respect your work and although now a warrior in the service of the King, I too was once a monk so know full well how such things can prove unsettling in a community such as this.'

What I said was clearly no surprise to him. 'My Lord, I wondered whether you had once been in Holy Orders when you told me that you were used to life in an Abbey,' he said.

'I never progressed beyond being a novice,' I admitted.

'Even so, my Lord, leaving your order to make your way in the world is a great change for any man.'

'I believe it is God's will,' I explained. 'Just as I believe he would have me support your work. As I told you, the woman who came here saved my life and, although a Celt, is a skilled and learned healer. She needs care which I hope the good people she now lodges with may provide. I've told them to inform you of anything she needs and will willingly meet whatever cost is involved. I should like also to repay you in some way for all you've done for her.'

He looked a little hurt.

'In offering this, I mean no offence to your creed of hospitality but am grateful for that which you've already provided for Aelred and myself.'

'Tell me, my Lord. Do you regard this woman's welfare as so important because she bears your child?' he asked. 'If so, is your offer intended merely to salve your own conscience?'

I wasn't quite sure how to respond, for I saw nothing in Ingar's condition for which I needed to reproach myself and thus my conscience was clear in that respect. 'No, Father, I assure you it's nothing of the sort. I seek only to make good whatever harm has been done in her coming here, for I can well understand what effect her presence has had on an otherwise tranquil and celibate order.'

'I see,' he said. 'And you have no other motive in mind?'

I assured him that I hadn't. 'Will you therefore allow me to make some modest restitution?'

He thought about that for a moment. 'I shall pray on this, my Lord,' he said. 'And I shall also offer prayers for this woman and for her child who is as yet unborn. But I would not normally accept payment for that which we are already sworn to provide. However, if I find that your offer is meant as an act of generosity and doesn't stem from self-interest, I may be minded to accept it as it would then accord with our own creed in such matters. But none here shall benefit as a result, be assured of that. If any do I shall require them to do penance and to seek forgiveness.'

*****

It was later that same evening that one of the monks returned from having visited a number of the farmsteads, including Wilfrid's, taking a charitable donation of food and produce. He seemed much troubled. 'You must go there, my Lord. And I pray that you make what haste you can.'

'Why? What's happened?'

'They would not say my Lord, but implored me to tell you that you are both much needed there,' he told me, his voice filled with concern.

Aelred and I grabbed our weapons and left at once. Carrying torches to light our way, we rode hard towards the farmstead and, as soon as we were near enough to be heard, I called out. As there came no reply, I hurriedly dismounted and drew my sword, then rushed inside where I found Wilfrid cowering in one corner with his wife beside him, his arm around her as if to comfort her. 'Where's Ingar?' I demanded.

Wilfrid pointed outside but otherwise made no attempt to move. I went around behind the hovel where I found Ingar standing over the body of a man. I raised the torch to see more clearly, but his was not a face I recognised. Moments later Aelred joined me.

Ingar was clearly much troubled by whatever had transpired. She was shaking and her face looked as pale as death. 'He came here to kill me,' she muttered. 'Why would he do that? What have I done to deserve such treatment from a man I've never even seen before?'

I bent down to look at the body more closely and could see that he'd been stabbed with a pitchfork which still lay on the ground to one side of him, the prongs bloodied and one of them bent.

'What happened?' I asked.

Ingar composed herself. 'I don't know, but I believe he came to kill me. Thankfully Wilfrid saw him and also saw that he had a sword in his hand so slew him before he could harm anyone here.'

'Then he did well,' I said, though the weapon he'd been carrying was not a sword but a seax.

'God's truth!' muttered Aelred. 'To take on a man armed with a seax with nothing but a pitchfork. That takes guts!'

'I took him by surprise,' said a voice from behind us. 'What will come of it, my Lord? Will I hang for having killed this man?' pleaded Wilfrid who was clearly very frightened.

I shook my head. 'No, you'll not hang for what happened here,' I assured him.

'Then what of my soul, will that not be tarnished by the crime?'

'You acted in defence of another not for profit or for any advantage to yourself, so have no fear for your soul. Yet you should concern yourself in this world for he may have friends who'll seek revenge. It's therefore best we be rid of him and say nothing.'

Wilfrid looked worried. 'But how, my Lord? What of the body and…?'

'Don't worry about the body. We'll take it away from here and leave it somewhere in the forest. By the time the crows and the wolves are done with it none will recognise it and therefore there'll be no way of knowing of your hand in this.'

Aelred sneered. 'They won't think it strange that the wolves used a pitchfork to kill him?' he queried.

It was a good point. 'Fetch three arrows,' I ordered.

'Why, what are planning?' asked Aelred.

'You'll see.'

When Wilfrid had fetched the arrows, I took them and inserted one into each of the holes made by the prongs of the pitchfork, pushing them in hard then snapping off the shafts.

'What purpose does that serve?' queried Aelred. 'All you've done is to spoil three perfectly good arrows!'

'You and I will report that we were attacked by a bowman and have his arrow to prove it. If the remains of this knave are ever discovered whoever shot at us will take the blame for his death as well.'

Aelred grinned, clearly liking the plan. 'Well, whoever this bowman is he must be a very good shot.'

'Why do you say that?' I asked.

'To land three arrows in a man's chest in such a perfect line and so evenly spaced is well beyond the skill of most men, myself included.'

I had to admit he had a point, but could think of no other option.

'So what do we do now?' asked Aelred.

'You stay here in case anyone comes back to finish the job this fool made such a mess of. I'll get rid of the body whilst it's dark. I'll take it to the forest and just dump it somewhere far from the track and leave it there for the wild beasts to do with as they will.'

'But, my Lord, will I not need to make confession for my crime?' asked Wilfrid, clearly still not at ease with all I'd said.

'If you feel the need for confession, go to your priest and tell him all that transpired. He'll tell no one for his calling forbids him to speak of anything told to him within the sanctity of the confessional.'

We all agreed it was a good plan so we returned to join Aleesa in order to set about putting it into effect.

'Are you all right?' I asked Ingar.

She looked at me and nodded, though still seemed very distant.

'Had he any cause to harm you?' asked Aelred.

She shook her head, still having no idea who the man was or why he wanted her dead.

'To get at me,' I reasoned. 'This is the handiwork of those who would see us gone from here. Does anyone recognise this man?'

Nobody did. Even Wilfrid who said he'd lived in the Shire all his life had never seen the man before.

'A stranger then,' I said. 'So perhaps he was a paid assassin.'

'Do you think he's the one who shot the arrow at us earlier?' asked Aelred.

I shrugged, for neither of us could say for certain as we didn't get much of a chance to see the rogue at the time.

'Well, he's not dressed the same,' ventured Aelred. 'That could mean we still have another knave to worry about. So what do we do now?'

'For a start we have to get Ingar away from here. If they've tried to kill her once they may do so again now they know where she is.'

'But where to?' asked Aelred. 'Apart from the Monastery, this is as safe a place as could be devised.'

I thought for a moment. 'To Winchester,' I said at last. 'You could take her there where Lord Alfred could keep her safe and she could also receive what help she needs.'

'How am I supposed to do that?'

'I'll give you letters that will ensure you can speak to Lord Alfred in person. It'll take you no more than four or perhaps five days so I can manage here until you return.'

'I'm supposed to be minding your back!'

'I'll be fine. If they'd meant to kill me I'd surely be dead by now. All this is intended just to warn me.'

It was Wilfrid who then spoke. 'I'm sorry I've caused you this problem, my Lord. I meant only...'

I put my hand on his shoulder. 'You did well and I thank you for it. Have no concern about the consequence of your actions, I shall ensure no blame attaches to you. With your permission once I've rid you of this worthless corpse Aelred and I will stay here tonight in case this wretch wasn't working alone.'

With that I went outside and, with Aelred's help, dragged the body over to where our horses waited and together we laid it over Aelred's saddle. I then mounted my own horse and turned to leave. 'I shall be back shortly,' I said. 'Stay here till I return.'

Leading Aelred's horse, I rode back towards the forest and, once a good way from the farmstead, cut the ropes securing the body and let it fall to the ground. I made a token effort to cover the remains with leaves then rode back to join the others.

Chapter Nine

Leaving Aelred to watch over Ingar, I returned to the Monastery the next morning, there to see Father Gregory. In private, I told him part of what had transpired, omitting to mention that it was Wilfrid who had actually killed the stranger, knowing he'd assume it had been either Aelred or myself.

'And you say that no one recognised this man, my Lord?' he asked.

'No, Father, even Wilfrid has never seen him before.'

'Is it not possible then that he was just a wastrel or a thief?'

'Perhaps, though it seems unlikely that old Wilfrid and Aleesa would have much worth stealing,' I reasoned. 'Also, he was armed so I think his intentions were plain enough.'

I could tell that the good father was particularly concerned about something – something he seemed almost afraid to mention. 'My Lord, I pray that I'm mistaken in this, but I fear that some of the good people of this Shire may have learned of Ingar's pagan ways and taken it upon themselves to drive her away from here.'

It was a possibility I hadn't even considered, but, if true, the implications could be very serious indeed, particularly if it had resulted in the death of a man – even if he was a stranger. I knew well enough that fear and superstition could make people behave in such a way, particularly in defence of their faith. Indeed, I recalled how Aelred and I had experienced something similar whilst trying to find our way back to Chippenham having escaped from the slavers. We'd been turned away without compassion from several settlements simply because they believed I'd consorted with pagans and had returned from the dead. Despite that, I dismissed the thought as I remained convinced that harming Ingar was intended as a warning to me, yet I admit that it suited my purpose to have the abbot believe otherwise. 'Well, whatever the truth of it,' I told him, 'I must now move her to a place of safety for she could be much at risk if she remains where she is.'

'So where will you take her?' he asked.

'If your fears are right, I think it best that I don't say and thereby keep her whereabouts a secret. I mean no offence, Father, but someone must have told others where she was staying. If you'll allow me to borrow the cart once more I'll have Aelred take her as far from here as we can manage.'

He agreed without hesitation. 'But are you sure you've told me all?' he pressed.

'Father, I've told you all I can,' I assured him.

He didn't answer at first. 'My Lord, if it was you who killed this stranger you must repent the sin,' he managed at last, sounding even more sombre than usual. 'The salvation of your soul depends on it.'

I hesitated before speaking, anxious not to say more than was needed about what had actually happened. 'Father, I've killed many men,' I admitted. 'But always with good cause. Whilst I regret the death of each and every one of them, in this matter my conscience is clear.'

He hurriedly made the sign of the cross. 'Just be wary in what you say, my Lord,' he warned. 'You've indeed come a long way since being a novice, but always remember that God can look into our hearts and see us for what we truly are. You cannot hide your sin from Him, any more than you can shield your soul with lies and denials.'

I acknowledged the truth of that but said nothing more. Even so, it seemed that the abbot was far from done.

'Very well, my Lord. I don't know what really happened last night and perhaps I never will,' he said as if resigned to that. 'But as you well know, without confession you cannot be absolved of whatever part you played.'

'Thank you, Father. But there's nothing I need to confess about what transpired last night. Whilst my part in what was done was against the laws of man, it was not against the laws of God.'

* * * * *

I borrowed the cart and, with my horse tethered behind it, set off towards Wilfrid's farmstead. My thought was that it would be easier for Ingar to travel in the cart, so I rendered it as comfortable as possible with straw to serve as cushioning and woollen blankets to keep her warm. When I reached Wilfrid's farmstead Ingar was ready and waiting, her few belongings having been placed in a sack.

'I've given Aelred a letter for him to take to Lord Alfred explaining your plight,' I told her. 'He already knows all that which passed between us and is a good and wise man. I'm sure he'll help you and you should be safe enough once away from here.'

'I'd prefer to stay with you,' she said simply.

'You can't. I have enemies here and am likely to make yet more. Any harm they could do to you will be a way of hurting me. If they now know where you are you're far from safe.'

Wilfrid still looked worried about having killed the man so I did what I could to reassure him. 'They'll never find the body,' I told him. 'And even if they do, there won't be much left of it and certainly nothing that will lead them to your door.'

He seemed more at ease with that then offered back the coins I'd given him to cover Ingar's keep, but I refused to accept them. 'Your task was to keep her safe and you've done all any man could in that respect. In fact, it's only thanks to you that she's still alive.'

'But it's blood money!' hissed Aleesa bitterly. 'No good can come of it!'

'It's nothing of the sort,' I assured them. 'It's simply what was offered for the care you agreed to provide. You've done what was asked of you so have earned what was promised. Besides, from all I've seen, you're honest Saxon folk who've been poorly treated. Perhaps this will help to provide some small measure of comfort for you both.'

For a moment they still looked uncertain as to whether they should accept it, but, in the end, just nodded their agreement.

'That was generous,' said Aelred once we'd left the farmstead. He was driving the cart with Ingar resting in the back whilst I rode alongside them.

'I think they deserve something for all they've suffered,' I said. 'You and I have grown used to having blood on our hands and sometimes forget that for many such a thing is a huge burden even in these wretched times – and one which will surely trouble them.'

'Killing never comes easy,' said Aelred.

'Aye,' I agreed. 'It still troubles me to take a life even when it's warranted, but then I seldom seem to have much choice.'

'So, do you still reckon the man who was killed back there was the one who attacked us in the forest?' he asked.

I shrugged, for it was impossible to say. 'As like as not it was,' I managed. 'For I doubt Oeric would pay for two assassins, but we'll find out the truth of that soon enough.'

'That's what worries me,' said Aelred. 'Are you're certain it's safe to remain here on your own?'

'Don't worry, I can look after myself,' I assured him.

'Matthew,' said Ingar, joining the conversation. 'Have you told Lord Alfred about what to do when the time comes for me to give birth?'

'No,' I admitted. 'He would neither understand nor approve. But Aelred here will do what's needed if anything should happen to me.'

'And you'll do that?' she asked Aelred pointedly. 'You'll ease my path from this world then cut both babies from my womb and ensure they're separated from the moment they're born?'

I left Aelred to answer for himself, but he seemed to be struggling to find the words. 'I'll oblige if I can,' he promised somewhat reluctantly. 'No man can say more than that. But I'm hoping to keep Matthew alive long enough for him to do it so I won't have to.'

'Don't worry, I'll be there,' I said laughing. 'My wound barely troubles me at all these days, though I know you still believe it will yet be the death of me.'

'I do,' she said firmly. 'But only fate knows where and when that will happen. Until then just take care. You're a good man, Matthew, and there are now few enough of those in this troubled realm.'

* * * * *

I reckoned that travelling by cart, the journey to Winchester and back would take Aelred at least five days, possibly longer if the weather turned against them or if Ingar was unwell during the journey. I gave him coin so that he could secure food and accommodation for them both each night and thereby render Ingar as much comfort as possible. He also carried a bow and his spear – not to hunt, but to defend himself if needed. I rode with them as far as Leatherhead and saw them safe on to the Harroway. Then, having bid them farewell, I had duties enough of my own to attend to.

* * * * *

Recalling all Alfred had told me about Lord Werhard being so well trusted, I was anxious to speak with him again in private, but could never seem to do so. Whenever I'd enquired after him I'd been told that he was either resting or that he couldn't be disturbed. Without any evidence to the contrary, I couldn't clear him of neglecting his responsibility to protect the people of his Shire, yet I was convinced that all the blame lay with his greedy stepson. Even so, it was for him to appoint someone competent to administer matters in his stead and I was anxious to know why he hadn't done so.

'I think he's frightened of his stepson,' Aelred had told me when we'd discussed the matter a day or so earlier. 'So much so that the greedy bastard gets away with everything.'

Before attempting to speak with Lord Werhard on these matters and thereby ascertain the truth of them, I went again to see the blacksmith who I'd asked to make up the spear points, arrowheads and all the items which would be needed to construct the fortifications.

'You were missed at the training session last night,' I pointed out.

For once he actually looked up at me before answering. 'I spoke with Leonfrith about that and told him that I needed every hour of daylight God sends just to prepare all you need from me. He agreed my time would be better spent here than in training.'

I knew as much for Leonfrith had already cleared that with me, so acknowledged the explanation. 'That's all to the good,' I told him. 'So how many have you finished?'

He promptly fetched half a dozen spears all of which he'd fitted with shafts cut from ash. He assured me he would have others ready in time to bring to the training session that evening. 'I shall also attend in person, for it's some time since I did so,' he offered.

I examined the spears and could not help but admire his handiwork. The spear points were all keenly sharpened and the shafts were long and straight. I told him I was impressed. 'But what of all the other gear Leonfrith needs for the stockade?' I asked.

'I've already given him nails and such like to be going on with and have lent him chains and pulleys to serve as lifting gear. I'll start working on the arrowheads and forge more nails tomorrow.'

I thanked him, but as I turned to walk away he said something which puzzled me.

'My Lord Matthew, are you leading us all to our deaths or to yet more glory for yourself?' he asked.

It was a fair question, but beyond anything he had the right to ask. More importantly, he was taking a liberty in addressing me by name. I took no offence, but couldn't let it pass lest that degree of familiarity should become common to others. 'Though I fancy that you and I would stand well together in battle, you must remember your station,' I advised.

He looked at me long and hard then seemed to take my point. 'I call a man by his name as a sign of respect, not use his title to infer undue deference.'

It was a good answer so I found it hard to rebuke him. 'Even so,' I said. 'I must retain the respect of all the men here. But in answer to your question, I already have enough glory as it is. What I need now is good men who will stand firm beside me when the time comes. Thus I mean to ensure that as few of them as possible are slain or even injured.'

*****

Having left the forge, I went directly to Lord Werhard's Vill and, knowing I would be offered the usual excuses as to why I couldn't see him, I ignored the guards and simply marched past them without so much as a word. Given my authority, none of them tried to stop me except one. Needless to say, it was Otto who challenged me.

Even the sight of Otto was enough to rile me so I walked over and stood directly in front of him. 'The other day in the forest a man tried to cut me down with this arrow,' I said, producing the arrow and using the point of it to prod his chest.

'So, what's that to do with me, my Lord?' he asked.

'That's what I mean to find out. And if I find proof that you or anyone else here had a hand in it, I'll take my sword and drive it deep into their belly. Is that clear enough or shall I give you a taste of how that might feel?'

'My Lord…' he protested.

'You've been warned. In the meantime, I'm growing weary of your insolence. From now on, if even your shadow so much as crosses my path without my consent, I'll thrash you to within a hair's breadth of your life. Do I make myself clear?'

He swallowed hard then nodded.

'Good. Now get out of my sight before my wrath forces me to do something I may later regret.'

To push my way in thus was, in itself, a gross discourtesy, but at that point I saw no cause to show Oeric any respect and anyway, I was still intent on provoking him.

'The arrangements for the fyrd are a disgrace!' I shouted as I burst into the main Hall where I expected him to be. 'Have you no concern for the safety of the Shire?'

All the shutters were closed and the Hall was in darkness save for a few torches which flickered lamely in the entrance so that I could barely see him or indeed anything else in there. But I heard him right enough. 'Such impudence!' he bellowed struggling to his feet but remaining in the shadows. 'You've been here for what – barely a week, yet already you think you know the way of things!'

'I know what I've seen,' I said, moving deeper into the Hall. 'And I think you do as well.'

'Be gone from here, you've no right to barge in like this!'

I ignored him and moved closer. From there I could see a girl who was all but naked. She grabbed her clothes and tried to cover herself, then cowered in one corner, pressing herself back against one wall.

'Oh, so that's what keeps you so busy!' I said accusingly.

He looked at the girl then back at me. He was only part dressed himself and certainly wasn't armed. That being so he called for the guards.

I drew my sword in anticipation of their arrival. 'That's right,' I challenged. 'Call for help. And much good may it do you!'

'Mind your tongue or I'll have them remove you from here by force! This is my Hall and you've not been invited! I'll have the guards throw you out like a common thief!'

'Your Hall?' I queried. 'I thought we'd established that it belongs to your stepfather, not to you. But have it your own way. Summon your men and with luck you may find at least one of them not asleep at his post. Oh, and don't worry, if any do come running I shall make very quick work of them!'

With that I left. As I reached the small entrance lobby I noticed Lord Werhard following me from the Hall having no doubt been disturbed by all the noise.

'What's this?' he demanded looking at my still drawn sword. 'Matthew, you've no right to draw a blade in my Hall!' he said angrily. 'Alfred shall hear of this; you mark my words!'

'Alfred shall hear of many things, my Lord,' I said calmly. 'He shall hear how your Vill is so poorly guarded, how the fyrd have no proper weapons and how the man who is supposed to train them barely bothers to call them to arms even though you suffer more raids than any other Shire in the realm.'

'I'm still Ealdorman here,' said Lord Werhard. 'And I run this Shire as I see fit.'

'Then I'm sorry, for I gather you were once much trusted by the King.'

'What of it?' he challenged.

I'd calmed down by then and, remembering my station, sheathed my sword and carefully secured the peace tie to make it clear that I was no longer intent on violence. 'I'm sorry to be so blunt, my Lord, but all my attempts to see you have been thwarted by that oaf you call a stepson. Or at least, by those acting under his orders.'

Lord Werhard came closer and seemed unsure of what to say. He knew I had cause, but to burst into his Hall, with or without a drawn sword, was a grave offence. As Ealdorman, even if only in name, he was entitled to more respect than I'd shown him.

'My Lord, it is incumbent on you to ensure that those you appoint to run affairs in your stead do so diligently and in accordance with the responsibilities of your office. From all I've seen that duty has been neglected and—'

I stopped abruptly as he stepped closer and the light from one of the torches near the entrance made him suddenly more visible. As it did so, I noticed that the side of his face was bruised and heavily swollen beneath one eye. It was then that I realised what was really happening within the Vill.

'My Lord,' I muttered under my breath. 'Who treated you thus?' Of course, I already knew the answer.

The old man looked at me defiantly. 'This is nothing! I got what I deserved for I should never have said anything to you when first you came here. All I've done is brought trouble to our doors.'

'I thought you wanted help,' I reasoned.

'Well I don't!' he snapped. 'Just leave us be for there's nothing you can do here.'

'But Lord Alfred…'

'If Alfred is so concerned why does he send a mere boy and a wretched coerl to resolve matters? Most likely he needed something useful for the pair of you to do and so sent you here for no other reason than it's a goodly way from Winchester.'

'Believe what you will,' I said, realising that the fault was mine, for I'd not recognised that the old man was being controlled by violence. It also explained why he was always 'resting', for Oeric had good cause to ensure that none could see the markings of his temper. I decided to say no more, for he would soon see what a mere boy could do, but one thing was certain, his stepson wasn't going to like it.

*****

Unsettled by all I'd discovered at Lord Werhard's Vill, I went back to see what progress had been made at the mill. Knowing nothing of my argument with his Lord, Leonfrith greeted me warmly and proudly reported all he'd achieved. Already some posts had been prepared and were stacked on the bank of the river, ready to be set into place. Leonfrith was marking out the position for them by pegging out a line in the dirt.

'We'll start work on building the stockade itself once all the stakes are here as all hands can then be applied to the task,' he said. 'But you and Aelred should be able to reside here within a day or so.'

That was indeed good news so I began to look around more closely, commenting on what seemed to be excellent progress.

'We'll need a large supply of arrows,' I said. 'If besieged, they and sling shot will be the only weapons we can use to fend off the attackers.'

Leonfrith agreed and said he would set the women to making them as soon as the arrowheads were ready. 'With regard to the sling shot, there are plenty of pebbles in the river we can use. I'll have the children gather as many as they can. The slings should be easy enough for every man to fashion for himself.'

Pleased with all that, I began to think beyond the immediate problems of keeping the Vikings at bay. 'Have you attended to the beacons yet as we'll need to rely on those to summon reinforcements when the time comes?' I asked.

Leonfrith pointed to a brazier on the high ground above the settlement and another beside the ford, both of which he assured me were already supplied with firewood and had a stack of kindling and more dry logs set beside them. 'More beacons are being placed where they can be seen by all,' he confirmed.

I nodded approvingly. 'And once completed, the stockade should accommodate how many men?' I asked.

'I think fifty at least,' he said. 'Just as you advised. And provided they hold the ford, the men here can be supplied and reinforced from the other side of the river.' With that he led me down to stand on the bank. 'When more men arrive they can wait on the far side where they'll form a shield wall as Aelred suggested. That and with the hail of arrows we let fly from the stockade should make it very difficult for Hakon's men to cross.'

All in all it seemed a good plan. 'Can we fashion a bridge from the stockade to the island?' I asked. 'It need only be a narrow walkway so that the men can use it to escape if we're overwhelmed. It will also allow reinforcements to join us if needed.'

Leonfrith said it could be done. 'Perhaps a temporary bridge would be better, my Lord,' he suggested. 'That way if the stockade is taken by the Vikings we can quickly remove it, forcing them to find another to way to reach the island. The water wheel has scoured the riverbed there, making it too deep and much too dangerous for them to wade across, particularly if they're wearing mail or carrying heavy arms.'

'Could they not scramble across using the water wheel?' I asked.

He smiled. 'I'd like to see them try, my Lord. It's as slippery as hell and anyway, they could only manage it one at a time.'

I acknowledged what he'd said and turned my attention to the defences on the other side of the river. 'So the people from this settlement and any others under attack can shelter safely behind the shield wall,' I observed, thinking aloud for my own benefit rather than his. 'And if that's breached they can, as a last resort, disperse and seek safety within the hills.'

'Exactly, my Lord.'

With all that agreed I commended Leonfrith on his efforts and was about to walk over to the Common Field for the training session when Lord Werhard arrived in person.

'Matthew, my apologies,' he said extending his hand. 'I spoke out of turn and in anger. I think you know what a disappointment my stepson is to me and all you've said and done has only served to make me more aware of his failings.'

I clasped his hand warmly. 'It's of no matter, my Lord,' I said. 'I was wrong to barge in as I did. I also acted in rage as, like you, I find him wanting in all respects and feel he's working against all that we strive to achieve here.'

With that Lord Werhard surveyed the progress and, like me, seemed much impressed. 'All this should have been done sooner,' he admitted. 'I trust Leonfrith has served you well?'

'He has,' I said. 'He's a good man. We need skills such as his as much as we do warriors.'

'And the training of the fyrd continues?' he asked.

'It does. In fact, they should assemble shortly. We lack proper war gear, but will soon have enough weapons for them all.'

'So if the raiders strike again you'll be ready?'

'Not quite yet, my Lord, though we'd fare better than we would've done a week ago. But if Jarl Hakon and his horde were to strike now I fear there's little we could do to stop them.'

* * * * *

Aelred had been particularly anxious to ensure that, in his absence, I didn't press the men too hard. 'If they lack training and arms to the point where they can't protect themselves it's the fault of their betters and you should treat them more kindly,' he'd advised.

'And you think the Vikings will do as much when they confront us?' I'd reasoned, though I knew he was right. Given they were all freemen, we would likely get more from the men if we allowed them due respect.

However, as the men gathered for fyrd training late that afternoon, it seemed that word had spread about my argument with Otto and rumours of what I'd said to Oeric were also rife. I ignored all that and, as Aelred wasn't there, had Osmund usher them into line.

I was pleased to note that they seemed to find their place more readily and all at least stood proud and tall, just as I'd ordered. Eagbert, the blacksmith, had come to attend and, as promised, he'd brought with him the supply of freshly crafted spears. Osmund gave one to each of the men. Most had brought what war gear they had as well, though it still didn't amount to very much and there were barely enough shields to form a proper wall.

'Right, form up!' ordered Osmund and the men began to sort themselves into two ranks, each to stand one behind the other. I just watched in silence then, when they seemed to have settled down, I walked along the line. 'Much better,' I said quietly, heeding what Aelred had advised about treating them less severely. 'But moving so slowly I think you'd have earned the rare distinction of all being slain even before you found your place in the line!' With that I began moving men, adjusting their position according to height and placing the bigger men to the back where their weight would give them every advantage. 'Ideally you'd each have a helmet and would carry a shield and a seax as well as a spear,' I said once they were mustered into some sort of line. 'We shall do what we can to provide all that as soon as possible.'

As I spoke I looked to the blacksmith who acknowledged what I'd said. 'My Lord, helmets will involve more work than

I can manage on my own,' he admitted. 'I won't have time or resources enough to make them. Shields are something the men can make for themselves. If they bring them to me I'll fit a metal boss and some sort of rim to keep them sound. As for those who don't have a seax, surely any blade will suffice so long as it's properly sharpened.'

It was a good point so I charged the men to attend to those matters. In the meantime, Aelred and I had agreed that Osmund would be best placed to organise the training for, although not overly experienced, he was at least a trained warrior. He was also used to the people so would know how to get the best from them. With a little instruction from me and his own instinct for a fight he seemed to be doing well enough. I therefore stood aside and let him get on with it.

He started by giving the order to raise the shields they shared between them. Needless to say it was a slow and clumsy manoeuvre. 'Right,' he said. 'Remember your positions. When I give the word I want you all to take three steps forward. And try to move as one!'

They tried that and it actually worked quite well given that no one actually tripped over. He then ordered them to take three steps to the left and then to the right. Again it was reasonably successful.

'Good,' he acknowledged. 'We're going to practise that every night, hopefully with shields once everyone has one. We can then learn how to properly protect ourselves from arrows and such like by raising some shields above us and holding others in front at the same time. It'll take practice to do that swiftly but it's a lesson all must learn. In the meantime, I want you to remember this. You do not break rank for any reason whatsoever unless ordered to do so. I don't care if the enemy is in full flight or lying dead at your feet. You remain in the shield wall until I give the order to break.'

It was all sound advice and in particular I recalled how at the battle with Torstein I'd seen for myself what happens when the shield wall breaks too soon to follow an enemy in retreat. I knew all too well the carnage which could follow as a result.

Osmund then divided the men into pairs and had them practise with whatever weapons they had. 'Strike and prevail,' he said, echoing what I'd been told by my brother. 'A battle is not the time for clever strokes or guises. Put your man down, finish him if you can and move on.' He then showed how the spear was a favoured weapon against the Vikings, for they tended to prefer to fight with an axe or a sword. 'With this you can hold them at bay,' he said, showing them how to do so. 'Use the length of it to keep them at a distance. If they come in close they'll kill you, for as like as not they'll have more skill than you can ever hope to manage.' He watched as they each tried this then continued. 'Jab, then drive it home with all the force you can muster. A foe with a sword or an axe will try to cut the shaft, so tonight add leather as binding where you can; that way they will need at least two blows to break it.'

He then walked among them, adjusting the grip of some and prompting others to keep further apart or to get lower. 'You'll not readily pierce mail or even leather with a spear even if you put your shoulder to the task,' he advised. 'So, aim for any part which is left exposed to bring a man down then use the seax or a knife to slit his throat or stab him. At the very least ensure that he can't fight on.'

As the men continued to practise I noticed that Aethelbert, the younger of the two brothers – the one who had so little to say for himself – seemed to have a particular skill with the spear. 'Have you trained before?' I asked him.

'He hasn't, my Lord, but he has a natural way with a spear as he does with a staff,' said his brother, answering for him.

Osmund came over and had Aethelbert demonstrate his skill to all so that others could learn from him.

'There,' said Osmund when he'd finished. 'I pity the poor Viking who has to fight a man who can handle a spear like that!'

'It's those that bring an axe to the fray that worry him,' explained Aethelred, once again speaking on his brother's behalf.

'Why so?' I asked, stepping forward.

'My Lord, because it's such a fearful weapon to come against.'

'It may seem that way, and that's their intent. The Vikings use it to intimidate their foes and in so doing hope to win every contest even before the battle begins. But remember this, the axe is a good weapon with which to attack, but can be a liability when it comes to defence. If you can avoid the first blow from one, you'll have your foe at your mercy, particularly if his axe becomes embedded in your shield, for that leaves him helpless and exposed.'

They all considered this and some even began to practise what I'd said.

As they did so, I asked for those who considered themselves to be good with the bow. Five men stepped forward and each took turns to shoot at a target of straw I'd arranged to be set up at some distance. They all proved they could shoot well enough with only a few arrows passing wide of the mark, but it was soon clear that Godric the forester had exceptional skill. Having raised his bow, he drew it back whilst keeping his eye on the target the whole time before letting the arrow fly. As a result, it found its mark every time.

'So, Godric, it seems you have a way with the bow,' I said loud enough for all to hear.

'And so I should, my Lord, for I've now no other means to put meat on my table.'

'Then I'd have you command the bowmen and train these four men to match your skill. Can you do that?'

Godric seemed pleased with the promotion. 'I can and I will, my Lord,' he said proudly.

'Good. Your men must also learn hand-to-hand combat as well, but will be excused duty in the shield wall. Instead, at each session they must devote that time to practising with the bow.'

I was certain that Godric was an inspired choice, not only because he had the necessary skills but also having been deprived of his home, he thirsted for revenge. Satisfied with that, I reminded everyone to report at the same hour the next day and to bring their weapons with them. I then released them from training and, as they left, it was clear that they were all much happier about serving in the fyrd. In fact, I'd dare say that some of them even enjoyed it.

'They'll get better,' said Osmund as the last of the men departed. 'But you can see how their training has been neglected.'

That was certainly true. 'The important thing now is to ensure that they're properly armed. We need those shields plus a plentiful supply of arrows and sling shot if we're to put up a reasonable defence,' I said.

'We also need war gear, my Lord. Leather jerkins and helmets at the very least.'

'Well, one step at a time,' I mused. 'We now have enough spears, let's see what else we can muster in the way of equipment.'

Osmund looked at me. 'Agreed, my Lord, but, in the meantime, we should pray that the raiders don't strike again too soon, for I fear we still wouldn't last long if we came up against them as we are.'

Chapter Ten

With Aelred away, I pressed on with the training and did what I could to hasten along the works needed to fortify the watermill. The pile of stakes which would form the stockade wall was growing ever higher and, after just two days, Leonfrith reported that both stores were as ready as they'd ever be and that I was welcome to stay in the one which had been prepared as a place where Aelred and I could lodge.

Although there had been no further attempts on my life, I felt that staying at the mill would not only be safer, but would also save me travelling back and forth from the Monastery. So I thanked Father Gregory for his hospitality and persuaded him to accept a small donation plus a modest sum for the compensation I'd offered to pay for the inconvenience and distraction caused by Ingar's presence. That done, I loaded our few possessions on to our pack horse and moved the very next day.

The store hadn't changed much, as they'd done little more to convert it than was needed to keep out the wind and rain, plus sweep the floor and put down some fresh straw. Two cots had been formed, one in each of the far corners, and a few candles had been provided from the Vill plus a piss bucket and a basin at which we could wash. Leonfrith looked somewhat embarrassed when he showed me round, but I assured him it was no worse than where we were staying at the Monastery.

'Lord Werhard has twice suggested you should stay at the Vill,' he offered.

'I need to be here,' I assured him. 'And both Aelred and I are used to lodgings such as this. The only thing I would ask is that our horses are stabled with Lord Werhard's where they can be properly groomed and fed. Apart from that this will suffice.'

I quickly realised that I'd spoken too soon. My first night at the mill was very uncomfortable as the wind seemed to find every gap in the walls and doorway. With winter approaching, I needed to have those sealed and some sort of brazier provided, plus more blankets, as proof against the cold. I also found it difficult to sleep, perhaps missing the routine of the Monastery where the gentle sound of the prayers and incantations had provided a soothing background which, to me at least, was both familiar and comforting. All I had at the lodge was the noise of the water wheel which seemed to grate and creak as it turned in the water. Despite all that, I resolved to stay there and settle in as best I could.

I have to say that I missed Aelred's company and, most of all, having someone I could talk to and confide in. I consoled myself with the fact that he'd be back within a few days and we could then press ahead with all that still needed to be done.

Then, late on the second night I was there, I was woken by someone entering the room. As had become my habit, I slept with my sword by my side so gripped it and waited to see what would happen, my eyes only half open but with all my other senses stirred.

I heard whoever the intruder was cross towards me and, fearing it was an assassin, swung my legs from the cot and was on my feet in an instant. As the room was in darkness, I could barely make out who was there, but already I had my sword raised.

'My Lord, I mean no harm,' said the voice of what sounded like a young girl.

'Step away!' I ordered. Then, as she did so, I lit a candle and waited for it to light the room enough for me to see her clearly. I was surprised to find the girl I'd seen with Oeric on several occasions. She was standing naked before me – her clothes in an untidy pile on the floor.

I couldn't deny that she was both young and pretty, with long fair hair that hung below her shoulders. She looked as embarrassed at being there as I was.

'What are you doing?' I demanded.

'Lord Oeric sent me,' she managed. 'He said I was to do whatever was needed to please you, my Lord.'

I could barely believe what I was hearing. 'Cover yourself, girl,' I ordered, then looked away as she began to dress.

'My Lord, I didn't mean to offend you I...'

'You what? You thought I'd treat you as does that bastard Oeric?'

She said nothing, but lowered her head in shame.

'What are you? His whore?'

'Not by inclination, my Lord. I had no choice but to become as I am. My father sold me to him lest his farmstead was taken in settlement of his debts.'

'Dear God, are we come to that? What are you called?'

'Mildred, my Lord. I'm sorry if I...'

'It's not your fault,' I assured her, regretting having been so harsh. 'Now be on your way and we'll speak no more of this.'

She made no attempt to move. 'What's the matter?' I asked.

'My Lord, he'll beat me if he thinks I've failed to please you.'

'Will he by God! I'll have his miserable hide flayed from his body if he does!'

Still she didn't move. 'My Lord, take me if you will. I'd much prefer that than to suffer what he'll do to me whether you later avenge me or not.'

I wasn't sure what to do. I'd spent many nights in want of a woman's company and though sorely tempted by Mildred, I knew I had to resist her charms. 'Tell him that I've bedded you and seemed well pleased,' I advised her. 'Make up whatever story you will for he'll be none the wiser.'

'Then may I stay here tonight?' she pleaded. 'That will add weight to my story.'

I could see how frightened she was of Oeric so agreed on condition that she sleep alone in the other cot. Given how long it had been since I'd lain with a woman, I confess that her presence stirred me so much that it took all my resolve to resist her. Somehow I managed, reminding myself of Emelda's plight when she had been forced to become a whore through no fault of her own. As such I couldn't bring myself to take advantage of Mildred's position, yet I cannot say that I slept well or easily that night. Fortunately, she made no other attempt to fulfil her orders and I was almost grateful when, at first light, she rose and hurriedly dressed herself. Before leaving she bent over me as I pretended to sleep and gently kissed me on the forehead and whispered her thanks.

*****

Leonfrith seemed to be making good progress with the fortifications and the training of the fyrd was going well. I was much cheered by all that until Aelred returned from Winchester. Whereas I should have been pleased to greet him, the moment I saw him I knew at once that something was wrong.

At first he looked almost afraid to speak. It was as if the words he needed were beyond him and he struggled to get them out. In the end he put his hand on my shoulder and led me to a stool where he made me sit before telling me the news which he knew would cut me deeper than any sword ever could. As was his way, he decided that his best course was to come straight out with it.

'Matthew, I have to tell you that Emelda is dead,' he managed.

The words seemed to bite me so hard that I could scarce believe them. Even as I gradually grasped the truth of them, all I could do was stare at him, not knowing what to say.

'She died in childbirth,' he explained. 'It happened the day before I arrived at Winchester. Alfred was already preparing to send word, but I said it would be better coming from me.'

'Surely this can't be so?' I pleaded. 'She was not yet due and…'

'The child came too soon,' he said consolingly. 'According to the nuns who attended her, the boy was all too anxious to be born and wouldn't wait. Because of that the poor girl was in labour for two full days and nights.'

Stunned by the news, I somehow found the words I needed, or rather those I thought were expected of me. 'What of the child?' I asked.

'The child is well,' he said. 'I didn't see him, but I gather he's whole and healthy.'

'He? So I have a son?'

Aelred hesitated.

'He is of my blood,' I assured him. 'Of that I'm certain.'

Aelred nodded as if to accept that. 'They've named him Edward in recognition of that,' he said.

I can't explain what I felt at that moment. I was torn between my concern for the child and the pain I felt for the loss of Emelda. It was as though I could still hardly believe what Aelred was saying and was too distraught to ask the questions I later wished I'd raised. I looked at Aelred who seemed to understand my pain.

'The boy is small for having been born too soon,' he said. 'But I gather he fares well enough. Emelda had time to bless him, but then died a few hours later. Her last words were that she was going to join you in Heaven.'

Suddenly the full weight of all I'd withheld from her seemed to settle on my shoulders. 'I should have gone to her,' I wailed, fighting back the tears. 'I shouldn't have let her think me killed. It was a betrayal; a cowardice of which I'm now ashamed. I must return to see the child and acknowledge him as my own.'

'Is that wise?' asked Aelred. 'Alfred would have me assure you that he'll deal with everything on your behalf and see that the child is well cared for. He's already found a man whose wife is barren but desperately craves a child. They're both overjoyed at the prospect of caring for the boy and will love him as if he were their own. He's recorded their names and left word of it with that abbot you took me to see...'

'Father Constantine you mean?'

'Aye, Father Constantine. But he has instructions to reveal the details to you only with the King's consent.'

'But surely I'm allowed to see my son?'

'Alfred expressly told me to advise you against returning too soon. Is it not your duty to—'

'My duty!' I stormed. 'It was my duty to support and care for the woman I love. Instead of that I'm here trying to do God knows what to secure this realm when I should have been there by her side. I'm sick of doing my duty!'

'Is there anything I can do?' he asked quietly.

'No! No, just leave me. I'd rather be alone.'

With that Aelred reluctantly left. I gather that he went to the Vill and explained what had happened to Leonfrith who, with Lord Werhard's blessing, arranged for him to remain there for a few nights in order to give me time and space to grieve.

*****

I rejected all visitors, even turning Aelred away when he came to see how I fared the following day. Then, once alone, I seemed to settle into a dark abyss of remorse and self-confession. All those doubts which had dogged me throughout my life seemed to surface once more as I tried to recall the things I'd done to deserve what was, to my mind at least, God's just and deserved punishment.

Of course I recalled all that dear Brother Benedict had told me about how God doesn't punish, but my sorrow seemed to outweigh his counsel. I prayed in earnest, getting down on my knees as I searched my soul. The list of my sins which needed to be redressed seemed endless, but I readily confessed them all, desperately seeking redemption.

To make my condition worse, I took to drink and, once started, found it hard to resist as it seemed to ease the pain of my loss. For the first time in my life my mind was clouded by ale and strong mead, and the more I drank the more morbid I became. Strange that having been so undecided about my true feelings towards Emelda she soon became the focus of my sorrow and I realised that I'd loved her all along.

Whilst thus depleted, I continued to pray repeatedly, craving forgiveness for my soul and particularly for the one sin which seemed to cut much deeper than all the others I'd committed – the betrayal and deception of the woman I loved in letting her believe me killed and thereby failing her when she needed me most.

All this time I took no interest in how the works were progressing. I still refused to see anyone and instead kept myself confined to the lodge, living like a hermit, forgoing both food and company. After three days I at last began to take a hold of myself, but, by then, I felt both low and dejected and regretted having been so foolish. I resolved to set matters right and, as I lay in my cot that night, I determined that whilst nothing could relieve my sorrow, I would rise early and find Aelred, there to make amends for my behaviour. I was sure he'd understand and hoped he'd forgive me so that we could put it all behind us and set about our duty as before.

With those thoughts fresh in my mind, there came a light knock at the door. Hoping it was him, I called out for whoever it was to enter. But it wasn't Aelred; it was Mildred,

Oeric's whore, come to see if there was anything I needed, carrying a torch to light her way.

'Tell Oeric to go to hell!' I told her, still abed and not bothering to get up on her account.

'He doesn't know I'm here,' she said softly.

'Then why have you come?' I demanded.

'My Lord, I've come of my own accord,' she said. 'I would have come sooner, but only learned of your sad news yesterday which Aelred said you've taken badly. I've come to see if I can help.'

'There's no need,' I said ungratefully. 'I'm all but recovered now.'

Mildred glanced around the room and could see at once the state it had become. She started to gather up all that which I'd discarded on the floor, emptied my piss bucket and then took away the wash basin to fetch fresh water from the river. She also washed the cups I'd used for drinking and began to tidy away all that which was out of place. 'It stinks in here!' she said. 'In fact, my Lord, you stink as well!'

It wasn't her right to speak so plainly to me, but I did manage a smile for the first time in several days. 'Very well,' I said. 'Then leave me to wash myself.'

'First give me your clothes and I'll wash them as well,' she said, then turned away clearly expecting me to undress. I did so, removing my tunic and leggings which I'd not taken off for several days. As she took them away and placed them ready to be washed, I used the basin to cleanse myself, splashing the cold water on to my face to clear my head then washing my body as well. By the time she returned I'd finished and had covered myself with a cloak, shivering but feeling better. As she continued to tidy, I lay on the cot and watched.

'What are you doing now?' I asked as she stood before me and slowly removed all her clothes.

She was naked as she moved towards me and then lay herself down beside me. 'I've done what any woman worth her salt would do to help restore you, now I must help to comfort you as well.'

'But you can't! You must...'

I was lost from the moment she put her arms around me and drew me close. I couldn't help but recall when first I lay with Emelda and, if truth be told, as we embraced it was her I was making love to, as if saying my goodbyes.

We lay together afterwards, still entwined and feeling a closeness I can barely describe. It had never been that way with Ingar as she'd simply used me in a hurried and purposeful manner so that all was accomplished so quickly that I barely had time to know what had happened. Mildred had been tender and loving, just as Emelda had been, so I was content to lay with her for longer than was needed.

'I'm sorry,' I said as she got up to dress herself.

'What for?' she asked.

'I should not have taken advantage of you,' I explained.

She laughed. 'Taken advantage of me! You are the one man who has never tried to do that. I offered myself to you when I was ordered to by Oeric yet you refused. It was a kindness I've not forgotten and one which few men would have shown. This time I came of my own free will and am glad to have done so. You have taken nothing from me which others haven't taken before, but, for the first time, I gave myself willingly and completely. In that I hope I've helped to ease your pain. Whoever your woman was, if in dying she's lost you then she's lost more than most women will ever know.'

With that she bent over me and kissed me once more before leaving.

*****

Mildred returned later with some fresh clothes for me to wear and, having dressed myself, I went to find Aelred. I guessed he'd gone to stay at the Vill, so went there first and was told that he and Lord Werhard were taking breakfast together. I was shown through to join them and was grateful to find that Oeric wasn't with them.

Lord Werhard offered me his condolences whilst Aelred enquired whether I was yet able to continue with our plans. I said I was, but of course said nothing of what had transpired the previous night. 'How are things progressing?' I asked as I took my seat. Having not eaten for several days I was indeed hungry and so helped myself to meats and smoked fish.

'All is progressing well,' said Aelred. 'I assumed you needed time to yourself so we stopped work on the stockade – but don't worry, we found plenty more to do.'

I must have shown that the prospect of them stopping work on my account concerned me.

'We've now cut all the stakes which are needed and have carried them to the mill. As you will have seen, some have already been set into place. The signal beacons are also completed and I've had the men training hard. They now seem to work as one and should give a good account of themselves. In fact, it would be useful if the raiders did strike soon as it would give them a taste of battle and a chance to prove their skills.'

'Are you sure they're ready yet?' I asked.

'As ready as they'll ever be. We still lack helmets and protective gear but most have fashioned something for themselves in that regard. They all have shields and Eagbert has provided weapons.'

'Including arrows?' I asked.

'There are now ten baskets crammed full of them plus we have thirty bows. True, not all the arrows are well made or even properly fletched, but they'll do well enough, particularly at close range.'

It was all good news. 'My Lord, are you satisfied with all that's been done?'

Lord Werhard smiled. 'More than satisfied. I can scarce believe that all has been achieved so quickly.'

'We have Leonfrith to thank for that,' mused Aelred. 'He's worked tirelessly to ensure that everything is as it should be.'

'He is indeed a good man,' I agreed. 'Perhaps we can go to inspect the works together?'

With that we finished our breakfast and Aelred and I walked back towards the mill.

'Was Alfred prepared to help Ingar?' I asked quietly.

'He seemed to understand her plight,' he assured me. 'Perhaps even more so than I do. He asked to see her and though they met in private, I gather they seemed to get on well. In fact, I was told that Alfred was very interested in all she had to tell him about her "Earth Mother". She even prescribed a remedy for a pain he suffers in his gut from time to time.'

'Alfred is always quick to listen to new ways of doing things. He'll take the best of what she can teach him and thereby put her knowledge to good use.'

With that we arrived back at the mill where Leonfrith had already resumed work. I went across and thanked him for his efforts. He made no mention of my grief as to do so would have been beyond his station, but the look in his eyes was enough for me to know what he might otherwise have said.

'So, what next?' I asked.

'With your permission, my Lord, I'll now have the men start to erect the remainder of the stakes to form the stockade,' he said. 'It should take us no more than three or four days given that all can now assist with that.'

'And what about the gates?' I asked remembering my promise to ensure that the miller's work was not interrupted.

'I plan to put them in the part of the stockade which is closest to the ford.'

'Why?' I asked.

'Because, my Lord, they'll be the weakest part of the defences. The Vikings will know that and try to force them in order to gain entry to the stockade. If they succeed then all is lost. As like as not they'll try to burn them down or break them open, but by siting the gates there, those trying to breach them will make easy targets for our bowmen positioned behind the shield wall on the opposite bank.'

I smiled as I could see the logic of that. 'Yes, so charging the gates wouldn't be a very healthy place to be!' I agreed. 'So what else remains to be done?'

'We must erect the hides on the island to help protect the bowmen there and also fashion the makeshift bridge as you requested. I also plan to lift all the stepping stones at the ford, but will leave that until last as we'll need to get all the people who live here across the river to safety once we know the attack is coming. Apart from that we're all but done.'

'I'd still prefer to have chains drawn across the river in case they come by boat,' I said.

'Not chains, my Lord. As I said, we have no resources for that. But as agreed stout ropes will be used instead and should suffice equally as well.'

It was indeed good news. 'Also, the bridge must be sited as far away from the mill as you can manage for it may be our only escape if the stockade is taken. We need to ensure that we can still reach it even if the mill is ablaze.'

Leonfrith saw the sense of that at once.

'Excellent. So more training and more arrows. Then all we have to do is wait.'

*****

'You're very quiet,' said Aelred as we stood together and watched the men setting stakes upright within a trench, then backfilling and levelling that before lashing and nailing the stakes tightly together.

'I'm sorry,' I said. 'But it was such a blow to learn…'

'That's to be expected. But tell me, is there really some doubt as to whether you're the father of the child?' he asked.

I realised it was time to tell him how I came to be with Emelda. 'I first met her on the retreat from Chippenham,' I explained. 'Her father was a traitor who, when exposed and punished, begged Alfred to take her with him as a slave. When we reached Athelney Alfred forced her to become a whore to satisfy all the men's baser cravings.'

'Christ! And you married her after that!'

I shook my head. 'No, I never took her to wife. I had intended to but never got the chance. But you must understand that she was not a whore by nature or intent, rather she was forced to become one as penance for her father's crimes.'

'And you took advantage of her favours but fell for her charms,' he said knowingly.

'I think it was more that she took advantage of my innocence in such matters, but once sampled, I couldn't help myself.'

'Ah! First taste!' remarked Aelred laughing. 'You're not the only man to be smitten by the first woman who offers him her favours.'

'Perhaps,' I nodded. 'I was certainly eager enough at the time. But I didn't know she was with child until I returned to Winchester and Alfred told me. He persuaded me to leave her be on the grounds that he'd sent her to a nunnery where none knew of her past and where she thought me dead. That way her reputation remained intact.'

'But you think the child is yours?'

'I know so,' I said.

'So you'll acknowledge it when we return?'

'I will. Though when that will be I can't say as there still seems so much we need to do here.'

'Then what about Ingar? Alfred seemed to know that you're the father of her child as well. Though I said nothing about that bastard Ljot having sired the other one.'

'Good.'

'Alfred said he'd speak to you further when you return about what's to be done, but, in the meantime, he's sent her to a place where they care for women in her condition.'

'Not into the care of Father Constantine at my old Abbey I hope! He'd no more understand her ways than he would her condition, and would approve of neither.'

'No, he's sent her to a nunnery in Wareham. I think it could be the same one to which he sent Emelda.'

'Then I wish them luck! Whatever their intent, Ingar will know more about what's needed than they ever will!'

Aelred managed a laugh. 'By the way,' he said. 'I told Alfred about the man who tried to kill Ingar as I thought he should know that her life might be in danger. I didn't mention that Wilfrid had killed the man. I trust that's what you intended?'

'Thank you. I doubt anyone will question what took place that night. In fact, I doubt they'll ever find the body or, even if they do, none will put a name to what's left of it.'

Aelred seemed satisfied at that. 'So as you can see, things have progressed here apace,' he said, changing the subject.

He was right about that. 'We'll need to stockpile provisions such as salted meats and fish, plus fruits and other items which might be needed in the event of this becoming a siege,' I pointed out. 'That, with water from the river, would mean we could hold out here for a week if we have to and even then more supplies and reinforcements could be provided by those on the far bank.'

'Leonfrith mentioned something about a bridge from the island to the stockade,' queried Aelred. 'Do we have time to build something like that?'

'All I have in mind is a simple footbridge, hewn from a single tree and lain from one bank to the other. It would only afford access in single file but could be easily rolled aside if the stockade falls into Hakon's hands.'

Aelred seemed much impressed with that idea. 'That means we could indeed hold out here for a goodly while – provided we've not all been killed by then.'

I glanced at him as if to check he was joking about us all being killed, but quickly realised he wasn't. 'We'll survive whatever Hakon throws at us,' I said to reassure him.

'Let's hope so,' was all he managed.

'You say the training has gone well. Has Osmund stepped up to the mark?' I asked, tactfully changing the subject.

'He's done well and was a good choice,' said Aelred. 'The men are quick to acknowledge his lead and are now inclined to follow his orders. Like I said, they need to be tested in battle, but I think they'll hold up well enough.'

Thus it seemed we'd reached a stage where the first part of my plan was all but ready. We had only to await news of the next raid at which point our skills would indeed be tested and, assuming we prevailed, all we'd need to do after that was wait for Hakon to make his move. When he did, we could be certain of giving him a rough reception.

So, it seemed everyone had done all that was asked of them and more. Unfortunately, it was left to me to let them down.

Chapter Eleven

Two days later, Leonfrith was setting up the protective hides on the island to provide cover for the bowmen when Aelred and I went to speak with him. The job of those stationed there would be to kill any Vikings trying to cross the ford and thus reduce the number of those reaching our shield wall on the other side of the river, which was to be our last line of our defence.

'My Lord, we should also consider placing a bowman on the upper part of the mill,' suggested Leonfrith. 'That would be a good place from which to pick off senior members of Hakon's horde, perhaps even Hakon himself.'

There was a gantry to the front of building which was used to haul up sacks of grain and such like, together with an access hatch let into the eaves which I agreed would make an excellent vantage point for a skilled bowman.

'That's all very well,' warned Aelred. 'But I wouldn't want to be up there if they set the place ablaze!'

'That is a worry, my Lord,' agreed Leonfrith. 'We'll have pails on hand in case they try to burn down the gates or the stockade itself, but we'll have no way of reaching the flames if the roof of the mill is set on fire.'

I listened to all that as best I could, but I have to admit that my mind was elsewhere at the time, thinking about my newborn son who I yearned to see. Although I knew Alfred had counselled against it, he had not expressly forbidden me from returning to Winchester and it was therefore only my sense of duty which kept me from doing so.

Thus engrossed, I delayed responding when summoned by Oeric to attend him. In my defence, given my birthright and my position, I was well within my rights to expect a more courteous request for a meeting, but it was only when I did eventually go soon after midday that I found I'd committed a grave error of judgement. In so doing, I'd let everyone down.

'There are reports of a small band of Vikings headed towards a farmstead north of here near a place called Bleakley Wood,' said Oeric without bothering with anything which resembled a greeting. 'Now we'll see what wonders you've managed to work with the fyrd.'

'How many men?' I asked.

'Ten I'm told. No more. But all armed and their intentions made plain.'

'And how big is the farmstead?'

He thought for a moment. 'Four households. Perhaps six men in total but two of them too old to fight and another barely off his mother's tits.'

I went to look at the rough map of the Shire on the table to one side of the Hall and studied it closely. 'When do you expect them to arrive?'

Oeric, who seemed unusually co-operative, came across to stand beside me. 'The report came in early this morning, which is why I sent word so promptly. But I gather you had more important matters in hand.'

I ignored the criticism and instead repeated the question.

'It placed them somewhere here,' he said pointing to the map. 'That means that by now they'll be well on their way. They'll probably rest tonight and strike at dawn tomorrow.'

'How do you know they're planning to strike at that particular farmstead?' I queried.

'We don't. But there's little else in Bleakley Wood beyond some Roman ruins and old abandoned brickworks, none of which would interest them.'

'So is it far from here?'

'A few hours' march, no more.'

Although I was the one who had cost us precious time, I realised it was not too late. Normally one of the beacons would be lit to summon the local fyrd in the event of a raid, but there was no need that day as the men would be assembling shortly for training. I decided that any signal might alert the Vikings to the fact that we were on to them so resolved to wait, thereby hopefully preserving an element of surprise.

'We'll leave tonight and be ready to greet them in the morning,' I told Aelred, having returned to the mill to set matters in hand. Although I didn't say it, I was still worried as to whether the men were truly ready, but I knew that neither he nor Osmund had any qualms on that account.

'Don't worry,' said Aelred, sensing my disquiet. 'If there are just ten of them we should fare well enough. With the Vill guards and the men from the fyrd we should number seventeen, plus of course there's you and I. That makes near twenty all told and we'll also have the benefit of surprise. It'll do the men good to score an easy victory and send word to any other would-be raiders that things here have changed.'

'Then we need to organise supplies for two or perhaps three days,' I suggested to Leonfrith. 'Aelred and I can march beside the men and leave our horses to carry the provisions and any spare weapons. We should make better time that way.'

Leonfrith went off to attend to that so all we had to do was await the men's arrival, brief them, then march to the farmstead. It would be fully dark by the time we reached it, which would help us to arrive unseen and prepare to fend off the attack. As we did so, we could send the folk who lived there to a place of safety.

* * * * *

It seemed word had already spread about the impending raid and the men arrived knowing what to expect. All came armed and wearing whatever war gear they had and stood together looking very anxious as they waited for me to address them.

Aelred and I had donned our own war gear – I was dressed in my mail vest and he in his leather jerkin, and we had our helmets and our weapons to hand. 'So it's time to put your training to the test,' I said as the men hurriedly formed their line in front of me. 'Our intelligence is that there are just ten raiders, but no doubt all are warriors so we'll not underestimate their strength or ability. My plan is simple. We shall march to the farmstead tonight and be prepared to greet the bastards when they attack at dawn, just as good Saxons should.'

I waited for anyone who had a mind to speak on the matter, just as Alfred often did when trying to raise the men's spirits. In truth I'd learned much from him, though couldn't find the words that would stir all into action as he always seemed to manage.

'Can we beat them, my Lord?' asked Eagbert.

I looked to Aelred to answer.

'If there are but ten of them then yes,' he said. 'In fact, we should do so with ease. The aim tomorrow will be to ensure that none of us are killed or even wounded. Thus you must do exactly as ordered, without question or delay.'

'But are we ready?' asked Aethelred, presumably speaking for his brother as well.

Aelred smiled. 'More so than you were a few weeks ago. The first battle is always the hardest, but once you come safely through it, that's a question you won't ask me again.'

'Right,' I ordered, conscious of the time. 'Collect what other arms and equipment you need from the store then form up into rank. We march at once, but keep your eyes open in case these raiders are not alone. Osmund, I would have you take two men to lead the way. Keep far enough ahead of the main column to warn us if there's anything that looks to be a trap, but leave enough distance to give us time to muster our defence if you're attacked.'

Osmund looked pleased at being given such responsibility. Thus assembled, we began the march to the farmstead. In fact, in the dark it took longer than expected and when we arrived we found that the people who lived there had already driven off their livestock then taken all they could carry and gone off in search of somewhere safe to hide.

The farmstead was set close to the edge of Bleakley Wood which was a large area of managed woodland, much of which had been thinned and cleared over the years as the excellent timber from there was used for building homes and such like. What remained of it lay to the rear of the farmstead, but there were open pastures to the front. The farmstead itself comprised just four main buildings all set around a sort of courtyard, two on one side, one opposite them and another at the far end. Beyond these were various byres and shelters, plus grain stores and a few other rough outbuildings. It had no defences to speak of, albeit the open pastures to the front offered a clear view of anyone approaching from there. It was therefore the woodland to the rear which worried me as that provided the perfect cover for attackers, hence I posted guards there to quietly keep watch during the night.

As the men started to settle into one of the buildings, Aelred looked at me but didn't need to say anything. We both knew that it was not an easy place to defend. 'We'll keep out of sight until the last moment and thereby take them by surprise,' I suggested, speaking aloud so that all could hear me. 'As the Vikings come in, howling and screaming as they surely will, we'll step out and form our shield wall right in front of them. So remember your positions. You'll need to find your place quickly and be ready to brace yourselves to receive them, just as we've practised so many times already. Is that clear?'

With that I urged the men to get some sleep, though I doubt if any of them managed to do so as the prospect of the battle loomed large in all our thoughts. Then, a few hours before dawn, we received the news that none of us wanted to hear.

'There are dozens of the bastards!' screamed one of the two men I'd set to keep watch.

With that the other man on watch also returned with a similar story. 'There must be near forty of them at least!' he declared. 'We have to be gone from here before they arrive or we'll all be slain like dogs!'

I realised in an instant what had happened. 'That bastard Oeric has set us up,' I said under my breath. 'The lying toad has tricked us!'

'He must have sent word to warn the people here as well,' suggested Aelred. 'I wondered why they left even before we arrived!'

It did make sense, but I could see that the prospect of fighting such a large force had unnerved the men. Aelred had the good sense to calm them. 'Stay put,' he ordered. 'We're safest here. If you rush out into the night you'll be slain for sure.'

I turned to the two men. 'How many did you actually see?' I asked.

Neither could answer accurately, but it seemed that an estimate of between thirty-five and forty warriors was about right, all of them lurking within the trees behind us.

'We should go now,' said one of the men. 'We should march out as one then get as far from here as we can so as to be ready to protect our own homes!'

Most of the others seemed to think that was a good idea and some of them even started to gather up their things.

'Don't be fools!' ordered Aelred. 'That open pasture will be their killing ground if you do. It might be tempting to run, but they'll quickly overtake you and when they do they'll put you all to the sword! Who will protect your families then?'

'Besides, there's a better way,' I announced. 'It won't be easy, but it could work to our advantage if we use their own ruse against them.'

'How do you mean to do that?' asked one of the men.

'They won't know our numbers, so some of you will form a shield wall in the courtyard whilst the rest of us wait here.

When the Vikings attack they'll come in from the woods and, thinking you an easy target, will just charge straight at you. Once they've fully engaged, the rest of us will emerge and attack their rear. They won't be expecting that and we should be able to reduce their numbers quickly enough and thereby even up the odds.'

'You mean we're to stab men in the back?' asked Eagbert.

I knew what worried him, for it was the Saxon way to look a man in the eye when we slew him, not creep up on him from behind. But all that had become a thing of the past as the wars with Vikings had forced us to fight them as they did us. It had been a hard lesson for many Saxon warriors but one which we'd all needed to grasp given what we were up against. 'That was the old way,' I said. 'I lament its passing as much as any man, but the nature of war has changed. You fight now not just for your homes and families, but for the right to live as Saxons. Therefore we must fight as they do and I assure you, they won't think twice about killing you whatever way they can.' I recalled that Alfred had said something similar before the battle at Combwich when some expressed doubts about fighting as he intended.

It was Aelred who spoke next. 'For my part, I don't much care whether I skewer Vikings from the front or from behind. My only concern is to strike hard enough to make certain that I kill the bastards.'

Looking round I could see that most were prepared to accept that, so I turned to Godric. 'Once the shield wall is formed we can't afford for the Vikings to get behind it. I'll need you to station one of your bowmen at either end of the wall so they can kill any who try. Then take your other two men and hide among the buildings. Pick off the Vikings with arrows where you can, particularly any carrying torches, for if they set fire to this building we may be forced to show our hand too soon. Can you do that?'

'I can, my Lord.'

'Good, when you run out of arrows come and join the fray.'

Aelred was considering the plan. 'It does make more sense than just running,' he said.

'But there could be near forty of them out there, all armed and looking for blood!' stormed one man. 'Are we to be slain defending an empty farmstead?'

'Those odds are not so bad,' I reasoned. 'I stood with those at Combwich when we took on worse than we face here – and they were all berserkers. We can manage this.'

'But how, my Lord?' asked Osmund. 'These men are mostly farmers, tradesmen and artisans, not warriors!'

Once again it was Aelred who calmed then. 'They're no longer just farmers, they're men trained for combat. What's more we can prevail. Matthew here should be good for six of the Vikings at least. I can manage three and the bowmen should put down seven or even eight between them. That leaves barely twenty men to stand against us and we have the advantage of surprise. Are those odds more to your liking?'

'We shall also offer prayers,' I said.

'Prayers!' said one man. 'Much as prayers are always welcome, my Lord, they'll be of little consolation when facing a Viking battle-axe!'

'I didn't mean that I'd pray for us,' I told him calmly. 'It's those poor sods out there who'll need our prayers. For they've come expecting to slaughter a few defenceless farmers and have no idea what's about to be set against them.'

At this the men seemed to settle. Then one of them stepped forward. 'My Lord, forgive me for asking, but who are you that even though so young, you can be reckoned to account for so many Vikings?' he asked.

There was silence as all waited for me to answer. I did so by removing my mail vest, fleece undershirt and tunic, thereby exposing the dreadful scar on my chest. A gasp went up from all of them.

'You're the…'

'Yes. I'm the so-called warrior with the pierced heart. They say that I died and then returned from the dead and that I cannot therefore be slain. I don't know if that's true, but if I did die before, then I recall very little about it so have no qualms about doing so again.'

*****

I considered moving some men to one of the other buildings so that we could attack from two positions at once, but was afraid that the raiders would be watching and thereby know there were more of us than we would have them believe.

'Shall I tell you the story about the boy who stood alone against a Viking warband?' asked Aelred.

It was not a tale I knew, but Aelred often had a way with his stories, as I'd found to my advantage when I fought Torstein, so I encouraged him to tell it.

The men gathered round him, grateful for anything which would take their minds from what they would have to face come the dawn. When they were settled, Aelred began.

'There was once a very fierce band of Vikings who no one dared to fight so they were always allowed to simply march in

and take whatever they wanted from all the settlements, one after another. Their warlord, a man named Ivar, was particularly cruel and let it be known that if anyone resisted they'd be killed – and he would sometimes kill a few people anyway just to show that he meant what he said. One day he arrived at a small settlement where all the people were so terrified that they decided not to resist and instead sent word inviting Ivar to help himself to whatever he wanted if he would spare their lives.

'Seemingly happy to oblige, Ivar and twenty battle-hardened Viking warriors marched down towards the settlement but suddenly found that a small boy was barring their path, armed with nothing but a sling.

'"Step aside!" ordered Ivar.

'"Why should I?" asked the boy, whose name was Oscar.

'"Because I'll kill you if you don't," answered the Viking who found it amusing that just one small boy had the courage to stand against him.

'"You'll kill me anyway," said Oscar. "And if that's the case I'd as soon die fighting."

'Ivar was impressed but still roared with laughter. "Boy, I have twenty well-trained warriors who are all thirsting for blood. What can you hope to do against so many?"

'"I can kill a few of you with my sling," replied the boy. "And if I do there's one thing that's certain, I'll be welcomed into Valhalla whereas they won't."

'"What do you mean?" demanded Ivar.

'"Only that when the Gods ask me how I died I shall tell them that I stood alone against twenty warriors and died fighting them. They'll certainly be impressed with that. What those of you I kill will tell them is that they all died fighting a small boy armed with nothing but a sling. I don't think any of

you are likely to be offered a place in Valhalla on the strength of that, do you?"

'Ivar could see that the boy had a point. "Don't be a fool. There's no need to die. Step aside and I'll order my men to spare you."

'Oscar shook his head. "Someone has to make a stand so it might as well be me. Besides, I think I'd like it in Valhalla."

'With that Ivar realised that his men were none too keen to risk being killed by a boy and thereby miss their chance of going to the Great Hall of Dead Warriors. "Then I'll have just three men fight you," challenged Ivar. "Those are the odds which the Gods may see as being fair."

'The boy shrugged. "I don't care if it's three men or three hundred men. I know I can kill at least two of them before they get close enough to strike me down with their axes. And I won't mind killing them because I won't have to meet them again in Valhalla, will I?"

'Ivar turned to his men before deciding what to do. "Will you fight this young upstart or shall we run away from here like craven cowards just because of a mere boy?"

'The men looked none too keen, but one of them stepped forward and, raising his bow, sent an arrow straight into Oscar's heart, killing him outright.

'"That's well done," roared Ivar but then, as he turned to look at the settlement, he saw a mob of very angry men coming towards him. The good people of the settlement had been shamed by the courage of the young boy and, incensed by his needless death, were craving vengeance. Far from stepping aside and letting the Vikings take what they wanted, they were so filled with rage that they set about them with so much violence that not one single Viking warrior was left alive. Oscar of course became a hero and they buried him in the centre of their settlement as a reminder of his courage.'

As Aelred finished there was utter silence for several moments before one of the men spoke out.

'But he was still dead!' he said.

Aelred acknowledged the point. 'But he died with honour. What's more, he showed the people that even when facing a much-feared enemy, you can prevail. Thus it is with us. We may be fewer in number and we're facing trained warriors, but we can prevail if we find the courage and hold our nerve, just as the people at that settlement did in the end.'

Whilst timely and well told, I was not convinced that Aelred's story had done much to lift the men's sprits. Certainly none of them were any keener to fight or were more at ease with our position.

* * * * *

It was indeed a long night but just before dawn I had them all kneel for prayers in which I asked God to see us safe through the coming battle. That done, I selected the men who were to go out into the courtyard and form the shield wall, which was to be commanded by Osmund. It would comprise only the guards from the Vill as I reckoned they would have the discipline to stand firm and also had the benefit of mail vests for protection, though that meant it would be only one row deep. 'You're to defend yourselves as best you can, but on no account break rank until ordered to do so, even if you think you have the advantage,' I reminded them as they prepared themselves. 'Just hold your position till we reach you.'

Even so, they all looked very frightened. 'I should go with them,' suggested Aelred. 'We'll need to ensure they remain firm.'

I had to admit it did make sense but decided against it given that he and I would be needed to lead the small remaining group who were to attack the Vikings' rear. Standing in the shield wall would be frightening enough, but to actually charge the Vikings would take more nerve than most untried men could muster.

'I suggest you and your remaining bowmen take up your positions now,' I said to Godric. 'Your job is to harry the Vikings with arrows in a running battle, using whatever cover you can find. If they can't see you, they'll believe there are more of you than there are so keep moving at all times. When all your arrows are spent, come and join the fray for we're going to need all the help we can get.'

He acknowledged the order then he and his remaining two bowmen slipped away into the half-light of the coming dawn.

* * * * *

Our small group didn't have long to wait before the raiders came down upon us, emerging almost silently from within the trees. 'Stand firm,' I ordered, my voice not much more than a whisper. 'Remember the plan!'

As I watched and waited, I was not sure what to make of things. None of the Vikings carried lighted torches with which to set the buildings ablaze, nor were they screaming and howling as they usually did, perhaps intending to take the farmstead by surprise. Were they slavers then, I wondered? I hoped not, for I'd had my fill of such men. Then, when they were close enough, Godric and his bowmen began to wreak their particular brand of havoc, picking off targets wherever they could.

'Go now!' I said, urging Osmund to lead his men out to form their shield wall. As he did so, they all followed him bravely and took up their positions right in front of the Vikings, thereby blocking their path. Meanwhile Godric and his men had felled at least four men with their arrows, forcing the raiders to abandon whatever plan they had and simply charge the shield wall instead.

As Osmund gave the order to form up, I was proud to see that the men did so with all the skill of practised warriors, locking their shields together and immediately bracing themselves for the impact. As the Vikings slammed home the noise was deafening with men screaming and shouting as they pressed up hard against the shields, hacking with their axes and probing with their swords and spears. Our men did well to hold them off, stabbing and jabbing with their own weapons where they could, though I saw no one actually fall at that point. Still Godric kept shooting, his men rushing from cover to cover, stopping only to loose an arrow before moving on.

Meanwhile I held the rest of the men ready, waiting for the attackers to fully engage before making our move. Only when I was sure they were fully committed did I give the order to move out. 'We go softly,' I said. 'You three go with Aelred, stay close and follow his lead. The rest of you stay with me. They've no idea we're here so we'll creep up close then take them by surprise, hitting them hard and killing as many as we can. That done, work your way around to join the shield wall, thereby reinforcing it. But remember, there's no time for mercy or for vengeance. Strike them down and move on, we can finish them later.'

With that we moved forward, any sound we made lost to the din of the battle as it raged in the courtyard. We were almost there when one of the Vikings saw us and tried to warn the others, but either he was too late or his comrades couldn't hear him. Paying him no mind, we tore into them like a gang of angry men.

Startled by our sudden appearance, some Vikings tried desperately to turn and engage us. Even as they did so we killed or wounded at least three before the rest could turn sufficiently to properly defend themselves. After that it was every man for himself, but they were at a disadvantage, for whichever way they turned they were exposed. I charged straight into the fray, ramming my shield into the back of one man, then cutting him down with my sword. Two others spun round as he fell, but I dealt with them both even before they realised what was happening. After that, I put aside any scruples I had about facing my enemy, and instead began hacking into their ranks without mercy. At that point I turned to ensure that others had followed my lead. I could hardly believe what I saw, for those Saxon farmers were doing far more than simply holding their own, they were setting about the raiders with zeal, skewering them with their spears and wreaking much terror as they did so.

The noise of men screaming in pain or howling their abuse was deafening as Aelred led his group to the left and I took mine to the right. We reached the edges of the shield wall without loss and there we joined with Osmund's men, locking our own shields with theirs.

When the Vikings saw this they were suddenly silent. I heard a man shouting what I was sure were orders and, almost as one, they stepped back to reform their rank, leaving a few men dead on the open ground between us.

I looked to Aelred as if to ask whether he'd heard what was said, but all he did was shout back at me as loudly as he could. 'Form up!' he screamed.

It was then that I realised what was coming next.

*****

A man stepped out from the Viking ranks carrying a dreaded daneaxe. Our men were terrified when they saw him, for the heavy long-handled axe was a dreadful weapon to come against and the one which every Saxon warrior feared most. It took two hands to wield it, which meant that whoever carried it did so without a shield, but it could rip through mail, flesh and bone. It could also haul aside a shield, thereby opening up a shield wall so the rest of the horde could then pour through and wreak their slaughter.

To make matters worse, the man with the daneaxe was like a giant, stripped to the waist and carrying the dreaded weapon on one shoulder. I shouted for everyone to stand firm, but I could tell that they were all but ready to falter and knew what would happen if they did. I looked to Godric hoping he could shoot the man, but he and his bowmen had already spent their arrows. That meant there was but one thing for me to do.

Pushing aside those who stood beside me, I stepped out of the shield wall and screamed my challenge. The giant looked at me and, relishing the chance to kill me, answered by striding towards me, brandishing his weapon. I rushed headlong towards him intending to crash into him with my shield, but barely got the chance before being knocked aside by a heavy blow from his daneaxe. As I lay there, I raised my shield to protect myself, but he struck again, this time so hard that it was like being crushed by a rock. The daneaxe blade embedded itself in the shield, smashing hard into my shoulder as it did so. To his horror, the giant then struggled to free the daneaxe, but I gave him no chance to do so. I simply drove my sword up into his belly. As he fell he was clutching his stomach, blood spewing forth from his gut. For my part, I just moaned in pain as I lay there, desperately nursing my injured shoulder.

In truth I remember very little about what happened next but was told later that the Vikings seemed to lose heart, not only because of the ease with which I'd killed the giant, but also because their numbers were already depleted. To protect me, Aelred ordered the shield wall to advance, taking half a dozen paces forward and stepping over me with their shields still locked together. As they did so the Vikings moved back still further.

As soon as they reached me, Aelred ordered two men to help me and, between them, they took me to the relative safety of one of the byres where I was given my sword and allowed to rest. One of them offered to stay with me, but I refused, knowing that all were needed by those still engaged in the battle. So, sword in hand, I made ready to defend myself, but dreaded the prospect of having to do so given that the wound to my shoulder had rendered me all but helpless.

As I sat there, I could at least see that by then the battle had turned fully in our favour. With so many of their men dead or wounded, the raiders had fallen back to form a line of their own.

I was in no state to count nor close enough to see clearly, but, if pressed, I would say that more than twenty-five raiders lay dead or dying. That meant that we'd done well enough, but there was no doubt that we'd taken casualties as well. Even so, my men, fired with a sudden lust for blood and emboldened by their success, were not about to let up the slaughter. At this, some of the raiders fled from the farmstead, but those few who stayed to fight were quickly overcome, being mercilessly speared or hacked to pieces where they fell, often being attacked by men from two sides at once. Then at last it seemed as though it was all over.

As I looked around at the bloody field I almost wept. Ten of my men lay broken and bleeding, five of them killed outright, including Cedric, one of the guards from the Vill. Apart from him, they were men who had no interest in war and should have been tending their farms or plying their trade, not dying in some pointless battle.

Aelred came over, his leather jerkin stained with blood. 'How is it?' he asked, looking at my shoulder.

I was in too much pain to speak but nodded my head to confirm that I was all right.

'Are you sure?' he pressed. 'You look very pale and drawn.'

I swallowed hard against the pain, then raised my hand as if to show that I wanted to be left alone.

'The battle's done,' he said solemnly. 'We prevailed despite the odds, thanks to you. The men are now putting the few wounded survivors to the sword.' I think he was worried that I wouldn't approve of the last part, but, in truth, I was past caring and could well understand that the men needed to vent their anger.

With that Aelred looked at my shoulder, carefully helping me to remove my mail vest by untying the lacings to the back. He then gingerly cut away my fleece undershirt and tunic to reveal the wound. 'Can you move your arm?' he asked as he tried to examine where the daneaxe had struck.

I cried out in agony as he did so.

'You're lucky,' he said. 'Your mail vest took most of the blow and saved you. You'll be bruised beyond reckoning, but there's no wound to speak of. All we have to do is reset your shoulder.'

I knew what that entailed for I'd seen it done once before whilst a novice at the Abbey. I started to protest, but even before I could do so, Aelred took my arm and, with his knee against my back, popped the shoulder joint back into place. 'There,' he said. 'That'll hurt like hell for a while, but you'll live.'

He was right about the pain, but I could at least then move my arm.

'I'll get you some more clothes from the people who live here. Yours can be taken back to be mended and I'll have Eagbert repair your mail vest. As he picked up the vest he showed me where the force of the axe had crushed some of the links. I knew then how lucky I was to have survived the blow.

*****

Later, as the men began to drag the dead Vikings from the battlefield, Aelred came across to speak to me again. 'Most of the raiders were indeed Vikings,' he told me. 'I heard several speak and it was always in their tongue.'

I remembered that he could speak their language so was sure he was right. It therefore put paid to any question about whether or not they'd been a band of robbers. With that news I straightened up a little, clutching my shoulder as I did so. The pain was beginning to subside by then, but I still felt very stiff and sore. 'So were they Hakon's men or just a band intent on plunder?' I asked.

'Pah! Who knows,' he said. 'But whoever they are, these rogues came in greater numbers than in previous raids and I don't think this time they intended not to harm anyone. My guess is that it was not the farmstead they came for, it was us.'

'Then was that bastard Oeric behind it?' Even as I spoke I got up and tried to flex my arm.

'As like as not he was. Particularly if, as you said, he has Viking blood in his veins.' With that Aelred noticed that the men had taken a prisoner. 'Ah!' he said. 'Now we'll get to the root of this.' Unfortunately, as he started towards them the Saxons who'd captured the man butchered him on the spot. Although angry at losing the chance to interrogate the prisoner himself, I hoped Aelred wouldn't rebuke those responsible, for they'd suffered much at the hands of the raiders and the battle had been their first chance for revenge. I'm not sure what he did say to them, but I noticed that he sent one man to find the people who lived at the farmstead, presumably intending to have the women return to help tend any wounds. I learned later that apart from those who'd died, only half a dozen were wounded and needed serious attention. Certainly the toll could have been much worse and I was grateful for that.

Having rested, I felt it was my duty to at least see the bodies of our fallen if only to pay my respects. The pain had eased a lot by then, but I still needed Aelred to support me lest I fell. Thus he and I went together to where the dead had been laid out. 'Find some sort of cart. We'll take them back with us so their bodies can be tended by their kin,' I ordered. I then told others to burn the bodies of the dead Vikings. 'First strip them of anything of value and bring it to me,' I added. 'There'll be equal shares for all, including the families of those who've fallen.'

I knew that we dare not delay much longer before returning to Leatherhead, but first I needed to rest some more. I therefore went back to the byre to do so. Once there, it wasn't long before the Saxons who lived at the farmstead returned. They brought me a rough tunic and a cloak to wear which I promised to have returned to them. Then one of the women fashioned a sling to help support my left arm. That done, they all knelt before me and thanked me. 'Go about your business,' I urged them. 'Help with what's needed to clear away the dead. We've done no more than provide the protection which it's your right to expect.'

Aelred overheard what I said. 'Is that wise?' he asked. 'By my reckoning near half a dozen raiders got away from here and could return seeking vengeance.'

It was a good point. 'Then these people must return to Leatherhead with us,' I said.

With that I turned to look at the spoil taken from the dead Vikings which had been placed in a small heap on the ground near where I sat. It was actually quite a reasonable haul, for the raiders seemed to have a quantity of personal wealth, much of which looked to be too valuable to have been stolen from poor farmers. It included a number of silver armbands plus several rings and brooches. 'We'll divide it later,' I said. 'For now let's be grateful that we got away so lightly.'

Aelred sneered. 'I'm not so sure that you did get away so lightly,' he said. 'You still look very pale. Are you sure that blow hasn't disturbed the wound to your chest?'

'I'll be all right,' I assured him. 'Anyway, there's nothing more we can do here so we should return to Leatherhead as quickly as we can.'

'Agreed, but there's something you should see first.'

'What is it?' I asked.

'Over there among the bodies is one you'll recognise.'

I looked across, wondering who it could be but remained seated.

'It's your old friend, that bastard Otto. His body is well bloodied and quite disfigured, but it's definitely him.'

'You mean he was actually fighting alongside the raiders?'

Aelred nodded.

'Then he was a traitor as well as an insolent fool.' Even as I said it I realised that it was me who'd been made to look a fool. I'd allowed myself to be lured into a trap and risked the lives of all the men in the fyrd because of it. As things had turned out we'd actually fared well and our victory had done much to bolster the confidence of my small force, though it had cost the lives of five good men to do it.

'So that's how Oeric knew where the Vikings would strike!' I said.

'Aye,' said Aelred. 'Which means we were right, he's connected with the raids in some way. As like as not, he and Otto planned the whole thing. They showed the raiders where and when to strike, then told us they'd be few in number knowing we'd want to test the men in battle…'

'You mean the treacherous snake set us up to be butchered!' said Osmund who was standing with us.

Aelred put his hand on Osmund's shoulder. 'It's worse than that, my friend. He's been draining the people of the settlement of all they own thereby turning freemen into all but slaves.'

I thought carefully for a moment then realised that I had to stop things getting out of hand. 'I'm sure you're right, but Otto being here proves nothing of Oeric's involvement,' I pointed out. 'He'll deny it if we accuse him.'

Several of the men had overheard what was being said. 'It's proof enough for us!' they insisted. 'We should hang the bastard and be done with it!'

'Hanging's too good for him,' said another. 'We should string him up and cut out his greedy, treacherous heart and feed it to the crows!'

'You'll do nothing of the sort,' I said as loudly as I could manage. 'The punishment for raising your hand against your betters is death, whether he's guilty or not. I'll not see any of you punished for doing that which you've every right to do.'

'You mean he'll get away with it?' said Osmund

'Oh no. I'll personally see that justice is done.'

'Pah! You mean he'll be reprimanded and told to mend his ways?' said Eagbert. 'He'll not pay for his crimes, his sort never do, however much harm he's done and however much we've suffered for his greed!'

'I'll see him punished severely, be assured of that,' I promised them. 'And if he's guilty you can be sure of one thing: he stands closer to his grave than any man alive.'

Chapter Twelve

'How's your shoulder?' asked Aelred as we watched the men preparing to cremate the Viking bodies. The plan was to build a single pyre on which they could all be burned as one.

'Still sore,' I said, flexing it as best I could.

'Don't worry, it'll mend soon enough and at least you'll have a bruise big enough to impress the ladies,' he teased.

'Where did you learn how to put joints back into place like that?' I asked.

'Ah, actually I didn't,' he confessed. 'I've seen it done once or twice by others but that was the first time I've ever tried it myself.'

'Then all I can say is that I'm glad you didn't mention that at the time!' I said. 'Now if only you could settle my conscience as easily.'

He looked at me, curious to know what I meant.

'It's just that I'm sickened by all the blood that's been shed,' I explained.

'Well, it's not over yet as you still have to deal with Oeric now that you've got proof of his treachery. Whatever else he's done he deserves to be punished for his involvement in the raids alone.'

'Otto's being here doesn't prove that Oeric was involved,' I pointed out.

Aelred looked doubtful. 'The greedy sod is as guilty as sin, and well you know it.'

'Yes, but knowing it isn't the same as proving it,' I reasoned.

'Yet he must be dealt with. And if you don't do it the people from the settlement at Leatherhead surely will. They've suffered too long from his abuse.'

'Which is why we have to hurry back,' I said. 'Once they hear of his treachery it'll be hard to stop them taking matters into their own hands. If they get hold of him they'll string him up for certain.'

'He deserves no less if you ask me. In fact, given half a chance I'd do it for them.'

'Don't worry,' I assured him. 'If I can find proof I'll act, otherwise all I have is suspicion which may turn out to be unfounded.'

'At the very least he deserves to stand trial. Surely there's enough evidence to warrant that?'

I didn't answer, recalling Alfred's instructions that I was to deal with Oeric as I saw fit. The crimes which he would stand accused of would merit nothing less than a sentence of death – and I knew it would fall to me to ensure that was carried out.

'At least the men did well,' said Aelred, sensing my disquiet and changing the subject. 'Shall I tell them you thought as much?'

'Do, and give them my thanks for their support. You also put up a good fight yourself,' I acknowledged, recalling his quick thinking in having the shield wall advance to cover me as I lay on the ground all but helpless and in pain. For that I owed him my life, and not for the first time. 'And that tale you told before the battle was inspired. I don't think it served to stiffen the men's resolve as much as you hoped it would, but your point was well made. If you ever tire of fighting you could become a storyteller instead.'

'Ha! Well, we each do the best we can.'

'Amen to that. I just regret all that slaughter, particularly as so much Saxon blood was shed. Five good men have died for nothing.'

'It could have been a lot worse, that's for sure. Besides, you're a warrior. Slaughter's your business.'

I recalled the conversation I'd had with Lord Ethelnorth after the battle at Edington when even he seemed full of remorse for all the men he'd slain. 'I never set out to be a warrior,' I said ruefully. 'It just sort of happened.'

'Well, you're a good one, like it or not. That plan you came up with was truly inspired and your own contribution to the battle was crucial. That bastard with the daneaxe would have broken the shield wall soon enough, so killing him saved all our lives. I suppose you learned those skills from your brother?'

'And others. But Edwin had more skill than I'll ever manage.'

'Well, from what I saw of it, you fought like a true warrior, turning and slashing with such speed it was hard to know where you'd strike next. I think he'd be very proud of you for that.'

*****

Having started to cremate the bodies of the Vikings, we left the pyre still burning as we prepared to return to Leatherhead. We borrowed a small hay wagon from the people who lived at the farmstead and used it to carry our Saxon dead so they could be returned to their families for a Christian burial. Most of the wounded could still walk, but the two who couldn't were placed on a makeshift litter. We knew Oeric would be waiting for news of the battle, though probably not expecting to learn of our success.

'So 'tis true, my Lord,' said Osmund as he walked beside me thereby proudly leading our small column. He'd done well in holding his nerve whilst commanding the shield wall and had thereby fully justified my faith in him.

'What is?' I asked wearily.

'Why, that you can't be killed. Not many men would have survived a blow like that from a daneaxe.'

I scoffed. 'Don't you believe it,' I admitted. 'I can bleed and die as easily as the next man.'

He looked at me as if the words made no sense. 'But that can't be so, my Lord. For you're the warrior with the pierced heart. You showed us the scar!'

'All that means is that I was lucky – both when first shot by the arrow and also back there when I was struck by the daneaxe. Believe me, that's the truth of it.'

He seemed reluctant to accept that, but said no more. Instead, we marched on until we reached Leatherhead where many people came out from their homes to greet us. Those who then learned that their menfolk had died were comforted by others whilst the rest were just grateful for those who'd survived and for our triumph.

I noted that the tyrant Oeric was conspicuous by his absence so went straight to Lord Werhard's Vill where Aelred and I burst our way in. We had no cause to wait given that we already knew that the only guard, Otto, had been slain, and there were therefore only a few servants to prevent us and they showed no inclination to do so.

Oeric was seated at his chair with a small table of pastries in front of him. Mildred was on his lap, but as he tried to get up she was tipped on to the floor and scurried off without a murmur.

'Well done,' said Oeric struggling to haul his bloated body from the chair. 'I take it then you were victorious?'

'No thanks to you!' I said.

Without breaking step, Aelred grabbed him roughly, heaved him fully to his feet then threw him to the floor. 'Grovel you treacherous bastard,' he shouted, then stepped back so I could move in closer.

Oeric looked up at me, fear in his eyes. 'But... But...'

'There are no "buts", for I know what you've done. You've grown fat on the profits of those raiding the very people you were sworn to protect.'

That's not true! I've done nothing...'

'Exactly, you've done nothing, and that's the crime for which you must answer.'

With that he turned and started to crawl away from us on his hands and knees. Once clear of us, he got up and thought to make a run for it, but quickly realised his mistake. Outside he found the members of the fyrd were waiting, all of them intent on vengeance.

As soon as they saw Oeric they surged forward and quickly enveloped him. Before I could stop them, he was hustled and half dragged towards the Common Field where others from the settlement had gathered. It seemed that word of his involvement in the raids had already spread and all were baying for his blood. I heard Oeric call out, ordering his guards to protect him, but they were unable or unwilling to intervene.

I followed as quickly as I could and forced my way through the crowd to stand beside the wretch. 'This treacherous bastard has betrayed you all,' I announced, shouting to be heard above all the noise and accusations. 'I believe that he was behind the raids which have made many of you homeless. He then indentured others to repay what he loaned them, rendering them as slaves in all but name. Such treachery is unforgivable and not within the remit that he holds from Lord Werhard.' Then I pointed to the wagon. 'Those good men died because of that treachery. Now, by the power vested in me by Lord Alfred, I shall take him and commit him to trial.'

Several people called out asking for the right to kill him themselves.

'No, none of you can have a hand in this, for the punishment for you if you set against him is too severe. He'll die readily enough once the accusations against him have been proved.'

Even as I spoke I could see that the people were barely satisfied with that. They had only to look at their dead still laid out on the wagon for their blood to be stirred. One by one they began to call for Oeric to be handed over to them. With the crowd growing ever more hostile and crying out for justice, I signalled for Aelred to come and stand beside me.

'I'll not raise my hand against these people,' he said to me under his breath. 'Not for Lord Alfred and not even for you. They have a right to see justice done.'

I looked at him and could see he was in earnest. 'They'll tear him limb from limb if we don't protect him!' I warned. 'And they'll pay for that with their lives if they do.'

'Then so be it. He deserves all he'll get and more besides. His crimes are such that if you drag him back to Lord Alfred he'll only execute him anyway. We should therefore just let the crowd have him and thereby save the King and you the trouble.'

'That's not justice,' I reasoned. 'Besides, he's the son of an Ealdorman and Alfred cannot allow them to raise arms against him, whatever he's done.'

'Then let me do it,' said Aelred. 'I'll happily draw a blade across his throat and take whatever consequences come from that.'

With that Osmund and the guards formed a line in front of us thereby holding back the crowd. Lord Werhard was with them but showed no inclination to speak on his stepson's behalf. Instead, he came to stand beside me as if to endorse my authority. Someone in the crowd then threw a stone that struck Oeric on the head. It was followed by several more and then someone else produced a rope in which a noose had been formed. On seeing that, Oeric dropped to his knees, imploring me to stop them as they jostled closer, trying to reach him. When he realised that pleading with me was to no avail, he turned to his stepfather and begged him to intervene, but Lord Werhard refused as well, though I could see that it pained him to do so. In fact, there was nothing either of us could do against so many, yet I was determined not to execute him without proof. I nodded to Aelred who seized Oeric and hauled him to his feet, then, with the guards on either side of us, we tried to push him through the crowd so we could take him back to the Vill.

Still they cried for blood and I knew that if they got hold of him they'd string him up there and then. Getting him away from there in one piece clearly wasn't going to be easy.

'I know of this man's guilt,' I shouted to be heard above the noise. 'But I have no proof.'

'No, but I do,' called a voice from the crowd.

Suddenly there was silence and, when I looked, I could see it was Godric who'd spoken. As he edged towards me the crowd parted to let him through.

'What is your proof?' I asked.

Godric reached out and grasped a pin that Oeric was using to secure his cloak, tearing it roughly from the rogue's clothing. He looked at it then spat at Oeric. Holding up the pin for all to see, he spoke firmly. 'This pin belongs to my wife. Lord Werhard here will vouch for that, for it was given to her by his late wife as thanks for having cared for the dear lady in her final years.'

All then waited as Lord Werhard took the pin and examined it. With tears in his eyes he confirmed that all Godric had said was true.

'The pin was among that which was taken when my home was raided and burned,' continued Godric. 'Now it serves to pin the cloak of this treacherous snake. Have him explain how he came by it!'

That was enough to ensure that Oeric's fate was sealed. The people again began shouting and calling for his miserable hide to be handed over. I realised then that I had to act and that any hope of a fair trial had gone. I remembered again what Alfred had said about dispensing justice as I saw fit. I had no wish to do what was needed, but realised that I no longer had a choice.

'By the power vested in me by Lord Alfred, King and Bretwalda of all Wessex, I call upon this man to answer the charges made against him and explain how he came by this pin.'

Oeric looked flustered. 'I…I found it,' he tried. 'W…whilst out hunting. The rogue who stole it must have thrown it away or lost it. I thought it pretty enough but had no idea…'

The crowd were not convinced and began shouting once more. I raised my hand for silence then turned to Lord Werhard. 'I have to act,' I said. 'His guilt is now plain enough and if we leave it to the crowd he'll be torn apart. I can hasten his end if you wish it.'

I could see that the prospect of what I suggested troubled him, but neither he nor I could let the people carry the responsibility for hanging Oeric, even though he deserved to die at the hands of those he'd abused.

'It's down to me then,' I said. With that I removed the sling from my arm and tossed it aside. 'You lie like a treacherous toad and have abused your position of privilege and wealth. Your greed has cost the lives of all those good men over there and others besides, men it was your duty to protect. Also, you've reduced free men to a life of poverty and done nothing to ease the troubles of your people. There's but one sentence which can be passed.' With that I drew my sword and held it where he could see it. 'Therefore how do you plead?'

He snivelled like a frightened girl, but instead of answering, he dropped to his knees and begged again for mercy.

'Explain yourself or prepare to die! How do you plead?' I entreated him.

Still there was silence from the crowd.

Oeric mumbled something which sounded like a denial, but the words were lost to my ears as the crowd all screamed as one to answer for him. 'Guilty!' they cried so loud that I could hear nothing else. 'He's guilty! Kill him now and avenge us all!'

I looked at the sorry, bloated fool as he cowered at my feet. 'You can't do this!' he pleaded, shaking at the prospect of what would follow. 'I'm of noble birth and demand the right to be tried by my equals, as is my due!'

'You're not of noble birth. And your equals are the rats which run in the latrines and I doubt that even they'd have much to say on your behalf, so prepare yourself and make your peace with God!'

As he crouched there he looked up at me, fear and pleading in his eyes.

'Would you go to your maker unresolved?' I demanded, but still he made no answer. I remembered how Ethelnorth had been obliged to execute the farmer who'd paid taxes to the Vikings, but who also refused to repent before being slain. My dilemma was now the same as his. 'Resolve yourself!' I demanded. 'Make your confession to God before you die!'

Still he said nothing. Instead, he just burbled and snivelled like a cowardly wretch. He crouched so low that I wasn't certain I could make a clean sweep with my sword so instead I took it in both hands and raised it high above my head. Even as I did so I felt a sharp pain which I at first thought was coming from my shoulder, but then realised it was much more intense than that. I winced as it seemed to bite deep into my chest and was forced to lower the sword, but knew I had to carry on.

'Are you all right?' asked Aelred.

I ignored him and raised the sword again. It took all my strength to do it, but I realised that I had to strike or would no longer have the ability or resolve to do so. 'God have mercy on your soul,' I muttered, then drove the blade down through his shoulder, so deep that the tip of it reached his heart.

Blood pulsed from the wound and dribbled from his mouth and nose. There was no doubt that he died instantly but his body seemed to remain there, shaking as the life left it – or perhaps it was his soul anxious to be free from such a vile carcass. Only as I put my foot on his shoulder to withdraw the sword did he topple over and then lie on the ground, still bleeding but otherwise still.

The crowd was suddenly silent again as if in awe of what they'd witnessed. Many of the people walked over, spat on the body then moved away, more sated than satisfied and probably realising the horror of what it was they'd obliged me to do.

Aelred was also strangely quiet. 'You now carry the blame for them all,' he said at last. 'It's a heavy burden and, if I know you, it's one that may well trouble your soul. Yet you had no choice it—' He stopped suddenly when he realised I was in agony. 'What's the matter?' he demanded.

I lacked the strength to answer as a second wave of pain ripped through my chest. It was so intense that it was all I could do not to cry out and I even allowed my sword to fall to the ground as I no longer seemed to have the strength to hold it.

Aelred quickly tucked his arm under mine to support me. 'Is it the wound to your shoulder or your chest?' he asked.

I couldn't answer for by then the pain seemed to consume my very being.

Aelred signalled to the nearest guard to help him and, between them, they all but carried me back to the Vill.

* * * * *

'You've pushed yourself too hard,' warned Aelred as he helped me settle on a cot. I was still unable to speak, but was vaguely aware of all that was going on. He and the guard removed my clothes and, with the shutters closed and the room in darkness, covered me with a warm blanket. Aelred remained with me as I endured the pain as best I could. I have no idea how long I lay there, but I must have slept eventually for when I awoke the pain had largely gone.

'That blow to your shoulder did more harm than you realised,' warned Aelred when he noticed I was awake. 'I fear it unsettled your old wound.'

I knew it right enough. 'I just need to rest,' I reasoned, my voice not much more than a whisper. In reality I feared it was more than that. Normally, having exerted myself, any pain I felt from the wound to my chest subsided quickly enough, though left me weak and exhausted. But that time was different. The first pang had come upon me so suddenly that I could scarce determine what had happened. Those that followed were even more intense and seemed to pulse through me in waves. As such they all but took my breath away – but I dared say nothing of that to Aelred.

'Then do so,' he advised. 'There's nothing more you need do for now.'

'Tell Lord Werhard I'm sorry,' I managed, my voice still weak.

'I've spoken with him and he understands that you had no choice,' Aelred assured me. 'His heart is troubled, but he knows that the mob would have strung up his stepson if you hadn't intervened. At least this way the wretch got a better death than he deserved.'

I nodded to acknowledge the truth of that. 'And Lord Alfred must be told…'

He put his hand on my arm. 'All is being dealt with. Leonfrith has already sent word to him and we'll speak more about this later but, like I say, you must rest for now.'

There was so much I wanted to say at that time but lacked the strength to do so. In particular, whilst there was no outward mark to indicate that the wound to my chest had been disturbed, I was certain that Ingar's prophecy would soon come true for something within me had changed – and it was not the sort of change which should be welcomed.

*****

I was surprised when Aelred brought Mildred to visit me the next day and charged her with responsibility for caring for me. I was feeling much better by then, though was still sorely tired.

'I trust you'll approve my choice?' he said, smiling as though he knew there'd been something between Mildred and I.

I said nothing but he was not done with teasing me. 'There is of course an old crone who lives nearby who is said to have a way with bruises. I can send for her if you'd prefer...'

Mildred gave a little laugh then immediately set about making me more comfortable. She started by examining my shoulder and applying a balm to help reduce the bruising. I winced a little when I felt it cold against my skin. She then looked at the scar on my chest and applied a little balm to help soothe that as well.

'Be careful,' warned Aelred. 'Matthew is not a good patient and doesn't always know how to behave in the company of those who would help him.'

'Oh, I think Matthew knows full well how best to please a lady,' said Mildred cheekily.

'Ah,' said Aelred. 'Then I think it best that I leave him to your tender care.' With that he left us.

*****

Lord Werhard came in person to see me the next day. Although feeling much stronger, I'd resolved to rest a little longer, not only to give myself a chance to fully recover but also to allow things to calm down within the settlement. I still felt that in allowing myself to be drawn into the trap by Oeric, I was at least in part to blame for the loss of the men who'd died.

'My Lord,' I said, trying to get up as the Ealdorman entered the chamber where I'd been allowed to remain. He looked drawn and tired, his features somehow diminished. 'I'm so sorry that all should have transpired as it did. I...'

He raised his hand to stop me saying more and insisted that I remain abed. 'You did what was needed. Had you not slain him the crowd would have had him hang like a common criminal. Though perhaps that's what he deserved.'

'Even so, it was a cruel way to die, but I had no other option given how things were developing.'

'The fault is as much mine as yours, for I should have seen what he was about and not allowed him the freedom to act as he did. It's therefore high time that I set matters right.'

'In what way, my Lord?'

'I shall cancel the debts incurred by those who've suffered from the raids. I shall allow time for payment of all dues and excuse others from some of their obligations in order to give those who've struggled under the heavy yoke he placed upon their shoulders a chance to restore their lives.'

It was a generous offer which I knew would come as a great relief to all. 'I'm sure Lord Alfred would approve of that,' I said.

He acknowledged the point. 'There is another matter of which I think Lord Alfred will approve and which I would discuss with you if you've yet recovered enough,' he said.

'What is it, my Lord?' I asked.

'Matthew, I fear that I've been remiss in not recognising that I've grown too old to fulfil my responsibilities as Ealdorman within this Shire. I see that now and recognise how much harm has been done by allowing my stepson to run things because I felt too old and frail to do so myself. That was an error of judgement on my part which only serves to prove that I am indeed no longer fit or able to oversee all that happens here.'

'My Lord, I'm sure you acted for the best…' I managed.

He shook his head. 'It's kind of you to say as much but my best is no longer good enough.'

'So will you send word to Alfred and have him appoint a new Ealdorman?' I asked, not sure if that's what he meant.

'Yes,' he said firmly. 'But I'll also suggest a man who I think can take on that role.'

'Who do you have in mind, my Lord? I see none here worthy of the role and…'

'Matthew, you've achieved so much in the short time you've been here and whilst much has been resolved, the greatest challenge of all is yet to come. When Hakon and his horde descend upon us I fear I'm not the man to lead these people. You are the only one who could manage that, for they now much respect you and will follow where you lead.'

'My Lord, what are you saying…?'

'I'm saying that I would have you act as Ealdorman in my stead. Alfred will, I'm sure, see that as a wise and sensible step, though of course it will be for him to confirm it as a permanent appointment in due course.'

I didn't know quite what to say. 'My Lord I'm honoured that you should think highly enough of me to suggest such a thing…'

He smiled at me. 'For now, what I'm proposing is to let you finish the job you've started. Hopefully my stepson's death will mean the raids will cease or become less blatant. Of course we cannot be sure of that, but even if not, thanks to you we could now reasonably expect to see them off if they do deign to attack any of the farmsteads here again. More importantly, from what I hear of it, all the thanes are much impressed with your victory and your courage and will willingly support you when needed. Also, the fyrd will proudly follow the man they recognise as the warrior with the pierced heart. That just leaves the thorny problem of how to tackle Jarl Hakon and I've no doubt you'll have plans for how best to deal with him when the time comes.'

'I'm relying on the support of the thanes and on the fortifications which are all but complete. My concern is that the raid on that farmstead was intended as a trap. Hakon sent those men to tempt us into a fight which he expected to win thereby depleting our trained forces prior to securing the ford.'

'You mean that having slain the members of the fyrd, the raiders would have moved on to take and hold the ford until Hakon arrived?'

'Exactly, my Lord. And with the fyrd defeated there'd be nothing we could do to stop them.'

'Which is all the more reason for you to assume command. So think upon it, Matthew. Acting as Ealdorman carries a heavy burden, but no man I have ever met is more suited or capable of doing what's needed.'

'Thank you, my Lord. I…'

'If you accept then I'm no longer your Lord, for our roles would be reversed,' he said smiling.

I was thinking how strange it would seem not to address Werhard by his title when I realised I was expected to say something more. 'The appointment will do much to help me organise matters here so I accept it with thanks,' I managed. 'But you will of course retain all due respect and privilege.'

He thanked me then began to address various matters. 'I will have Leonfrith send word to Lord Alfred at once and to all the thanes and nobles within the Shire. Once Alfred agrees, as I'm sure he will, the position can be made permanent. In the meantime, you and Aelred will of course reside here at the Vill. If you will allow me to retain a chamber for some comfort in my old age, that would be much appreciated.'

'Of course. And I'd welcome any advice you can offer.'

'I suspect you'll need little in the way of help from me.'

'Except that no one knows this Shire better than you and I still have much to do to prepare against the likelihood of Hakon's attack.'

'Thank you. I appreciate the respect you've shown. Tomorrow, with your permission, I shall cremate Oeric's remains. Although against our creed to do so, I fear that feelings still run deep in the settlement and if I bury him his grave may not be left undisturbed.'

'I suspect that whether his remains are buried or cremated will make little difference in the eyes of God,' I said, meaning to ease his conscience in that respect, but he mistook my meaning.

'I fear my stepson will not have to worry about what God thinks of him,' he said ruefully. 'Given all his crimes I doubt he can reasonably expect to stand before Him or St Peter. He'll be more at home in the other place where he can spend eternity in the company of those who have, like him, followed the path to damnation.'

*****

'I thought you were already set to become an Ealdorman,' said Aelred as the next day he helped me to walk as far as the Common Field where we were to witness Oeric's cremation. I was feeling much stronger and was grateful for the chance to breathe fresh air and stretch my legs.

'That's true,' I acknowledged. 'It had been mentioned that I would become one, but I expected that to stem from my late father's estates, not here at Leatherhead. Anyway, it's only a temporary arrangement and still requires the King to agree.'

'I imagine there can be little doubt about that. Hopefully you'll still have need of a retainer like me to keep you out of trouble?'

I laughed. 'No, I have no need of retainers. But I do need a friend I can rely on to speak his mind and watch my back. Can you think of anyone who could manage that?'

Aelred inhaled deeply. 'Phew, that would be a difficult role indeed. You'll need a truly good man for that.'

'Exactly,' I said. 'Let me know if anyone comes to mind, but, in the meantime, perhaps I'd best keep you in tow – at least until someone more suited comes along.'

We both laughed. As we did so, I put my arm on his shoulder then grimaced as I felt the remnants of the pain in my chest once more.

'Are you sure you're yet well enough to be up and about?'

I nodded. 'I have to be. I'm not sure what Mildred has in mind for me next, but I have a feeling it'll be a lot more strenuous than simply walking about!'

*****

'Lord Werhard seems ill at ease with the prospect of a cremation,' said Aelred as we waited to witness the event.

'I think he's just conscious that the Church doesn't normally permit it, though given how many men and women have burned during raids and such like I can hardly see that it can make much difference to anyone's soul.'

'He's lucky that the vain bastard didn't end up with his head on a stake.'

With that it was deemed that all who intended to be there had arrived. The place set aside for the cremation was therefore sealed off by Lord Werhard's guards – or I suppose they were technically my guards by then. Their role was to ensure that no one could get too close, though many people from the settlement and surrounding farmsteads had gathered to witness it, some of whom might yet wish to despoil the body or even curse it. A large funeral pyre had been built and Oeric's bloated body had been lain atop it, dressed in simple robes with no finery. His body reminded me of Cedric, the traitor I'd slain whilst on my way to spy on Guthrum. Like Cedric, once dead Oeric's body looked much smaller than it had in life.

A priest had been summoned who offered prayers and spoke a few words, none of which seemed either eloquent or sincere. Then, when he'd done, Lord Werhard stepped forward carrying a burning torch. He hesitated for just a moment before setting light to the brushwood and kindling then stepped back. Like us he watched for a few moments more then turned away, stopping only to return the pin Oeric had taken from Godric. Then he walked away looking very dejected and alone.

*****

'So what now?' asked Aelred. We had both been given chambers in the Vill which were better appointed than anything he and I had known before. So much so that Aelred seemed to have taken on a new demeanour, striding around the Vill with his head held high.

'What do you think we should do?' I asked. I'd been thinking of Emelda a lot as I recovered and couldn't seem to shake her from my mind or indeed my prayers.

'Well, you've sorted things out here,' he ventured. 'We've seen off the raiders for the time being at least and I don't think they'll be coming back anytime soon. Oeric has been fairly punished, the thanes respect you and the people now regard you as their Lord. Add to that the fact that the stockade is all but finished and the fyrd is beginning to look like a force to be reckoned with. What else was it you were supposed to do?'

I laughed. 'You know full well what else. All that you've said is true, but none of it was the real purpose in our coming here.'

'You mean the little matter of two hundred Viking warriors who may decide to visit us?'

'Exactly. I'm worried that there's been no word from Alfred's spies and the winter is now fast approaching. I'm surprised they didn't send word when that raiding party left Hakon's camp. You'd have thought it was big enough to warrant their attention.'

'That's true,' agreed Aelred. 'But perhaps they had more to do at the time. Do you think I was right in suggesting that the raid on the farmstead was intended to weaken our position here?'

'I do. In fact, if they'd defeated the fyrd I'm certain they'd have moved on to take and hold the ford. If so, that could mean that the attack is now imminent despite the weather. It wouldn't be the first time that Vikings strike when you least expect it.'

'Then what's your plan?' asked Aelred. 'And don't tell me you haven't got one. I know you well enough by now to know that you always have a plan.'

'I think we should go to London and judge for ourselves what's happening there.'

'You mean risk our necks by walking back into that nest of vipers?'

'Exactly that,' I said.

He shrugged. 'I was afraid that's what you'd say. But are you yet well enough to travel?' he asked.

'Don't worry, my shoulder remains sore from the axe blow but will heal quickly enough if only Mildred would leave me alone long enough to rest it!'

'You should be so lucky! But I'm more worried about the wound to your chest.'

'As ever it'll recover, have no qualms on that account,' I lied.

'So when do we leave?'

'Tomorrow,' I said. 'We'll leave Leonfrith in charge of completing all the works here and order Osmund to carry on training the fyrd. If we travel light we should be there and back within three days.'

'I don't much relish venturing into that Viking camp,' admitted Aelred. 'You got away last time, but we might not be so lucky if we go there again.'

'Then we won't go to the Viking camp. We'll go to the Saxon side of the river instead and learn what we can from there.'

Aelred didn't look happy even at that. 'That'll take longer as it'll mean travelling upriver until we can find a way to cross. That could add several days to our journey there and back.'

'Then so be it,' I said. 'Besides, I've never been to London and look forward to seeing it for myself.'

Aelred shook his head as if to dismiss the idea. 'Well you won't like it when you do. For one thing it stinks and for another it's stock full of rogues and wretches intent on violence.'

'It's also in Mercia,' I pointed out. 'And whilst we have a sort of uneasy truce with them at present, they may not take too kindly to us being there, particularly if we're discovered by the Vikings and that upsets the rather awkward peace they seem to have achieved.'

'Yes,' said Aelred. 'And as like as not that's what will happen as most of it seems to be controlled by the Vikings one way or another.'

I considered all he'd said but had already made my decision. 'We have to go there,' I announced. 'I need to see what's happening and find out why Alfred's spies didn't warn us. For all I know they've been discovered and killed by now, in which case we can no longer rely on any warning from them if Hakon starts to make his move.'

'Phew, that sounds like we could be walking into a trap.'

'Exactly. That's why I suggest we go in at night, keep our heads down, then take up a position beside the river from where we can see Hakon's camp and observe what's happening, particularly with regard to the ships he's building.'

Aelred seemed to agree. 'I knew that coming along with you was a mistake,' he muttered. 'I've never known anyone who manages to persuade me to risk my neck as many times as you do.'

Chapter Thirteen

I was worried lest in travelling to London we might not get back before Hakon deigned to make his move. I therefore needed to find the quickest route there and back so as not to be away for longer than was needed.

Werhard said that he'd been to London several times and told us of a route he'd used which skirted south of the Vikings' camp and led to a ferry which we could use to cross the river. Once across, there was an old Roman road we could then follow eastwards all the way to the Saxon settlement itself.

With that in mind, Aelred and I determined to travel light, taking just one horse each and strapping whatever we'd need for the journey to the saddles. It was Werhard who suggested that we also leave our weapons behind and that we disguise ourselves as merchants intent on trade.

'It's an unruly place,' he warned. 'And if you venture into it dressed as you are and with such a valuable sword at your side, I fear you'll quickly attract unwelcome attention.'

Both Aelred and I were at first unhappy about travelling unarmed, but what Werhard said did make sense. 'We've no intention of staying for long,' I reasoned. 'So we'll go in, observe what we can and then leave. Hopefully that will mean just one night there, two at the most.'

Aelred still seemed far from convinced. 'And if anyone challenges us, what would you have us do?'

'We'll each carry a knife,' I suggested. 'That should suffice and none will think it strange that we do.'

In the end he agreed that it was probably our best option given that, by rights, we had no business being in such a hostile place. Thus we borrowed simple robes and cloaks that were not of the highest quality and selected more suitable horses than our own from the Vill's stables. Thus fitted out, we prepared to set off at first light, hoping to reach London before dark, though we expected to be hampered by the weather given that it was cold and raining heavily.

Apart from the weather, all went much as planned until we reached the edge of the marshes which lay to the south of London. They stretched further than I'd realised so the journey around them looked as though it would take much longer than I'd hoped. Also, it wasn't long before we came to a part of the road which was guarded by two Viking warriors.

'That's all we need!' said Aelred.

'Why on earth have they been posted here?' I wondered.

It was only as we drew closer that the answer became clear. There was a track which led from the road down through the marshes and thence to the river. We therefore assumed that they were there to direct any wagons needed to supply the ships or possibly the Viking camp itself.

'Leave it to me,' said Aelred. 'They won't delay us much.'

Neither of the men seemed all that interested in our being there. Instead, they sat idly beside the road with their horses tethered nearby. They'd formed a makeshift camp of their own and were sheltering from the rain beneath an awning with only a brazier for warmth. Perhaps because Aelred greeted them in their own tongue they were unconcerned by our presence or perhaps they were used to seeing travellers on that road. Either way they didn't even trouble to get up as Aelred approached them. After exchanging a few words, the guards laughed heartily at something he said and, with that, we were allowed to continue on our way.

'What did you say to them?' I asked, intrigued as to how he'd managed to persuade them into letting us pass so readily.

Aelred grinned broadly. 'They were only interested in what my young master might be carrying,' he explained.

'I'll bet they were! So what did you tell them?'

'I said that like a fool you'd lost all your wares and money gambling with a band of swindlers some days ago and now have nothing left.'

'Then why did they find that so funny?' I asked.

'I told them that they might as well stay where they are, warm and dry, then rob you when you return in a few days' time as you might by then have something worth stealing!'

'Was that really their intent?' I asked. 'To rob strangers who happened to be passing whilst supposed to be standing guard?'

He shrugged. 'What do you think? If we'd been carrying anything of obvious value I can't believe they wouldn't have tried.'

He had a point. I'd assumed that the fragile peace which existed between the Vikings on the southern bank of the river and the Saxon settlement on the northern one would ensure that we could travel safely enough as neither would be inclined to do anything which might upset that arrangement. However, as Aelred had surmised, hassling and even robbing a few hapless travellers was probably an accepted part of that and I began to wish that we'd kept our weapons.

Once past the guards, we travelled a little further before heading north towards the river, hoping to find the ferry which Werhard had told us about. As it turned out we didn't have to go far as we came across it quickly enough.

Even though the rain had stopped by then, the river looked very cold and grey on such a bleak day. It was not as wide at that point as I'd expected and had gently sloping banks on either shore. Gangways had been built leading down into the water in order that those intending to cross could board the ferry without muddying their feet, but there was nothing in the way of a shelter.

As for the ferry itself, it didn't look to be much more than a large raft which was operated by two men who I took to be father and son. The father was a stout ruddy-faced fellow and his son, who was taller, looked to be equally as strong, no doubt from the work needed for them to ply their trade. Although it had a steering oar which could be shifted from one side to the other if needed, the raft was moved by both men rowing whilst standing on either side of it. It looked to be hard work and the ferrymen therefore charged well for the crossing, and for anything they could sell to travellers besides. Not surprisingly they wanted payment before allowing us aboard so I took a few coins from my purse and gave them what was due, though it seemed a lot for such a simple service. I noticed how closely they watched as I began to count out the coins, so turned away from them as I did so.

That done, it seemed that Aelred and I were their only trade that morning and before setting off they warned us that we'd either have to wait until the tide fell further or we could leave at once if we were prepared to help, particularly if the current proved too strong at any point. Aelred said he'd be happy to do his share, but reminded me that I should not exert myself too much lest I again disturb the wound to my chest or even the one to my shoulder. We used the latter as an excuse but doubted the ferrymen believed it, particularly when we had to invent a story about my having fallen from my horse to explain the injury. After all, we could hardly say that a young merchant had been injured whilst fighting Viking raiders!

Having coaxed the horses aboard the raft, I was left to calm them whilst the others set about the task of tackling the river.

'You'd best cover their eyes,' advised the older ferryman when the horses seemed unnerved by the movement of the raft. 'We can't risk them getting riled if the river gets rough.' With that, the younger ferryman gave me sacks which I placed over the horses' heads and also two bags of feed, though once again he charged us dearly for those.

Seeing this, Aelred came across and spoke to me quietly. 'The bastards are rooking us!' he said. 'They're taking us for fools!'

I'd already realised as much, but had decided to let it pass as it suited our purpose. In any event, they didn't look to be the sort of men it would be wise to cross, particularly as we were both unarmed. 'It's not worth getting tossed into the river for the sake of a few coins,' I told him. 'And anyway, we don't want to draw attention to ourselves.'

Aelred saw the sense of that so went across to join the two ferrymen and help with the oars. 'You seem to know your trade well enough,' he observed amiably.

'As indeed I should,' said the older man. 'For I've been doing it long enough.'

'And you go across the river like this every day?'

'Aye, that we do,' said the man. 'We cross come rain or shine and sometimes several times in a single day.'

'That's a hard way to make a living,' I observed, joining the conversation.

He smiled. 'I can think of worse, my friend. No one causes us much trouble as most will need to use our services again, for there's no other way to cross the river hereabouts. Unless that is you've a mind to swim.'

He seemed to find that funny, but I didn't like to tell him that both Aelred and I knew all about that from when we'd swum ashore having capsized Torstein's boat, albeit that was a good way downstream from there. Instead, I laughed and continued tending the horses, stroking and patting them to calm them as best I could.

'No doubt you've business in London?' said the older man as his son took to the steering oar to keep our course against the flow.

I didn't answer.

'We've things to do once we get there,' said Aelred.

'Well, you mind you keep an eye on your young master,' warned the ferryman.

'Why, what's there which should concern us?' I asked.

He chuckled away to himself. 'It's just that we see many men safe across this river, but when they come back a few days later they seldom seem to have as much to carry as when they went.' So saying, he looked across to his son as though to share the jest with him.

Aelred glanced at the ferryman. 'Don't worry,' he said. 'We can look after ourselves.'

The ferryman looked doubtful about that. 'I hope that's so,' he replied. 'I've heard others say as much, but if you've a mind to come back this way you might choose to pay me now for the journey whilst you still have coin in your purse.

We don't work for free and often those that come back from London find they've been relieved of all they once had.'

We ignored the advice and finished the crossing in silence. Then, once safely on the north bank, Aelred took a few moments to rest before we set off along what looked to be a well-travelled road which, the ferryman assured us, would lead directly to the settlement at London.

As we followed the road we crossed several other much smaller rivers using bridges and fords until we reached the first of the homesteads which were situated on the outskirts of the main settlement itself, all of them clustered together for protection. As we got closer to London, we found that the road itself changed, being paved and lined with tombs, many of them Roman and most in need of repair with tall grasses growing between them. We stopped so I could read the Latin inscriptions on some of them, but most were too weathered to be legible. From there we continued until we reached the main settlement itself.

*****

Having been formed just to the west of what remained of an old Roman garrison, the settlement at London was a muddle of buildings and stores, all separated by narrow muddy paths. We dismounted and led the horses by their reins as we followed the widest of these and then turned down towards the river hoping that we would there be able to find a place from which we could clearly see the Viking camp on the opposite bank.

London was a large settlement – in terms of numbers it was much bigger than Chippenham and not much smaller than even Winchester, but the homes, workshops and trading stalls were huddled close together.

Even though it was late on a cold night, there were a surprising number of people still up and about, including some who sat outside their homes tending braziers. Groups of men and women were also gathered on corners, some of them gambling or talking, and there were stalls selling mead or hot spiced wine, all of which seemed to be doing a goodly trade. Aelred and I ignored these as we passed, keeping our faces covered against the cold and hoping no one would recognise us as strangers. At length we reached the river, but needed to follow it back along the bank towards the east until we could clearly see the lights from the Viking camp. There we stopped and settled down to wait out the dawn, anxious not to stay in that place for longer than was needed.

*****

We took it in turns to keep watch as we huddled against a wall with our cloaks wrapped around us as proof against the cold and with our still-saddled horses tethered close beside us. It was an uncomfortable place in which to rest as the stench from the river was an offence to our noses and there was considerable waste and rubbish strewn almost everywhere we looked, with rats running free amid the debris. It was also hard to sleep as however late it grew, there was the sound of people shouting and arguing somewhere in the distance.

When it was my turn to sleep, I'd barely closed my eyes before being wakened by Aelred prodding me in the ribs. 'We've got company,' he whispered.

As I looked up I could see three men with torches standing just a little way off who were obviously trying to decide whether we had anything worth stealing. I'd kept my knife concealed beneath my cloak, as had Aelred, so as far as the men were concerned we looked to be unarmed. Still they seemed wary as they edged closer, holding out their torches so they could see us more clearly.

I cursed when I realised what they intended. We'd hoped to slip into the settlement unnoticed and be away again without meeting or becoming embroiled with anyone, but already I knew that was not to be. I therefore decided to act swiftly and try to end the matter. Getting to my feet, I pushed my cloak aside and held the knife where they could all see it.

'Is there something you want from us?' I challenged.

The three men stopped in their tracks. I could see them more clearly by then and knew at once that the matter would not end there. One of them had already drawn a rusty seax and the other two were also armed – one with a heavy club and the other with a staff.

Aelred also got up and together we moved across to stand beside the horses.

'Stay where you are!' ordered one of the men.

'And why should we do that?' I asked boldly.

He raised the seax as if to threaten me. 'Because strangers aren't welcome here,' said the man. 'You've yet to pay the tariff for having stayed the night.'

'Ah!' I said. 'And I take it you're the one who's come to collect what's due?'

He turned to look at the others. 'Don't be a fool, boy,' he said. 'What have you got that's worth dying for?'

'Oh, I don't intend to die,' I assured him. 'And if you're of the same mind then I'd advise you not to try my hand. You'll regret it if you do!'

He was creeping closer by then and I could smell the drink on his rancid breath. That worried me as men confused by ale or mead often do things which, had they been sober, they wouldn't have thought of trying.

One of the others seemed to sense the danger and moved as though to restrain him, but was rudely shrugged aside. Then the man with the seax lurched towards me but seemed to stumble on something, lashing out wildly as he did so. Instinctively, I caught his arm by the wrist and made to defend myself, turning him away from me whilst holding him fast. As he struggled to free himself I felt my blade grind against something hard. Shocked, I looked at the man's face which showed that he was as surprised by what had happened as I was.

For a moment he stood there, then he fell to his knees clutching his side. He held out his hands, staring down at the blood which all but covered them, then fell forwards and lay face down in the grime.

'Christ you've killed him!' said Aelred.

'I didn't intend to,' I pleaded. 'The fool impaled himself on my knife!'

'We best get out of here,' he said. 'And fast.'

He was right about that. The other two had backed off several paces, but I couldn't be sure what they'd do next. In the end they seemed to retreat into the darkness and were quickly gone. Whether they simply ran or went to fetch more men I couldn't say, but we weren't about to wait around long enough to find out.

*****

'Leave the horses,' said Aelred clearly worried by what had happened. 'If they've gone to fetch others they'll be looking for two men who are mounted.'

'We'll have a long walk back to Leatherhead if we do!' I pointed out. 'Let's try to find a quiet corner of this wretched place and hide them. As soon as it gets light we can check out the Viking camp and then be gone from here in haste.'

It wasn't much of a plan and already we could hear raised voices and see flickering torches somewhere behind us.

'Perhaps we should go back and explain ourselves,' I suggested. 'I didn't mean to kill him, but given that he intended to rob us, he got only what he deserved.'

'They'll string us up if you do!' warned Aelred. 'And don't forget where we are. This is Mercia, not Wessex, so you can't rely on Alfred to intervene. We'll be hung like common knaves if they get hold of us!'

'You're right. But they'll be looking for two men. Perhaps we should split up and arrange to meet later,' I suggested. With that, a man appeared from the shadows. He carried no torch and approached us warily. 'Follow me, my Lord,' he said quietly.

'Who are you?' I demanded.

'A friend,' he said, his eyes everywhere at once.

I was suspicious in case it was a trap. 'I don't know you,' I said.

'No, but I recognise you, my Lord, from when you were at Winchester. You're Matthew, are you not? I was watching you to be sure of that when I saw what happened.'

I didn't answer.

'Look, I was also sent here by Lord Alfred to watch and report on that Viking camp over there,' he said, pointing across the river. 'Now we must be gone from here, for I fear you've stirred up more trouble than even you can manage.'

'What do you mean?' I asked.

'I mean that there's no law here beyond cold-blooded vengeance, so as strangers you're much at risk and mounted you won't be hard to find. I've a place where you can hide and once there we can talk some more, but if you stay here the mob will have you soon enough. And trust me, they'll look to hang you whether you're guilty or not!'

*****

The man took us to a hovel which was close beside the river. He led the horses into a small yard behind it and, having removed their saddles and brought them and our belongings inside, closed the door behind him. It was pitch dark in there, but he lit a single taper, worried lest even that should attract attention. From all I could see it was a squalid place, sparsely furnished and stinking of sweat and piss, but there was a window to the front which, though shuttered tight, looked as though it would have a good view of all on the far bank of the river. It was thus the perfect place for one of Alfred's spies to keep watch on all that was going on there.

'Wait here and I'll try to see what's what,' said the man in earnest. 'Don't make a sound or speak to anyone till I return. And be sure to bar the door behind me.' With that he was gone.

'Can we trust him?' asked Aelred.

In truth I wasn't sure. 'We don't seem to have much choice. But if he betrays us and returns with others he'll be the first to die,' I promised, tucking my knife into my belt.

When at last the man returned, the news he brought was far from good.

'You've stirred up a nest of hornets out there,' he warned. 'We'll need to keep you hidden.'

'But it was self-defence,' I argued. 'The man came at me with a seax. I didn't mean to kill him and even warned him, but he was intent on robbing us…'

'That's not what his brother's saying, my Lord. He claims you attacked them for no good cause and if they find you I don't imagine you'll get a chance to tell your side of the story. The bastards who run with these bands of robbers here in London think themselves above the law and have their own brand of justice.'

'So why did they try to rob us; surely we don't look as though we've anything worth stealing?'

'Did you cross by the ferry upstream of here?' he asked.

When I told him we did he seemed to know exactly what had happened. 'Those two rogues who work the ferry will have passed the word that you were ripe for the picking.'

'You mean they had a hand in it!'

'Not directly, my Lord. But they'd expect a share of whatever was taken from you.'

'The bastards!' said Aelred. 'And they've already fleeced us for the cost of the crossing! We should have taught them a lesson when we had the chance!'

'It's as well you didn't, for as like as not you'll need to use that ferry again to get away from here.'

'So what's to be done?' I asked.

'As I say, keep out of sight and I'll try to find a way to get you out of here.' With that he seemed to remember his station. 'By the way, whilst here I'm known as Radnor,' he explained. 'Like I said my Lord, I was sent here by Lord Alfred to watch the Viking camp.'

'And what are you called in Winchester?' I asked.

He hesitated then seemed reluctant to say more. 'That doesn't matter. Refer to me as Radnor for I need to keep myself from being known as anything else. There are spies everywhere – even in Winchester – and I've family there so would rather not have others learn of my reason for being here.'

Whatever his real name, Radnor seemed able enough. He was a small, wiry little man, wan faced from having lived in the settlement in secret for some time and probably thin from having eaten little whilst there.

'So how do you manage to keep your purpose here a secret?' I asked.

'I keep my head down and speak only to those I know,' he explained. 'Most here think I'm half Viking by birth so I'm left to myself by both sides, which suits my purpose well enough.'

I accepted that and introduced Aelred as my friend.

'My Lord, I'm sorry for the state of things here but keeping a tidy house is the least of my concerns.'

'No matter,' I said. 'But what have you to report?'

'All remains as when I sent word to you just over a week ago,' he said. 'Hopefully the man I sent then went on to report all to Lord Alfred.'

'A week ago?' queried Aelred. 'Then my friend I have to tell you that he never reached us.'

'So you never got my warning?'

I shook my head. 'No, what warning?'

'That a warband was going to attack a farmstead and hopefully draw you into a fight you couldn't hope to win. One of Hakon's spies there had set things up and having beaten you, the plan was to then secure the ford and…'

'That's just as I feared. But don't worry, we managed to make short work of them and I'm fairly sure we've dealt with the spy as well.'

'Then it seems the poor soul I sent never made it. That means Lord Alfred has not received my report either.'

'What did that say?' I asked.

'That the numbers at Hakon's camp are growing and that several ships have already left.'

'Then we can only assume that Alfred doesn't yet know that. You'll have to despatch another runner and have him set off in haste.'

'That's easier said than done, my Lord, for I've no one else to send,' he explained. 'There were three of us here – myself, the man I sent to you and one other, a man named Edwulf. He was discovered, but took his own life before the bastards could question him, fortunately for him and for me.'

'We can send word from Leatherhead,' I said. 'A rider should be able to get through from there. That's assuming we can get away from here.'

'Well, then you'll need to hurry. As I say, I fear Hakon is already preparing to make his move.'

'I feared as much,' I reasoned. 'That's why we've come. You say several ships have already left? Yet I didn't expect Hakon to risk his fleet in the winter storms.'

Radnor looked doubtful. 'You forget, my Lord, that these men are born to ride the storms and have their longships in which to do it. Even foul weather won't deter them from setting forth,' he said. 'Those left here are just coastal supply ships and I'll wager that they'll follow as soon as there's even the slightest break in the weather.'

'Well, don't worry. We're all but ready to take on two hundred Vikings!' I assured him.

'Two hundred?' queried Radnor. 'My Lord, there's many more than that to contend with now! Or at least there were. Some left aboard the ships which have already sailed, but at one time I counted near twice that number in the camp all told.'

Aelred and I were both stunned.

'That's many more than we expected,' I managed, a sense of fear seeping into my bones.

'I can only tell you what I've seen,' said Radnor.

'Do you know where the ships were headed?' I asked.

He shook his head. 'I had no way of telling. Word was that they were going abroad, but that could be a ruse. You know what these Vikings are like when it comes to being cunning.'

'So how many ships left?' I asked.

'Just three, all well laden with men,' said Radnor.

'They were laden with men?' I queried. 'That's strange. Why would he send men to wait at the coast? We assumed the ships were needed to carry his supplies and such like.'

Radnor realised at once what I was saying. 'No, as I said, they were all longships meant for raids and war. The ones remaining are more likely what he'll use for supplies, for they're all wider flat-bottomed boats, more suited to carrying cargo and such like. When they set sail they won't risk a storm and will need to keep close inshore, particularly if fully laden.'

'Then perhaps the other ships are indeed headed abroad. Three of them means what, a hundred men?'

Radnor agreed. 'Well, wherever they're headed it means trouble for someone.'

I knew the truth of that. 'They could be an advance force or perhaps they intend to launch a separate raid somewhere along the coast of Wessex on their own account,' I added.

'They could also be going north,' reasoned Aelred. 'The Vikings still have control there so it would be wise for them to go there rather than risk a raid in Wessex where they'd have limited support.'

'Either way Alfred must be warned. In the meantime, we must get back to Leatherhead with all speed and have the thanes send every man they can spare so we can hold off Hakon for as long as possible. Hopefully we can still delay him till Alfred can reach us.'

It was indeed a worrying position. 'So how many men do you think are still here with Hakon?' I asked.

'Perhaps three hundred, my Lord, including those who have recently arrived. Though they may not all be part of his warband.'

'That's more than we bargained for and what's worse, if Alfred has first to deal with the other raiders that will delay him arriving to reinforce us. But then perhaps that's what Hakon intends. If the men in those longships can keep Alfred busy somewhere on the south coast it means all Hakon has to do is breach our defences at Leatherhead. Given that all we have is a hundred men, he should manage that easily enough.'

Aelred looked truly worried. 'What you're saying is that we no longer have to delay them for a week, it could be much longer than that!'

'Or beat them,' I said, knowing that even with the thanes bringing their men we'd be outnumbered at least three to one and therefore couldn't hope to prevail against such odds.

Radnor listened in silence.

'Send us word as soon as Hakon moves,' I ordered.

'What good would that do, my Lord?' he asked. 'I'm on the wrong side of the river so he'll reach you long before I do.'

I realised he was right. 'Then all we can do is ensure that Alfred is told as quickly as possible. I suggest you leave at once, for there's nothing more you can do here. Go straight to Winchester and tell him to deal with the ships. He must then come to relieve us with all possible speed.'

'But, my Lord, we don't know where they're intending to strike! There are dozens of bays and inlets on the south coast they could use,' argued Radnor.

'Then he'll just have to search until he finds them. Do you know whether Hakon is still under Guthrum's command?'

He looked uncertain. 'From what I hear of it Guthrum still holds sway with all the Viking bands, but who can say what each of them intends. Certainly there are those warlords who would seek to take a small piece of Wessex for themselves if they can.'

'And is that Hakon's intent?'

'Who can say. But even if he can use all the men from his camp across the river and those he's sent on ahead in the longships, he couldn't hold whatever land he takes for long. Most likely he'll simply demand tribute and then leave.'

'Well, our orders are to delay him, so we'll do the best we can. Therefore you must go direct to Winchester. I'll send word as well as soon as we reach Leatherhead. Apart from that, all I can do is assume that his attack is imminent. I'll set lookouts to tell me when he approaches and make ready to receive him. That and pray that things are not as bleak as they appear.'

'There is one problem with that,' said Radnor. 'We need first to find a way of getting you both away from here alive.'

*****

As soon as it was light, Aelred and I looked out across the river and could see that all Radnor had said was true. Certainly some of the ships had gone and he was right, those which remained were more suited to ferrying supplies. Yet we still couldn't be sure where the longships he'd seen leaving were headed. Whether they intended to strike somewhere along the coast in order to draw Alfred away from Hakon's main attack or were simply out to raid on their own account, we couldn't say. If it was the latter, it was a very large group to be raiding, whether in Wessex or abroad. More likely they would join up with Hakon's main army sooner or later. Yet without supplies, such a large force wouldn't present much of a threat for long, so it was certain that the supply ships would need to set sail soon – and Hakon would then march south to meet them somewhere on the coast. That meant that his attack on Leatherhead was to be expected at any time. Therefore there was little point in watching further. We needed to get back to Leatherhead to prepare for battle – a battle we knew we couldn't possibly expect to win.

'You'll have to leave the horses here,' said Radnor. 'If I may, I'll borrow one of them and use it to ride to Winchester as I'll make better time that way. I'll leave it there for you to collect when time allows.'

'And what about the other one?'

'We'll turn it loose. There are many men here who'll steal it as soon as they see it. They'll hide it when they do to avoid any awkward questions about how they came by it.'

'And what are we supposed to do,' sneered Aelred. 'Would you have us walk back to Leatherhead?'

Radnor clearly assumed that's exactly what we'd do but it was a plan riddled with fault, not least because it would take us far too long and Hakon could well reach Leatherhead before we did.

'Look,' he said, having come up with a plan. 'I can get you to the ferry. There's a boatman I know who will take you there by river. He'll have to keep close inshore as the currents can be treacherous, but he knows them well enough.'

'What then? I asked.

'Use the ferry to cross the river then follow the road. That's the best I can offer, my Lord. At least from there you should be able to reach Leatherhead before Hakon does.'

'Or we could walk back from there to find those two guards,' suggested Aelred. 'They weren't posted far from the ferry and they had horses. We could "borrow" those and ride the rest of the way from there.'

'And you think they'll just let us take their horses and say nothing?' I said.

'Probably not. If needs be we'll just have to "persuade" them.'

It was Radnor's turn to look worried. 'My Lord, if you kill two Viking guards others will surely come after you looking for vengeance,' he warned.

I shrugged. 'Then we'll have to ride hard to ensure they don't catch us, won't we?' I said.

Aelred seemed amused. 'Why is it that whatever trouble you get me into, I find even more of it when you try to get us out of it?'

'Two guards won't be much trouble, particularly if we can catch them unawares,' I reasoned.

'No,' he said. 'That's true enough. But if what our friend here says is right, we could well find we then have a few hundred Vikings hard on our heels screaming for vengeance. They may not be quite so easy to deal with!'

*****

As Radnor went off to find the man who he said would take us upstream as far as the ferry, we began to make ourselves ready. We hurriedly took what we could from our saddle bags and placed it in a sack. Aelred then borrowed a stout staff from Radnor which he said might come in handy and, with that, we saddled one of the horses for Radnor to use. We first draped an old blanket across its back to help to disguise it then turned the other horse loose, just as Radnor had suggested.

When Radnor eventually came back he led us down to the river and along what served as a jetty to where a small boat was moored. I gave the boatman a coin which was probably more than he could earn in a week, then promised him another if we got there safely. It worried me that he would thereby know we had money about our persons but I gathered from our friend that he could be trusted.

We stressed to Radnor how important it was that he reach Winchester and tell Alfred about the boats and about how pressed we would be at Leatherhead until he arrived to relieve us. Even though I had no doubt that he would do all he could to ensure that his message got through, the thought was not lost on me that his chances of reaching Winchester alive were not good, but we seemed to have no other option.

The weather that day had turned into a wet sleet that seemed to chill us to the core. Nonetheless we could ill afford to wait for it to improve so, as Radnor rode away, Aelred and I settled into the small boat and waited for the boatman to push off and set about rowing us upstream. As Radnor had said, the boatman dared not risk the stronger currents when rowing alone in such a small boat so worked his way following close beside the bank. Many people stopped and stared as we passed but, as luck would have it, we were left to make the journey without incident.

Shortly before midday we arrived at the ferry hoping that the hardest part of our journey was done. From there all we had to do was use the ferry to cross the river, walk back along the road, kill two Viking guards, steal their horses and ride as though all the hounds of hell were at our heels.

*****

As I paid the boatman what I'd promised, it occurred to me that we might have asked him to take us as far as where the Emele joined the main river and then row us upstream from there all the way to Leatherhead. Although the miller had told us that parts of it were too shallow, with three us we could probably have carried such a small boat across any such areas we encountered.

The boatman laughed when I mentioned it.

'Lord help us, I've rowed all this way upstream for the best part of the morning without a rest and you'd have me go yet further? Well, I'm sorry my friend, but I'll not manage another stroke however much coin you pay me.'

It seemed reasonable enough, so I let the matter rest. Instead, Aelred and I went across to the gangway serving the ferry and signalled for it to come across to collect us.

When the ferrymen eventually arrived they doubtless assumed we'd no longer have enough money to pay them, believing that their friends had robbed us.

'Ha! I warned you they'd fleece a pair of innocents like you!' said the older man who seemed to find the whole thing amusing, as did his son.

'What makes you think they did?' I asked.

'Well if not, then what did you do with your horses?' sneered the older man. 'Did you not sell them when you found you'd not enough coin left to pay for food and lodging?'

They both laughed again. 'Perhaps they ate them instead,' quipped his son who was busy securing the raft. 'It's surprising what men will eat when they're hungry!'

Aelred and I went to stand beside the father. 'You might like to know that your "friends" in London were a little careless in choosing who to rob,' I told him. 'One of them in particular now has cause to regret that.' Even as I spoke, I drew my knife and fingered the blade.

The man said nothing, but watched with us as his son finished tying off the mooring rope. As he did so, Aelred stepped forward and produced his knife as well, thereby making our intentions clear to them both.

'The good thing is that we'll not need more coin for as I recall we were charged twice the fare last time,' I said, smiling. 'So why don't you and your young friend here make ready to set off again? Though if you'd rather stay here I'm sure we can manage the raft on our own.'

It was Aelred's turn to speak. 'Mind, how you'd get across to fetch it back again I wouldn't like to say, particularly if we were, shall we say, "careless" in how we secured it once on the other bank. As you said when last we met, there's no other means to cross hereabouts – unless of course you've a mind to swim!'

The man looked to his father, not sure what to do. 'But…?'

'Oh, don't worry, we made very short work of your friends in London, so unless you think you'd fare any better than they did, I suggest you take us back across or…'

'Or what?' said the older man, his face reddening with rage.

I raised my knife so he could see it plainly. 'Or my friend and I will cut out your gizzards and toss your miserable bodies into the river. So what's it to be?'

* * * * *

The two ferrymen decided not to call our bluff. After all, they had little to gain so challenging us wasn't worth the risk. Aelred stood beside one of them and I the other as we forced them to row the ferry across, making the journey in almost total silence. Once on the other bank, we bid them farewell and began the walk back to where the two Viking guards had been stationed, intent on stealing their horses.

'So do you think Oeric killed the messenger Radnor sent?' asked Aelred.

'Who can say, though you'd have to admit that it does seem likely given all that happened with the raid. Mind, I doubt he did it himself but rather paid others to do his dirty work for him.'

'Then he really was a treacherous rogue,' said Aelred. 'But where's that assassin now, that's what worries me?'

'Who can say? Most likely he left as soon as he learned of Oeric's fate, though of course we can't be sure of that.'

'God's truth, that means he could still be among us! Is there no end to this treachery?' asked Aelred. 'Do we still have to mind our backs at every turn?'

'I think we do, but, in the meantime, let's hope that Radnor gets through safely.'

'You'll presumably send another messenger once we reach Leatherhead, just in case?'

'I'm minded to go myself,' I said.

Aelred looked at me strangely. 'But you're needed at Leatherhead. It's your duty to lead the defence. Without you they won't stand a chance!'

'I know it! So once again I have to put duty before my own wants and needs.'

He thought for a moment. 'Ah! You want to see your son, I suppose. Is that why you want to go back to Winchester?'

'Is that so strange? You and I both know that there's every chance we may not survive this battle given what we now think we may be up against. I'd have liked to at least see him before I die.'

*****

The guards were still there – not the same ones we'd seen the day before but two men equally as bored and disinterested in the duty assigned to them. They were standing beside the brazier, warming their hands and paying us no mind as we approached.

'So what do we do?' asked Aelred.

I lifted back my cloak to reveal the hilt of my knife, thereby making it plain what I had in mind. 'We'll stroll up to them and you can distract them. Whilst their backs are turned, I'll seize the one nearest me and hold this to his throat. Hopefully that'll persuade them not to make a fight of it.'

'And if not?'

I looked at him, not needing to answer that.

'If you kill them they'll know it wasn't just a few horse thieves and, as Radnor said, you can't just leave dead Vikings on the road or others will come looking for vengeance.'

'So what's your suggestion?'

'Leave it to me,' said Aelred.

With that we approached slowly so as not to cause alarm. As we drew nearer they turned to look at us and Aelred asked them something, probably for directions, then went to stand beside their brazier. They seemed not to object to that and, for a moment, appeared to be discussing something. Then, when they least expected it, Aelred began to walk away. He'd taken no more than a few paces before he turned and, without warning, struck one of the men hard across his back with the staff. Taken by surprise, the man stiffened in pain, but before he could recover, Aelred struck him again, this time driving the staff into his side so hard that the Viking groaned then fell to the ground like a sack of grain.

The other guard reached for his sword, but when he saw me advance towards him with my knife already drawn, he seemed to think better of it. Two against one were not the sort of odds he relished, particularly if it might mean dying for nothing. Instead, he stood stock still, hardly daring to move.

Aelred shouted at them both, no doubt telling them to stay back as he went to untie their horses. Moments later we were mounted and riding hard towards Leatherhead for all we were worth.

Chapter Fourteen

As soon as we reached Leatherhead I summoned Leonfrith and, as a matter of courtesy, invited Werhard to join us as well even though he was no longer the Ealdorman. I first insisted that Leonfrith send a messenger to Alfred telling him about the longships laden with men which might be intending to strike somewhere along the south coast and also that I feared Hakon was about to make his move on us with a force of near three hundred warriors.

'Place two men on watch to warn us as soon as there's any sign that Hakon is coming,' I ordered. 'We must know the moment his men are sighted so that we can ready ourselves.'

'I thought word would come from Alfred's spies in London,' said Werhard, looking worried.

'That was the plan but the man they sent never reached us and was presumably killed whilst another took his own life rather than be taken by the Vikings. The third one, a man named Radnor, is even now on his way to Winchester, but we need to send a message from here in case he too is intercepted.'

'My Lord, we can post men on the hills to the north,' suggested Leonfrith. 'From there they'll have a clear view of the road from London and can light the beacons to warn us. That will also alert all the other settlements as well.'

'Good. But we can't afford to wait for that. Send word to all the thanes to attend at once and to bring every man they can spare, together with any weapons and all the war gear and provisions they can carry. Insist that they get here with all possible haste. Also advise those thanes who reside further afield that we may need their help, though I doubt they'll be able to reach us in time.'

Werhard looked worried. 'So what's to be done?' he asked.

'Whatever's needed,' I said simply. 'As the thanes arrive tell them to meet me here at the Vill and have their men muster at the Common Field. There's no time for delay.'

'But if Hakon doesn't come the men will have been drawn from their labours for no purpose!' said Werhard.

'That's a risk we have to take. But believe me, he's coming all right, and probably within a matter of days. All he's waiting for is a break in the weather so that he can risk his supply ships putting to sea. We have to be ready when he does.'

'Surely Alfred will march to relieve us as soon as he learns of this?' said Werhard. 'He could yet reach us in time.'

'Alfred will have more than enough to do if he's to deal with three ships laden with warriors. They may well have already landed so he'll have the devil's own job just to find them. My worry is that they're intended to draw him away from here so that Hakon can force his way past us more easily. If the two groups then join forces and are supported by Hakon's supply fleet, they'll be a force to be reckoned with, that's for sure. Either way it means that we're on our own for now.'

Werhard was suddenly silent. 'Then we're lost,' he said as though resigned to defeat.

'Not yet we're not. But we must act now. Is the stockade now complete?'

'It is, my Lord.'

'Then whilst we wait for the thanes to get here start to stockpile food and weapons there, particularly arrows and sling shot. This could well turn into a siege.'

Leonfrith didn't tarry a moment longer, but set off at once to carry out my orders.

'So Matthew, what's your plan?' asked Werhard.

I tried to sound as reassuring as I could. 'I won't know until I see what actually transpires,' I said. 'But I fear it's no longer just a case of delaying Hakon, we now have to find a way to defeat him.'

'What with just a hundred men at best? Surely we can have no hope of doing that!'

'All we can do is try,' I said.

'Then what can I do to help?' he offered.

'For a start we can evacuate the settlement. There won't be time for that once the Vikings are sighted. We need to get all the women and children to a place of safety on the other side of the river where they can remain behind the shield wall once we form it. The open pastures there should enable them to assemble together with all their livestock and belongings, but all the men must now help fight where they can regardless of age or ability. There can be no excuses.'

'Will the women and children be safe there?' he asked.

'We're none of us safe. But you're right. We should have them disperse into the hills taking all their provisions with them. Once Hakon gets past us he'll need to find food to feed his men so will plunder whatever supplies he can lay his hands on. I wouldn't put it past him to rape or butcher a few innocent bystanders whilst he's about it.'

'Then leave the evacuation to me,' he offered. 'The people know me well enough and will do as I say.'

'Thank you. That's one less thing for me to worry about. Heaven knows I'll have more than enough to do preparing our men for the battle once they learn what numbers they'll be up against.'

*****

The thanes started to arrive the very next day, not all at once as some had further to travel than others, but all responded without hesitation as soon as word reached them. They also brought men and weapons, though, as I'd feared, none of them were well armed.

'How many thanes have come?' I asked Leonfrith.

'So far just eight, my Lord,' he said. 'But we have word that the others are on their way.'

'I hope they know to hurry. How many men does that mean altogether?'

Leonfrith knew I wasn't going to like the answer. 'All told we should number about one hundred and twenty,' he advised, then waited for my reaction.

'Well, that's slightly better than we expected, but still nowhere near enough,' I said, trying to hide my disappointment. 'Our strategy must therefore remain defensive with our forces holed up in the stockade trying to cut down as many Vikings as they can. Are all the people now safely across the river?'

'Nearly, my Lord. They've been told not to leave anything behind that the Vikings can use, so progress may be slower than we'd like.'

'Well, don't let them hamper you in your work supplying the stockade, for there's still much to be done there.'

'What if the stockade is breached, my Lord?'

'Then we'll fall back to the island and destroy the bridge and the water wheel behind us. Once that becomes untenable everyone must join the shield wall on the other side of the river. We'll make our last stand there.'

'Against three hundred Vikings?' he mused. 'That's almost three to one.'

It was Aelred who then added his thoughts. 'Yes, but it could be worse. Remember we'll be fighting from cover so should be able to even up those odds a bit once the battle gets underway.'

'There are now twenty or so men from here who, although not part of the fyrd, are resolved to help, plus some of the women and boys. I've arranged for them to remain in the stockade to douse any fires, distribute arrows and also tend the wounded,' said Leonfrith.

'Good,' I said, hoping to reassure them both. 'Then we should fare well enough so long as the men's resolve remains firm.'

'Aye,' said Aelred. 'It's only if it comes down to hand-to-hand combat that we may prove inadequate. After all, our men's training has been brief whereas these Vikings were born to a life of violence and have had years in which to hone their skills.'

'What would you have me do next, my Lord?' asked Leonfrith.

'The men are already being mustered at the Common Field. Go there and deploy them as best you can. Send those who can shoot to the stockade or to the island and all the rest to make up the numbers in the shield wall.'

'Very good, my Lord.'

'Beyond that all we can do is hope that we've done enough to stop the bastards.'

* * * * *

I left Leonfrith to allocate the men whilst Aelred and I went to speak to those thanes who had arrived and were waiting at the Vill. I needed to be sure of their full support, but, as it turned out, they were more than willing to follow my lead as they'd been impressed at how we'd beaten the raiding party at Bleakley Wood even though outnumbered. They were also well aware that Werhard had appointed me to act as their Ealdorman and that it was likely the promotion would be made permanent. Thus they were all keen to curry favour with me where they could.

'We have a problem,' I said sounding as sombre as I felt. 'The messages from London were intercepted so never reached either us or Lord Alfred in Winchester. Had they done so they would have warned of an imminent attack by an even larger number of Vikings than we feared. Worse still, Hakon has already sent three ships laden with men. We can't be sure where they're headed, but have to assume they'll sail to the south coast to establish a bridgehead there. Lord Alfred will deal with them easily enough once he finds them, but that will delay him getting here to relieve us. I believe that's all part of Hakon's plan for it means he thinks his attack here will meet with only token resistance. I mean to show him he's wrong.'

There was a stunned silence.

'How many Vikings are coming?' asked one man.

'Possibly as many as three hundred,' I admitted. 'Hopefully less.'

A gasp went up from those assembled.

'We can beat them,' I assured them. 'I have a plan, but it allows that nothing can be left to chance.' With that I waited for them to settle before I spoke again.

'First we have to evacuate the settlement here. That's already underway so that the people who can't help with the fighting will take their belongings across the river and then hide in the hills where they should be safe. Werhard is overseeing that in person. We'll leave nothing the Vikings can use against us and certainly no food with which Hakon can feed his men.'

'They'll destroy this place anyway,' observed one man. 'You know what the bastards are like!'

'I know it, but there's nothing I can do about that. Once they have they'll march down to the river and try to cross. We'll hit them with everything we have from the safety of the stockade – arrows, sling shot and anything else we can throw at them – killing as many as we can. The stockade is already being provisioned and I'm placing fifty of our best bowmen there or on the island beyond it. The rest of the men will form a shield wall on the other side of the river to deal with any Vikings who manage to cross. Those men will need to be well trained and I'll leave Osmund, who is now chief of my guard here, to determine who shall serve where, but I want you to join them and keep them steadfast.'

'Where will you be?' asked a man who was standing to one side of me.

'Everywhere,' I assured him. 'Aelred and I will reinforce wherever the fighting is fiercest.'

'They'll simply push their way through! How can we stop them?'

'With arrows, then with blood. But remember, the water in the river is deep and already cold. They'll have to use the ford to cross, but can do so only three or four abreast. I've had hides built on the island to protect bowmen who will pick them off from there as they try. Once all the people are safely across we'll lift the stepping stones at the ford to make the water as deep as possible and plant sharpened stakes in the river to make crossing even more difficult. Ropes are also being put into place which can be drawn across in case they try to send men upriver by boat. The few Viking warriors who make it to the other side should then be easy enough for you to deal with. Hopefully some will flee, but those who don't must be killed. There can be no room for mercy.'

*****

From the Vill I went straight to speak with Osmund who was busy sorting out the men who were to form our shield wall, trying to place them to best effect. 'How bad?' I asked, knowing what he was going to say.

'They've all done some training, my Lord, though few have ever been in a full-blooded battle,' he said. 'I've divided them into groups. They'll form just two ranks to stand one behind the other. It won't withstand a full assault, but it's the best I can do. You'll have to keep up the barrage of arrows and such like for as long as you can.'

I must have looked concerned.

'Don't worry, my Lord. I've put men who seem to know what they're about to stand beside those who've never fought before. Where will you position the thanes?'

'I want them to stand with you behind the shield wall. That way they can shame or cajole their men into holding their nerve. They should also be able to deter any deserters.'

He nodded to acknowledge the sense of that. 'But am I to command, my Lord?'

'You are. I doubt we can match them if it comes to hand-to-hand fighting so keep the ranks tight and the shields raised. Godric will organise our bowmen and do his best to reduce their numbers where he can. Have you spoken with him?'

'I have, my Lord. He's in the stockade.'

I turned to leave, but then realised that I might not get another chance to speak with Osmund. 'Thank you,' I said. 'This won't be easy, but with men like you I'm sure we'll give a good account of ourselves.'

*****

Godric seemed much more at ease than most of the others. There were already thirty or forty men within the stockade and he was positioning them behind the fence in pairs, each with a basket of arrows set between them. Others were being stationed at various strategic points and on the island.

'How goes it?' I asked.

He grinned broadly, clearly enjoying his role. 'I wouldn't want to be one of the Vikings when this lot show themselves,' he joked.

'How will you use them?'

'I've ordered them to keep out of sight. As soon as the Vikings come within range we'll show ourselves and, on my command, will loose a volley of arrows directly into their ranks. That should slow them down a bit. My men will then continue to shoot at will as rapidly as they can. Not all are excellent shots but it won't much matter; the barrage should suffice to hit them hard. Those that do get past us will still have my men on the island to deal with when they try to cross the river.'

'Where will you stand?'

He turned and pointed to the hatchway on the upper floor of the mill. 'I'm going to position myself up there, my Lord. I'll be able to see the attack clearly from there and do what I can to pick off the senior Viking warriors. I have a few special arrows with long thin metal points which Eagbert has forged for me – ideal for piercing mail. I even have one reserved especially for Jarl Hakon himself.'

I smiled, something I hadn't had much inclination to do until then. 'Excellent,' I said. 'But do you know what he looks like?'

'I'm told he has hair the colour of copper and that he fights without a helmet so his men can recognise him in battle.'

'You'll also know him by his weapon. He carries a brutal club, which is why he's known as Hakon the Bonebreaker. If you can strike him down that will weaken the resolve of them all. But when the Vikings attack, rather than have the men deployed as you've suggested, have half of them shoot their arrows high into the air. It won't matter whether or not their aim is true; the Vikings will have to raise their shields to protect themselves from the onslaught and, as they do, will present an open target for the other half who can then aim directly at them.'

He seemed to like the idea. 'I will my, Lord.'

I put my hand on his shoulder and congratulated him on being so thorough.

'Thank you, my Lord. I shall serve as best I may.'

'I think you'll do more than that. I'm proud to have you with us.'

'My Lord,' he said, clearly flattered, 'I hope my having command here won't upset some of the thanes.'

'It may do,' I acknowledged. 'But I need men I can rely on and you, Aelred, Osmund and Leonfrith have already proved your worth. The thanes have only come lately to the fray and can best serve us by remaining with their men, but there is only room for one man to command each group lest our ranks become confused. I've chosen you all for that on merit.'

*****

Leonfrith was also busy at the stockade finalising the supply of provisions and such like. It was a task made more difficult by the men and women who were still ferrying their belongings across the river to safety on the other side. Some were using carts whereas others were simply dragging a litter, but all were in haste and clearly in fear for their lives.

'Has the settlement now been cleared?' I asked Leonfrith who had been tasked to ensure that all the food and provisions had been removed.

'There's not enough left in the settlement or the Vill to feed a rat, my Lord, never mind a horde of hungry Vikings,' he said cheerily.

'Good, then we'd best prepare ourselves.' So saying, Aelred joined me and, together, we went to don our own war gear as we felt that might help to impress upon the others that we were in earnest. My mail had been mended whilst we'd been in London and I noted that Eagbert's handiwork was as good as any I'd ever seen, so much so that it was hard to spot where links had been replaced.

As we returned to the stockade, Aelred noticed a few men who were setting the sharpened stakes into the riverbed either side of the ford with their pointed heads leaning towards where Hakon's men would be assembled waiting to cross. 'That should cause them a few problems,' he laughed. 'I'll go and tell them to set the stakes just below the surface so they can't be seen. That way when they stumble across them the Vikings will be forced to break rank and thus be sitting ducks!' With that he went to lend a hand.

By then, Leonfrith had finished storing the provisions and such like within the stockade. 'My Lord, all is ready,' he reported. 'Or at least as ready as it can be. Another week would have been better but…'

'Another month would have been better still. Will the stockade hold?' I asked.

'I think it will, my Lord. At least at first. My worry is they'll try to hack it down with their axes.'

'Warn Godric about that. Tell him to have his men do all they can to keep them at bay and prevent them from getting too close,' I suggested.

'Very well, my Lord. I also worry that they'll set fire to the mill as we discussed, but I can see no way of preventing that.'

I had to admit he was right. 'Then keep the pails to hand and make sure all who have agreed to help with that know what's needed. It'll be their job to fetch water to douse any flames. But remember, Godric will be up there so we'll need to warn him if the fire does take hold.'

'Where would you have me stand,' asked Leonfrith.

'I want you to finish what you're doing here then remain behind the shield wall and help to keep the people there out of our way.'

Leonfrith looked relieved as it meant he would be away from the main fighting.

'Are all the hides on the island prepared?' I asked.

'They are, my Lord. All is set.'

'Good. Then all we can do now is wait.'

'Yes, my Lord. That and pray to God that all goes as we intend.'

*****

The thanes all looked disgruntled as the men within their charge were allocated positions by either Osmund or Godric according to their skills.

'I would have you stay beside them,' I advised them all. 'They'll readily support you and therefore I've only to direct you for them to follow. That way I can despatch small groups to wherever they're needed most.'

I could tell they were not sure how to respond to that.

'Look, it will be bloody work once the Vikings reach the shield wall and I need men there who can handle themselves and inspire others to stand firm as well.'

They all seemed to relish that particular compliment, though in truth I had no idea how well any of them could fight, but I was anxious to leave the men I'd chosen to get on with things without interference. 'Are any of you good with a bow?' I asked.

Two of the thanes, Edgar and Coenred, both raised their hand. I didn't know either of them well but made a quick decision based on the fact that both seemed eager for the fray. 'Then Edgar, I would have you join the bowmen on the island so you can direct them, but you must follow Godric's lead.'

'Where will Godric be?' asked Coenred, the other thane.

'Up there, on the roof of the mill, hoping to pick off Hakon or any other chieftain he can spot.'

'Then, my Lord, I'd best join him. I can pick off a sparrow from a tree at thirty paces,' he boasted.

'Well, we're not after sparrows,' I quipped. 'But if you're as good as you say I don't doubt we can find a "raven" for you to shoot at. Aim for the man carrying the banner. Hit him and the Vikings will doubtless falter. Kill him and it'll stop them in their tracks,' I told him, recalling how Dudwine had turned the battle at Edington in our favour by seizing the raven banner. 'It won't take them long to rally themselves, but I have a feeling we'll much appreciate whatever respite that provides.'

* * * * *

As I inspected the preparations I was initially pleased that we seemed to be all but ready. It was Aelred who pointed out the one thing I'd overlooked.

'What about the monks at the Monastery?' he asked.

Even as he said it I realised I'd not sent word to warn them of what was about to transpire. My first thought was that they might be safe given that the Monastery was so well secluded. Leonfrith had sent word to all the outlying farmsteads and, for the most part, they'd come into the settlement, either bringing their livestock with them or having driven it to a place of safety. But the Monastery had been overlooked. 'Send word to them now!' I ordered. 'It's probably too late for them to join us here, but at least they can find somewhere safe to hide.'

A rider was despatched at once – I only hoped that he'd reach them in time. With that I instructed everyone to hurry the last of the people seeking shelter across the river.

There was then not much more I could do, but the thanes had brought priests with them and, whilst I didn't want to disrupt things by arranging for a Mass to be said, I had them go among the men to hear confessions.

'What about you?' asked Aelred. 'Is there nothing you wish to confess?'

I wasn't sure whether he was teasing me or not, but at that moment I did feel a desperate need to make my peace with God, fearing that it might be my last chance to do so. I therefore stopped to offer a silent prayer then crossed myself before turning to take one last look at all we'd achieved.

It was then that things began to go wrong.

The rider we'd sent to the Monastery returned much sooner than expected. As he rode back into the settlement he came straight to see me. 'We're too late, my Lord!' he shouted as he dismounted. 'The Monastery's under attack and already in flames!'

I cursed myself for the error, but could ill afford to waste time on remorse. 'So much for the beacons,' I said ruefully under my breath.

Only Aelred heard me. 'No doubt they killed the poor bastards before they could light them,' he said.

I realised he was right. It was too late to worry about that as all I could do was wait for the onslaught to begin and pray some more – but this time not for my own soul, but to ask God to ensure there was nothing else I'd overlooked.

*****

As Aelred and I stood together and waited, he seemed strangely ill at ease, not at all like the man I'd come to know. 'How do you feel?' he asked.

'Like I always do before a battle,' I said.

'You mean that sickness that seems to settle like a stone within your belly?'

I nodded, recognising the same symptoms myself. Suddenly I felt the need to tell Aelred what I wanted to happen to my remains if I should fall.

'Best not to think about it,' he advised.

'I have to. My estates are large and my death would be of consequence to many. First bury me somewhere in the forest where my grave won't be disturbed. I wouldn't want some Viking meddling with my bones or taking my head as some sort of trophy. Then take word to Alfred and give him my sword so that he can pass it on to my son. It was once my brother's and our father's before that. Tell him that I would have you look out for the boy and manage my lands in my stead. I'm sure he'll agree to that. And don't forget your promise to Ingar.'

'You're assuming that I survive the battle and you don't,' he said.

'You'll survive,' I assured him. 'But this may well be my last fight. I had a dream last night in which I recalled how it was when I was struck by the arrow, only this time my father and my brother were calling me to them, not ushering me away.'

He looked at me. 'Such dreams are nothing more than a mirror for all our fears,' he said. 'You carry the responsibility for what happens here so it's right that you should be concerned about all that which is about to unfold.'

'I hope you're right,' I said. 'Though I have a feeling that this time it will be different.'

* * * * *

It seemed that as she waited to cross the river, Mildred had been watching Aelred and I and had obviously overheard a little of what was said. She came over to speak with me, seeming almost coy about others seeing us together in public.

'Do you fear you won't survive this battle, my Lord?' she asked shyly.

'Who can say,' I said, anxious to reassure her despite all my own misgivings. 'I've fought in enough of them now to know that you can never be sure of anything when it comes to war, but I hope to survive as I have done so many times before. Yet as always, my fate is in God's hands, not mine.'

She seemed to accept that. 'Then I will pray for you, my Lord,' she offered, then kissed the tips of her fingers and pressed them to my lips.

I recalled how it was when I'd bid farewell to Emelda before going off to fight at Combwich. I'd given her a token to hold whilst I was away, but I had nothing of that sort which I could offer Mildred. Instead, I reached out and put my arms around her. 'If I do fall,' I whispered, still holding her. 'Find Aelred. He knows what you mean to me and will make provision for you.'

'I'd sooner you returned to me, safe and sound,' she said.

For a moment we stood there, looking at each other and almost afraid to say anything more. Then she turned away and walked towards the river, stopping only to look back and smile before joining others who were gathering on the far bank.

*****

I had hoped to avoid any undue panic, but as soon as word went round that the Vikings had reached the Monastery, we were engulfed in chaos. Looking round I realised that many people had failed to heed Werhard's insistence that they hide in the hills and far too many of them were still waiting on the other side of the river, perhaps hoping they could return to their homes more quickly from there. I could see the danger in that, for they could impede the movements of our men if we were forced to retreat in haste, so sent word to have them disperse.

Werhard rode across the river to speak to me on that point.

'We must move them back even further,' I advised. 'If the Vikings break through they'll all be slaughtered if they stay there. We have to get them as far away as possible.'

'Why worry,' said Werhard. 'Hakon will be more intent on reaching his supply ships as soon as he can. He daren't risk leaving them unprotected for long.'

'That won't concern him unduly,' I told him. 'He'll know that Alfred will be too busy dealing with the Viking advance party to worry about attacking a few supply ships. A hundred warriors landing somewhere on the coast is likely to be his first concern.'

'Exactly,' said Aelred. 'And he has to find them first. In my experience, finding Vikings who don't want to be discovered is no easy task. They seem to melt into the trees.'

'He'll find them,' I assured them. 'You can't move that many men without someone seeing. My worry is that if the advance party get to the supply ships first they could then form a secure bridgehead. If they do that and then Hakon joins them as well there'll be hell to pay.'

'So we can't expect to be relieved any time soon?' acknowledged Werhard.

'That's about the strength of it.'

'Well,' said Aelred. 'In the meantime, should we not send someone to assess the numbers Hakon has brought with him?'

'We should,' I agreed. 'But it's too late now. Besides, we'll be able to count them soon enough.' With that I turned to Werhard. 'You should go back across the river to be with your people,' I told him.

'My place is here,' he said boldly. 'If I'm to die I'd as soon do so here beside you and all these men who've served me so faithfully all these years.'

'Be that as it may, I need someone on the other side of the river who the people respect, someone they'll listen to,' I assured him.

'Leonfrith can manage that,' he said.

'Leonfrith is an excellent man who I much respect, but to most of them you are still their Ealdorman whatever you've pledged to me. Therefore they'll not only listen to you, they'll obey your every word.'

He could see the sense of that and nodded wisely. 'As you wish, Matthew,' he said, but barely had he turned to leave than we heard the sound that every Saxon truly dreaded – the hollow blast of the battle Lur as the Vikings charged into the settlement intent on slaughter and destruction.

Chapter Fifteen

We watched in silence as the Vikings ransacked the Vill and all the deserted homes at the settlement, then set everything ablaze. It was at that point that I realised just how terrified most of the men were as, although trained, many of them had never fought in a battle before and were therefore anxious about all that which they feared would follow.

'I'm not sure they'll stand once they see what's set against them,' warned Aelred as he stood beside me.

I knew he was right. The Vikings traded on fear and would surely test the resolve of even seasoned warriors as they appeared, screaming and howling their abuse. Terror would then spread through the assembled ranks like a plague. 'Help me with these,' I said as I started to remove my mail vest and fleece undershirt.

'What the hell are you doing?' he asked.

'You'll see. Just help me get these off. The men need to know who I am.'

'God's truth, Matthew, you can't fight whilst stripped to the waist!' he warned.

'I can and I will. And you'll soon see why.'

With his help I removed all my protective clothes and my helmet until I stood with my chest bared. That done, I drew a deep breath and walked out of the stockade as calmly as I could and went to stand beside the ford where I could be seen and heard by all. I shivered in the late autumn air, but gradually some of the men saw my scar and recognised it. Then, gradually, word of my being the warrior with the pierced heart spread to all those who were from the other settlements. With that I drew my sword and drove the point of it into the ground. I then knelt beside it and uttered a few prayers aloud, calling upon God to see us all safe through what was about to unfold and asking Him to receive our souls if we should fall. Others joined me by kneeling or repeating the words, some no doubt offering a few silent prayers of their own. When I'd finished, I crossed myself then got up to address them all.

'Hakon is coming!' I said as loudly as I could. 'Already he's made free with the homes of all those who live in this settlement and others besides. Have we come here to do no more than stand aside and watch?'

I paused there to allow the words to sink in, then continued. 'Or are we true Saxons? Are we worthy of that heritage and of the blood of our forefathers which courses through our veins? If so, then we must stand shoulder to shoulder like Saxons should and thereby keep this evil from our land. And pray don't tell me there are more of them than there are of us or that you fear them. Instead, look upon this scar on my chest and thereby know full well who I am. The Vikings know me well enough as indeed they should, not just because they believe I can't be slain but because they fear me and know that I'm a warrior worthy of the name. Already many of their kind have perished at the edge of my sword and many more shall likewise do the same.' Again I waited, just as I'd seen Alfred do whilst rousing his men before a battle. 'I'm not minded to turn away from this battle just because they've come in greater numbers, for that means only that more of them have come here to die,' I continued. 'Rather it's my intent to hold this ground and, in so doing, I shall not let up the slaughter until they all lie dead and the river runs red with their heathen blood.' I waited to see whether my words were wasted or whether they were serving to rouse those who were of less steadfast intent. What worried me was that they had all remained silent as I spoke, none of them uttering so much as a murmur. 'Remember,' I continued, 'we're fighting not just for our homes and our families; we're fighting for our freedom, for our religion and for the right to live as Saxons. The question is, must I fight them alone or will you stand with me?'

Still no one responded. Then, slowly at first, a few men began beating the backs of their shields. One by one others joined in. Then some started stamping their feet as others began calling out the Saxon battle cry of 'Out! Out! Out! Out!' Gradually, that call grew louder and louder until every man there joined in. 'OUT! OUT! OUT! OUT!' they shouted until the noise of it was almost deafening.

* * * * *

It was as I returned to the stockade that the first of the Viking warriors made their way down towards the river, having seemingly tired of destroying empty homes. I was about to give the order to 'form up', but the men needed no prompting from me – on seeing the Vikings everyone found their place and made themselves ready. Those who stood with Aelred and me in the stockade crouched low behind the defences, hidden but with their bows held ready. Godric and Coenred had taken their place on the upper part of the mill and I could see that they meant to strike quickly, hopefully killing a few Vikings even before the battle commenced. On the island they were also ready and waiting. Only the shield wall was not fully prepared, for they intended to form up only at the last moment rather than have to hold themselves braced and their shields raised for longer than was needed.

'Now what?' asked Aelred.

'Now we wait,' I said. 'Timing will be all and we can't afford to waste arrows. Delay is our best option as they'll be short of food, already tired, and will need Hakon to tell them when to attack.' With that I climbed up on to part of the mill where all could see me. 'Hold firm!' I shouted. 'All except Godric and Coenred should wait until Hakon attacks.' With that I looked up at Godric who was grinning broadly, clearly proud of the role he was about to play. Almost at once he loosed his first arrow, but it landed well short of where the Vikings were beginning to assemble.

Using that as a marker beyond which they were sure they'd be safe, the horde began swarming towards it, shouting and defiantly waving their weapons in the air. What they didn't know was that Godric had fooled them. As they formed up he and Coenred loosed more arrows in quick succession and three Viking warriors reeled back and then fell dead. The others hurriedly retreated a dozen steps or more, almost falling over themselves in their haste as my Saxon band jeered and mocked them. I looked up at Godric and acknowledged his ploy. With men like that I felt more confident that we might prevail. That was until the full extent of Hakon's warband appeared, a seething mass of men all armed and already baying for blood.

*****

'God's truth, there's hundreds of the bastards!' said Aelred as we looked out on the assembled horde.

With that Hakon himself rode forward mounted on a grey stallion with Ulf and a standard bearer on either side of him, also mounted. Then the standard bearer lowered his pennant: a sign that they wanted to talk.

'You'll not walk out and face them without your mail vest or at least a shield?' warned Aelred.

'Why not? Many of the Vikings there were present when I slew Torstein, therefore they've reason enough to fear me so let's remind them who it is they've come to fight.'

With that Aelred and I put our weapons aside. I slung a cloak over my shoulders for warmth and signalled for Godric and Coenred to honour the truce. We then walked out as boldly as we dared to meet Hakon the Bonebreaker face to face.

'Are you sure this is wise?' queried Aelred knowing we were, by then, well within range of the Viking bowmen.

'Don't worry,' I assured him. 'Jarl Hakon and I are old friends. He'll honour the truce and kill any of his men who deign to abuse it.'

'Ah well, that's all right then,' said Aelred. 'So long as they don't get away unpunished if they cut us down like dogs!'

With that we stopped and waited, thereby forcing Hakon and his party to take a similar risk by coming within range of our bowmen if they wanted to talk.

'My Lord sends greetings,' said Ulf when they reached us, all of them still mounted. 'It is good to see you again alive and well.'

'No thanks to you,' I said remembering the assassin they'd sent to accompany me back to Winchester. 'Is this a friendly visit or have you all come here to die?' I then asked.

As Ulf translated that Hakon roared with laughter.

'No one here needs to die,' said Ulf. 'You have only to stand aside and let us pass, we have no cause to harm anyone here.'

'Like you once told me you had no cause to invade Wessex, yet here you are, armed and having already sacked this settlement and burned the homes of these good people to the ground. And also the Monastery by all accounts.'

Ulf spoke again to Hakon. 'My Lord wishes you no ill. He has come to much admire you as a warrior.'

'Tell him he may regret that when the time comes for me to kill him,' I said boldly. As that was translated Hakon nodded knowingly, then called to several men who were standing somewhere within their ranks. They came forward to join us, dragging Father Gregory and two monks with them, all of whom were bound hand and foot.

'My Lord has ordered these men to be spared if you will let us pass unchallenged,' said Ulf.

I looked at Father Gregory, not sure what I could say. He could see my dilemma and was good enough to reassure me that he knew what would follow but was not afraid.

'My Lord, you must not prejudice your position on our account,' he said softly.

'Father, I fear they'll kill you if I don't do as they say but…'

'It's of no matter,' said the abbot. 'They've already butchered our brothers and destroyed our Monastery, burning it to the ground and thieving all we'd assembled there for the glory of God. If we must die it's because God wills it so and thus will meet our fate as readily and as meekly as Jesus Christ our Lord met his.'

I noticed that although his hands were tied he held a small reliquary between them. I recalled that it had once been set with jewels and bands of silver but all that had been prised away so that what remained was just a simple wooden casket, but I knew what it contained. He looked down at it and smiled, then held it out as if it were a gift. I looked at Hakon who seemed inclined to let me accept it.

'It's the bone from the finger of St Columba,' said Father Gregory. 'Pray take it my Lord and keep it safe. It's been of comfort to us and to many of those who've called upon us for succour and aid. It may therefore serve to protect you.'

I stepped forward and took the casket then passed it back to Aelred. 'You don't have to kill these men,' I said, speaking to Hakon direct. 'They've done you no harm.'

'As you know my Lord hates priests,' said Ulf. 'But he hoped that they might persuade you to see sense.'

'Tell Jarl Hakon that all I "see" are the butchers and rogues he's brought with him to this fray. Therefore if you kill these good men I shall show no mercy once I've claimed victory.'

'Do you not see the numbers ranged against you?' asked Ulf, seemingly surprised.

I shrugged. 'I've faced such odds before and shall answer as we did then – with courage and skill, and with our blood if we must. But be warned, we'll die defending this place, but many of you will die with us.' With that, realising there was little more to be said, both Aelred and I turned to walk away. As we went I half expected to feel an arrow between my shoulders, but nothing came. When we reached the stockade I turned and saw that both Ulf and Hakon had returned to their ranks, but that half a dozen men stood in their place and had forced Father Gregory and the two monks to their knees. One of them stood behind them and held up a knife with which he clearly meant to cut their throats. I quickly signalled to Godric and Coenred who didn't need telling twice. They shot the man with the knife and several others, but couldn't save the two monks, both of whom were promptly butchered and their bodies then despoiled. Angered at seeing some of his men slain, Hakon had the others retreat a short distance. They dragged Father Gregory with them and, once out of bow range, wrestled him to the ground and cut off the fingers from one of his hands. Laughing, one of the men held up the severed fingers for us to see then shouted something before throwing them towards us.

'What did he say?' I asked Aelred.

'He said something like here's a few more fingers for your little box,' replied Aelred.

With that they stretched out the abbot and cut of his head with an axe, a mercifully quick death but a brutal end for such a brave and gentle man nonetheless.

'Do you think there's any chance Alfred will get here in time?' asked Aelred.

'I doubt it. The ships will lead him a merry dance along the coast and he'll be forced to follow them. No doubt they'll draw him as far from here as they can.'

'Then it's going to be a bloody fray, is this one, that's for sure.'

All I could do was to acknowledge the truth of that. The trouble was, despite all I'd said to Hakon, I feared that most of the blood being shed would be ours.

* * * * *

I could see Hakon still mounted somewhere amid his throng of warriors. He seemed to be speaking to several men, no doubt urging them on or giving orders. Then, without warning, I saw him raise the heavy club on which his reputation was founded. As he lowered it I couldn't hear his shout above all the noise, but I knew it was his signal to attack.

The Vikings charged forward but, to my dismay, they mostly ignored the stockade and went hard towards the ford instead, presumably intending to surge across it by sheer force of numbers. I saw this at once and looked to Godric who immediately ordered first one group of men in the stockade to stand up and loose a volley of arrows, then the other. It was nothing like the swarm I'd witnessed at Combwich but still enough to stop some of the Vikings in their tracks – or at least force them to seek shelter behind their shields. I saw quite a few of them fall, either dead or wounded, but it made little impression on their numbers.

We kept loosing arrows and hurling sling shot into their ranks, but it was never going to be enough to daunt them. They crashed forward regardless, screaming and waving their axes and swords in the air, no doubt anxious not to miss their share of the slaughter.

By then the first few Vikings had started to cross at the ford. As I'd predicted, they could only do so three or at best four abreast, but Hakon had formed his plan well. The men all protected themselves by keeping in tight formation and holding their shields up to guard against arrows shot from the island or into the air by men positioned behind our shield wall. Some tried to wade into the deeper water either side of the ford, but hadn't bargained on the sharpened stakes we'd placed in the river. Several fell when exposed whilst trying to get around them, but, for the most part, our arrows had little effect. Given that the Vikings were so well protected, Osmund hurriedly told his men not to waste more arrows. Instead, they formed their shield wall and waited for the onslaught.

Most of the Vikings quickly realised that the ford was too narrow for them all to cross at once so turned their attention to the stockade. As they did so, we didn't let up with our barrage of arrows, but I began to wonder what more we could do. 'Keep shooting!' I ordered as they hit us hard and tried to breach our defences, hacking at the gates and at the walls of the stockade with their axes.

Some of the Viking bowmen had also set themselves up just within range and were shooting lighted arrows at the stockade, trying to set the fortifications ablaze. Several arrows embedded themselves in the timbers and whilst easily dealt with, kept us busy with pails of water to prevent any fire from taking hold. In doing so, several of our men made easy targets, but we had no choice but to do what we could to douse the flames. Then I saw to my horror that the thatch to the mill was ablaze and that flames were already licking at the weathered timbers. I looked up at Godric and Coenred who had both seen the fire, but seemed not to care. They kept loosing arrows at the Vikings who were shooting at us, picking them off where they could.

I began to wonder how long we could hold out. Certainly the battle wasn't going well and I knew that if even part of the stockade was weakened, the Vikings would quickly swarm through whatever breach they could establish and butcher us all. Yet if we abandoned it they could use it themselves for cover, which would mean that the day was lost. We therefore had to hold it for as long as we could whatever the cost.

Those on the island were similarly frustrated. They kept shooting their arrows but could inflict few casualties because of the Vikings' shields. Meanwhile our only consolation was that our shield wall was holding well given that the Vikings could only cross a few at a time. Those that did make it seemed inclined to hurl themselves directly at it, using their axes to hammer the shields in the hope of splitting them or driving their spears through any gaps they could find. It was bloody and tiring work for which they paid dearly as Osmund's men held firm.

Aelred came to stand beside me. 'It's not going well is it,' he shouted to make himself heard above the noise of the battle.

'No, that Hakon's a wily bastard. He has the measure of us, but we're not done yet. Organise the men who've come to deal with the fires. Have them concentrate on the stockade and leave the mill to burn, but try to get Godric and Coenred out before they burn with it.'

'Coenred's already dead,' said Aelred solemnly. 'He was surely a brave soul and no mistake. He stood there, as tall as a tree and loosed his arrows one after the other until struck down himself.'

We both looked up and could see that Godric was still picking off targets where he could, using to full effect the advantage he had in being so high up.

'He can't stay there much longer,' said Aelred. The truth of that was plain to see. The main roof of the mill was all but ablaze by then and might therefore collapse at any time.

'If they set fire to the gates like that we're as good as done for,' I said. 'All I can do is to have the men here keep shooting arrows, but they're not having much effect except to restrict the Vikings' ability to reach the ford in any sort of numbers.'

'What happens when we run out of arrows?' he asked.

I wasn't sure how to answer that so instead just shrugged, knowing it would then come down to hand-to-hand fighting which, given his superior numbers, was exactly what Hakon wanted.

With that Aelred put his hand on my shoulder. 'Then good luck, my friend,' he said, and started rounding up others to help him deal with the fires.

At that I split the remainder of the bowmen into two groups, one to cover the front and the other to harry the Vikings who were gathering at the side of the stockade waiting for their turn to cross the river. Even though fighting from cover, several of our men had been wounded and five had been killed outright. There was nothing I could do for the dead, but the wounded were of no use to us there and when the time came for us to retreat from the stockade in haste, they'd almost certainly be in our way. I therefore ordered them to retreat across the bridge, there to seek help or, if they could, assist those on the island. It was as I was giving that order that Godric turned the battle in our favour. He had seen Hakon urging his men on and, with a perfectly judged shot, took the Viking warlord down with an arrow to his throat. Hakon seemed to choke then slumped forward, desperately clinging to his horse, but then slid sideways and fell to the ground.

Godric's timing was perfect. As news that their leader had been killed went round, the Vikings' assault seemed to falter. In all the uncertainty which followed, some began trying to retreat whilst others were still intent on attack. In the melee of all that confusion our arrows at last began to exact a terrible toll. The Vikings screamed as they were struck, others just groaned as they fell to the ground.

Seeing that, Osmund ordered the shield wall to advance to the very edge of the river, pushing back the twenty or so Viking warriors who had made it across the ford and putting any of their wounded to the sword. Those Vikings who were in the water turned away as well, but, as they did so, left themselves exposed as the bowmen on the island loosed several volleys into their frightened ranks. As the bodies of the Vikings drifted away from the ford, the water became clouded with their blood.

The rest of the horde struggled in all the carnage and confusion. Eventually they began to retreat in numbers, leaving their dead and wounded behind them and forming their own rank with their shields raised, expecting us to counter-attack at any time.

'Hold!' I screamed, knowing that I needed to be sure their retreat wasn't a ruse. Besides, even though we then had a slight advantage, I knew that if it came to hand-to-hand fighting we'd be no match for so many tried and tested warriors.

Looking round, it seemed that Aelred had most of the fires under control by then – except the mill, most of which was burning fiercely. The heat from the flames was so intense that we had to abandon that section of the stockade and instead concentrate our defence on the area nearest the gates which was furthest from it. I couldn't see Godric at first, but hoped he'd managed to escape. Then my heart sank when someone pointed to him, still in his position but with his clothes on fire. With no way of escaping the flames, he leaped from the burning building and landed heavily on the ground below. Several men rushed to help him douse the flames, but I knew it was all too late. He couldn't possibly have survived the fall, never mind the flames.

As he lay there, his clothes and body still smouldering, I suddenly called to mind his mother's prediction when I'd met her that time in the forest.

'Beware the flames which may one day embrace you.'

I realised then that what she'd said had indeed come to pass. It was also a pointed reminder of what she'd said about my own fate.

'I see in you a man living beyond his years and searching for his grave.'

Recalling that sent a shiver down my spine, for I'd also not forgotten Ingar's prophecy. Even though I'd said little enough to Aelred at the time, all the pains which followed the exertion needed to execute Oeric had served to convince me that her prediction could well soon come to pass.

*****

The battle reached a sort of lull and both sides took the chance to regroup, tend the wounded and rest for a few moments. We were lucky that we could distribute food and scoop up enough water from the river to refresh ourselves whereas the Vikings seemed to have neither – or at least, not as much as they needed. Yet, even with Hakon dead, the outcome was far from certain.

Using the makeshift bridge, I went across to the island and spoke to Edgar who was commanding there, calling Osmund and the thanes who were fighting alongside the shield wall to come close enough to hear as well.

'What do we do now, my Lord,' asked Osmund. Both he and Edgar looked relieved at what we'd achieved thus far, but I knew that it had been a stroke of luck which had spared us – that and of course Godric's skill and sacrifice.

'For now we wait,' I said. 'Our task was to buy enough time for reinforcements to arrive.'

'But, my Lord, are you sure that help is still coming?' asked Osmund.

'To be honest I'm not. At least, not in time. But these Vikings are weary and have little in the way of food or water. They'll have to attack again – and soon.'

'So it's more of the same,' said Edgar wearily.

'No, the mill is now burning so fiercely that it can't remain standing for long. When it falls it'll likely take the walls of the stockade with it as well and thereby leave us defenceless.'

'So what's to be done?' asked Osmund.

'We'll be forced to abandon it so will do that now rather than wait until the last moment so we can get as many men out as we can. They can use the bridge to join you here on the island then wade across to the far bank to reinforce the shield wall. Edgar, I'll need you to cover their retreat.'

'But my men on the island will all be slaughtered once the stockade falls!' he said.

'I know it. But I need you and your men to keep killing any Vikings who are crossing the river or trying to assault the shield wall for as long as possible. Once you run out of arrows or your position becomes untenable, retreat to the far bank and join the shield wall as well. We'll make our last stand there.'

I think we all then knew that our position was hopeless, though none of us wanted to admit it. We'd stood bravely and held our own, but, with the numbers ranged against us, we were unlikely to prevail, especially as we would soon face combat at close quarters, the sort of fighting which the Vikings favoured.

*****

With all the buildings within the stockade on fire, our remaining supplies and weapons were effectively lost. I therefore ordered my men to withdraw as quickly and as quietly as they could, taking advantage of the fact that the Vikings were preoccupied in deciding who would lead them now that Hakon was dead. Once on the island, Aelred and two others destroyed the bridge behind us, rolling aside the huge log which had been used to form it. They decided not to worry about the water wheel as the mill was fully ablaze by then. Even as they stood there, we heard the remaining timbers which formed the mill creak and groan, then the whole structure toppled sideways and collapsed in a huge shower of sparks and flames, taking with it a large section of the stockade as well, just as I'd feared. We all stood and stared for a few moments knowing that we'd got out just in time – had we stayed any longer we would have been forced to leave the safety of the stockade or been burned alive within it.

As soon as we'd all crossed the river I went to speak with Osmund and the thanes. They all seemed relieved to be handing over command to me given that we expected the next onslaught to concentrate solely on our shield wall.

'Can we hold them?' asked Osmund sounding worried.

'We can for now, but it will be bloody work. Once they open up the shield wall it will be just a matter of time. Our only chance is to ensure that the men stand firm.'

There was silence as they all considered what I'd said. 'If any fall, be ready to fill the gap and do what you can to keep the rank tight. Have we any bowmen left here?'

Osmund looked doubtful. 'We have bowmen, my Lord, but few arrows.'

'Those on the island still have some. Send someone to fetch what they can spare. If we shoot them over the top of the shield wall and from the island at the same time that should slow down the attack, but remember, those on the island are probably better placed to kill the bastards so be sure to leave enough for them to use.'

He immediately sent someone across to organise that. I then spoke to Werhard and told him to get all those who weren't fighting away as soon as he could. Having seen our position and heard all we'd said, he didn't need telling twice.

That done, I turned to address the men, hoping to raise their spirits. 'Make ready,' I said walking along in front of the shield wall so all could see and hear me. 'Thus far we've given a good account of ourselves. Their leader is slain and many of his men have perished with him. That means there are now fewer of them than there were and all are tired and hungry, thus the battle begins to turn in our favour. Therefore now is the time for us to finish this. We'll stand together, shoulder to shoulder, and kill every Viking who dares to cross this river. We'll show them what Saxons can do and make them rue the day they dared to cross us.'

'What will become of us, my Lord?' asked one man.

It was a lone voice, but I knew it was the question they all wanted to ask. 'I don't know,' I admitted. 'But I do know this. No man can doubt the courage of any who were here this day and your names will be mentioned with pride whenever men speak of what it means to be a Saxon. I'm therefore proud to have fought beside you. As for the Vikings, all I would say is this. They came here and even though we were outnumbered, we matched them, blow for blow. In doing so we killed many and shall yet kill more. So many that already the ford runs red with their heathen blood.' It was then that I recalled something Alfred had said before the battle of Combwich. 'When we're done, be assured of this,' I said. 'The river shall have their bones as surely as the devil in hell shall have their souls.'

* * * * *

We didn't have to wait long before the Vikings came at us again. Knowing that the stockade had been abandoned, they marched straight down to the river, a seething rabble thirsting for blood. As they stood facing us on the far bank, I tried to assess their numbers, but, beyond the fact that a good many of them had been killed or wounded, it was impossible to count how many remained. We'd lost perhaps twenty men all told plus at least as many again who'd been wounded, though I knew that wouldn't be the final tally. I took some consolation from the fact that even if the next stage of the battle didn't go well, the Vikings were by then a spent force so Alfred would have no trouble mopping up the survivors when he eventually arrived. I then began to prepare myself knowing that without Jarl Hakon to lead them, they would just make a manic charge across the ford.

A few of our men started beating the backs of their shields once more. As others joined in they took up our chant of OUT! OUT! OUT! OUT! thereby almost daring the Vikings to cross the river. I at once took my place behind the shield wall and, as soon as the Vikings made their move, I gave the order to close up and for the men to brace themselves. Our bowmen sent several volleys of arrows into the air which slowed the Vikings down, but it was never going to be enough. What followed was utter carnage.

Even though they could still cross only three or four at a time, they hit us hard then quickly spread out along the bank. The fighting which followed was terrifying. Men were hacking and striking each other so fiercely that the wounds were as dreadful as any I'd ever seen, even at Edington.

Screams rang out as men were slain, but our ranks were packed so tight that even when killed there was no room for anyone to fall. Thus it seemed that even the dead were obliged to fight on beside us. Then several men did fall when their legs were cut from under them and the Vikings tried desperately to swarm through the breach. For the most part we held them off, skewering those who tried with spears or stabbing them with a seax.

As the slaughter showed no sign of abating I feared we could not keep up our defence much longer. I began to consider what best to do. Surrender would mean that as like as not all of us would be put to the sword and I could see no way of allowing even some of the men to withdraw. It was then I felt Aelred's hand on my shoulder. I couldn't hear what he was saying, but he was pointing to what remained of the burning settlement. When I looked, all I could see was a mass of men who had gathered there and were charging down the hill, presumably intending to join the battle. Fearing they were yet more Vikings my heart sank, but then I realised that what I was seeing was in fact the answer to all our prayers. For they were Alfred's reinforcements come at last to relieve us!

*****

At first it seemed as though the Vikings hadn't seen our reinforcements arrive. Then, as the realisation dawned on them, there was panic amid their ranks. Some turned to face the new attackers but were cut down even before they could do so. Others doggedly continued to press our shield wall, hacking at our shields with their axes, seemingly unaware.

'Hold firm!' I shouted trying to make myself heard above the din of the battle. Several of the thanes went and stood beside their men ensuring that no one broke rank. Some even bravely took the place of men who had fallen. Then, gradually, the Viking assault seemed to weaken as they began to realise what was happening, most of them already so weary that all the fight had gone out of them. Some managed to run, but most tried to fight their way through the attackers to their rear in order to escape the slaughter.

'Hold firm!' I screamed again as some of our men seemed inclined to follow the retreating Vikings. I knew they'd be killed if they did for although they'd done well, they were none of them a match for such seasoned warriors.

When at last the Vikings seemed to have abandoned their attack on our shield wall, I signalled for all to stand easy and rest, but insisted that they keep their lines ready to reform if needed. Aelred, Osmund and Edgar came across to speak with me.

'My Lord, you look cold,' said Osmund realising that I was still bare chested. It hadn't mattered in the heat of battle, but once the fighting stopped I did indeed feel distinctly chilled. He removed his cloak and wrapped it around my shoulders.

'We did well,' observed Aelred.

'We did,' I agreed. 'Though we couldn't have survived much longer.'

All there agreed, but we were too tired to say much more. In fact, when I looked at my men, it was clear that few of them had strength enough to stand, never mind fight again. Most were seated on the ground or leaning on their spears for support and I realised then just how close we'd come to being defeated.

*****

A man named Rufus came across the ford to speak with me. He introduced himself and explained that he'd commanded the reinforcements which, it transpired, had been sent at Alfred's insistence.

'You arrived just in time,' I told him. 'But is Lord Alfred not with you?'

He shook his head. 'No, but he'll come when he can. He first has to deal with Hakon's supply ships which landed on the south coast. They became stranded on the tide and by now all will have been taken or destroyed.'

'Then what of the other invaders? There were three ships all laden with men which we feared might also attack our shores.'

'God be praised for they haven't landed in Wessex. We have word that they went across to raid overseas instead. Lord Alfred has set men to keep watch and remains on hand in case they yet appear, but sent us to relieve you as he knew you'd be hard pressed here.'

'Thank God he did,' I explained. 'We couldn't have held them back much longer without you.'

He looked around at the carnage. The bank was strewn with bodies and many more still floated in the river having formed a sort of log jam there as the river washed the blood from their wounds. On the far bank, the Viking wounded were being put to the sword without mercy and the bodies of the dead were being stripped of anything of value. 'Whatever's taken must be shared with the men here,' I ordered.

He acknowledged the order. 'They deserve as much, for you surely did well given the odds against you,' he agreed.

With that Werhard came to join us and I asked him if he could send some women to tend our own wounded. 'And could you arrange for someone to bring us food and fresh water? Most here have eaten little since dawn.'

'So was the threatened invasion just a ruse?' asked Aelred.

'So it seems,' said Rufus.

'Then a lot of men have died here for no purpose.'

As always, I was sickened by the bloodshed, but was too exhausted to debate that further. Instead, I asked Rufus to assume command whilst I rested.

Almost at once Aelred seemed to know that something was wrong. 'Are you all right?' he asked quietly.

I nodded though couldn't deny that the pains in my chest were grumbling. They were not as severe as they had been in the past, but I knew that all was far from well.

'Let's get you back across the river and find a safe place for you to rest,' he advised. With that, he and I used the ford to cross, pushing our way between all the bodies which still floated there. As we did so, all the men rose and began to beat their shields as a sign of their respect. I wished I had the strength to say something, but in truth it was all I could do to raise my hand to acknowledge them.

Once on the other bank we could see the carnage which had been wrought. The dead were strewn across the field, many having suffered terrible wounds. A few Vikings were still fighting in the distance, probably hoping to find shelter in what remained of the settlement. To our right, the stockade and the mill still smouldered, though by then they were little more than charred and blackened ruins. I wanted to see the damage for myself, but Aelred wisely dissuaded me.

'Let's get you away from here,' he offered. 'You can inspect things later, but you've done all you can now.' With that he led me a little way upstream and set me down on a log to rest whilst he went to fetch water in his helmet for me to drink.

As I sat there I felt a shiver pass through me. I knew then that the pains in my chest would begin again in earnest. Gradually, they started to ripple through my body in waves, just as they had so many times before. To be fair, they were no worse than I'd experienced in the past, but the left side of my body was suddenly numb so that I could scarce move my arm at all.

I was therefore helpless as I watched Aelred go down to the river. As I did so, I became aware of someone running towards me, sword in hand. I recognised him at once as Arne, the Viking boy I'd tried to befriend but who still seemed intent on avenging his father whom my brother Edwin had slain so cruelly. As always, the little runt had held back and thereby avoided the worst of the fray.

As soon as I saw him I struggled to my feet and tried to draw my own weapon or at least raise my shield, but, with my left arm useless, I lacked the strength to do so. When he saw this he laughed then shook his sword at me – the one I'd returned to him when I'd offered to adopt him as my brother and which had once belonged to his father. I remembered it was called Red Viper, just as I remembered why it was given that name.

'Just wait until you see it thrust into some poor bastard's guts.'

I knew then that I was about to see that for myself, for there was no doubt about what he intended. I had only to look into his eyes to see the hatred that burned within his soul. Yet there was nothing I could do to defend myself.

I resolved to meet my fate as bravely as I could, not wanting to give him the satisfaction of seeing me plead for mercy. Instead, I stood and looked him straight in the eye which seemed to unnerve him, but then he started shouting at me. Though I had no idea what he was saying, I uttered a short prayer and waited for the blow which I knew would follow.

With that, Arne let out a cry as he thrust his sword deep into my belly then twisted the blade as was the Viking way.

In truth, my body was too numb to feel the full intensity of the pain. Instead, I just groaned and slumped to the ground. As I did so, he raised the sword again intending to finish me, but then noticed Aelred returning from the river. Realising he would soon be caught, the boy turned to run, but must have known that he could not escape. Others had seen him as well by then, but it was Aelred who reached him first. The boy turned to face him, but, as I suspected, he had no real skill with the sword so stood no chance against such an accomplished warrior. Aelred simply avoided the boy's blade then drove his spear point home. When I heard Arne cry out I knew that Aelred had prevailed.

Still helpless, I watched as Aelred picked up Arne's sword and admired it. 'At last a prize worth taking,' he shouted.

As Aelred tried a few short strokes with the sword I tried to call out to him, but my voice was not much more than a whisper. 'I know what you're thinking,' he called still without turning round. 'We should melt this down for there's likely to be much Saxon blood on the blade.'

With that he glanced over his shoulder and suddenly realised my plight. 'God's truth, Matthew, you're wounded! Why the hell didn't you say so?' With that he tossed the sword aside and came over to kneel beside me. He gently moved my hand aside so he could see the wound more clearly, then took off his cloak and pressed it against my belly to stem the bleeding. 'I'll go to get help,' he said, but I caught his arm to stop him, knowing there was nothing to be done.

As I lay on the cold hard ground I tried to endure the agony as best I could, though, in truth, it was not much worse than the pains in my chest. Aelred bent over me and tried to raise me up. Then I realised I was shaking, not shivering from the cold but quivering as I'd seen so many dying men do. I knew then that Ingar's prediction was about to come true.

I reached up and grasped his arm as tightly as I could. 'R…remember our p… promise to I…Ingar,' I stammered.

He nodded. 'I will, but you can look to her yourself when you're well.'

'No,' I implored him, shaking my head. 'G…go to see my s…son,' I urged. 'T…tell him of m…me. L…look o…out for him. Alfred will p…pay f…for y…your…'

'I need no payment for that,' he assured me.

I tightened my grip as a spasm of pain ripped through me. 'W…watch him g…grow,' I pleaded, tears forming in the corner of my eyes.

'I'll take you to him,' said Aelred.

I shook my head. 'No b…bury m…me as we s…said.'

With that I closed my eyes as if to sleep. In those final moments as I lay there, cold and still shaking, I saw Edwin again standing with my father to his side in the darkness, together with others I'd known beside them. This time they were calling me to them, not ushering me away and I seemed to have no choice but to follow.

*****

Thus I, Matthew, christened Edward, third born son of the noble Saxon Edwulf came to be buried in this lonely place. It was a cruel fate to be slain by one who should, by rights, have been my friend. Yet in truth the wound to my chest would have killed me soon enough, just as Ingar had predicted.

But I seek neither your pity nor your tears, for my short life had been filled with more love and friendship than those who had lived far longer than me. Not only that, but having begun my quest as a nervous boy and novice monk, I'd risen to become both a warrior and a counsellor to the greatest King who ever reigned, a King who I counted as a friend.

All I resent is having been taken when so close to making my mark upon the world. Having wrestled with my very soul over what should become of me in life I was taken when all at last had been resolved. Thus so much hope died with me and so many dreams perished as the blood emptied from my veins.

Such were matters which my very soul would not allow and, though dead, I could not rest, for even as my body went the way of all flesh, still my spirit lingered, clinging to the hope that the story of my life and the secret of my grave would one day be revealed.

For a thousand years I've waited for that chance and, now it's done, God grant that my soul may at last rest in peace.

Glossary

Whilst not all universally accepted, the following is an explanation of some of the terms as used in this story:

BERSERKERS Feared Viking warriors who were said to work themselves up into a frenzy prior to fighting, often by imbibing some form of hallucinogen. They sometimes fought bare-chested or wearing a symbolic bear skin and were said not to feel pain or fear anything, even death.

BRETWALDA A mainly honorary title given to a recognised overlord.

DANEAXE A brutal long-handled battle-axe wielded using both hands.

EALDORMAN A high-ranking nobleman usually appointed by the king to oversee a shire or group of shires.

FYRD A group of able-bodied freemen who could be mobilised for military service when required.

LUR A battle horn.

JARL A Viking nobleman or chieftain.

MOOT A meeting to determine local matters, both administrative and judicial.

REEVE An official appointed to oversee specific duties on behalf of the King or an Ealdorman. These included administrative and sometimes judicial responsibilities.

SEAX A short single-edged sword.

THANE A freeman holding land granted by the King or by an Ealdorman to whom he owed allegiance and for whom he provided military support when needed.

VILL The fortified estate of the King or an Ealdorman, usually comprising a large Hall plus other buildings to provide accommodation, administrative offices and stabling etc. It was usually supported by extensive holdings in terms of farmland, pastures and hunting grounds.

Acknowledgements

Having now completed the third book in the series, I am aware of just how many people I have to thank for their contribution – not only in terms of the research and publication, but also for their support and encouragement.

Research has always been an important part in writing the series and I am indebted to the many eminent historians whose work I have read and enjoyed, but not always slavishly followed, preferring to interpret events for myself. Therefore any mistakes, errors or omissions are mine, including the many 'liberties' I have taken throughout the story.

It would not be right to miss this opportunity to acknowledge the support of my wife without whose help I could not have managed. She has often been deprived of my full attention whilst I was 'away' with Matthew on his many adventures.

I should also like to thank the team at my publishers, RedDoor – particularly Clare, Anna, Julia and Heather, not just for their professionalism in producing this series but also for their help and guidance on so many aspects of writing.

Finally, I should like to thank my readers and my followers on both my mailing list and on social media, without whom this would have been a pointless endeavour. It is said that no man is an island and certainly that's true of writers like myself who rely on feedback to keep us on course.

A writer without readers is like a man talking to himself.
What he says may well be of interest, but what
good is that if no one can hear him.

C.B.

Author's Notes on the Series

One of the challenges facing any author writing historical fiction is that of achieving a balance between 'fact' and 'fiction' whilst not losing sight of the need to tell a good story. This is particularly so when writing a novel set in Anglo-Saxon England where many 'facts' have become lost to the mists of time. Even those we do have need to be treated with care as history is often written by the victor not the vanquished, giving us few unbiased contemporary accounts to rely on – after all, propaganda and fake news are nothing new. The mist thickens considerably where intervening generations have added their own embellishments and, in the case of such an iconic personage as Alfred the Great, there is the element of legend and folklore to contend with as well.

Given that I'm a writer and not an historian, my task has been to sift through all this information, thereby undertaking a huge amount of research. This proved no hardship for me as I have a lifelong interest in all things Anglo-Saxon, but it has given me the additional dilemma of deciding what to leave out rather than what to include. Therefore whilst I must confess to having taken some 'liberties' with the perceived facts (such as they are), I must also 'own up' to some deliberate omissions as well.

For example, almost all the characters in the Shadow of the Raven series spring from my own imagination rather than from the pages of history. One of the few exceptions is, perhaps, Alfred himself about whom a great deal has already been written by others. For my part, I've elected to portray him as a Churchillian figure, orator and far-sighted statesman, but with his share of human frailty as well. I hope I've done him justice in that respect.

With regard to the battles depicted in the series, I've tried to visualise the tactics and strategies employed but, in truth, we usually have little knowledge of what actually took place or, indeed, the numbers of men involved. Take for example the attack at Chippenham. There can be little doubt that it did take place and that Alfred's forces were all but annihilated. What intrigued me was why, after so many years of war, would such an experienced and battle-hardened commander as Alfred be taken by surprise, particularly given that Guthrum is thought to have launched his attack from Gloucester, over 30 miles away. For me, one obvious possibility was that of there being a traitor in his camp (my character Cedric in Book One) though I've no evidence to support this contention.

Similarly, we know little about the retreat to Athelney or how the survivors from Chippenham managed through the winter, but it is an important aspect of the story. It's from this wretched period that we have the tale of Alfred burning the cakes and also one which suggests that he ventured into the Vikings' camp disguised as a wandering minstrel to spy on them. Make what you will of his burning the cakes, but the story of him acting as a spy is one which almost beggar's belief when you consider what was at stake and that the reward for anyone prepared to betray him would have been wealth beyond reckoning. That said, I could readily see that Alfred would desperately need to know what Guthrum was planning to do next, so had Matthew fulfil the role of being a spy on his behalf.

Perhaps the most difficult aspect to portray was how Alfred managed to reassemble his army following the defeat at Chippenham. Most people at the time would have probably thought him killed or to have fled abroad, yet, within a few months, he managed to rally them and raise an army of sufficient size to beat Guthrum in open battle. How he achieved that remains an enigma but, in my view, he would have needed at least one decisive victory if only to show that the Vikings could be beaten and that he was the man to do it. I used my depiction of the battle at Combwich for that very purpose. This is loosely based on the Battle of Cynwit but, in reality, that encounter was fought between an Ealdorman of Devon named Odda and the Viking Ubba. I have to confess that my account of the events and the tactics employed have no basis in history (particularly as Alfred wasn't actually there!), but nonetheless it's intended to represent an important milestone in Alfred's comeback.

This is also true of the Battle of Edington, which I regard as possibly one of the most important ever fought on English soil, as had Alfred been defeated the whole of England would have come under Viking rule and history as we know it been changed for ever. There is uncertainty about where it actually took place and most of the accounts we have were written some years after the event. The tactics I've described are more dramatic than factual but are probably not so far from the truth given what we know about how battles were fought at that time.

Books Two and Three stray more towards the realms of fiction rather than fact but are intended to describe what I feel was probably going on in Wessex after the Battle of Edington. In writing them, I've been more concerned to capture the 'mood' of this critical turning point in English history. As the two leaders negotiated the very controversial Treaty of Wedmore, it seems likely that a fragile and uneasy peace would have existed but with various Viking factions continuing to raid hoping to secure their share of the prize. After all, there were many Vikings both in England and abroad who had taken no part in the invasion of Wessex and, as like as not, these included various splinter groups who were looking out for themselves. Raids and skirmishes are therefore likely to have continued and Matthew's adventures are intended to reflect what I believe remained a very unsettled and troubled realm.

Whilst this theme is continued in Book Three, I have to confess that I have no evidence of there having been a battle at Leatherhead. Yet it was an important Saxon settlement at the time (then called Leodridan), so much so that there is some evidence of a Vill having been there and possibly a Minster as well, though at the time of writing the locations for either of these has yet to be established. Leodridan controlled what we would now call 'the Mole Gap' in the North Downs, so it would have been a strategically important place and one which a Viking warlord might well seek to exploit. The Viking warband I refer to as having gathered in London was actually based at Fulham rather than where I've placed it and, whatever their intent, its mere presence must have intimidated Alfred to some extent during his peace negotiations with Guthrum. These Vikings eventually sailed off to raid abroad rather than march south as I've suggested but, if they had attacked Wessex, Leatherhead could well have come very much into focus.

I'm often asked about the detail which I've included in my writing and can say only that this is drawn from a store of useful 'snippets' which I seem to have accumulated over the years. In many cases I've long since forgotten how I came by them, but they include such items as the omens and portents seen in the sky before the Battle of Edington, the visitations from Saint Cuthbert, and Alfred's stomach problems (thought to be Crohn's disease). I've included them as a way of (hopefully) bringing the story to life.

Throughout the series I've tried to show the huge social divide between the nobles and the common man. In reality, I suspect that for most people the struggle to feed themselves and their families would have been much the same whether ruled by the Saxons or by the Vikings and certainly my overall impression is that life must have been extremely hard and, at times, brutal.

With regard to the Vikings, I hope I've portrayed them as something more than just the blood-crazed heathens they're normally depicted as being and given at least a glimpse of the adventurous and creative peoples I believe them to have been, albeit with some violent tendencies.

Finally, as I've relied on my own interpretation of events there are doubtless errors and inaccuracies for which I apologise and must acknowledge as my own. It was never my intention to write a history book as such, but rather to relate Matthew's story, a tale which came to me all but complete to the extent that it seemed almost as if he were there, guiding my pen as I wrote it. That's a rare and extraordinary experience of which

I've often spoken and for which I'm extremely thankful. I've thus followed the inspiration he provided even if it means that the series must inevitably sit on the fiction shelf of the bookcase rather than alongside the weightier tomes written by the many eminent historians who I much admire but have not the capacity nor inclination to emulate.

I very much hope you've enjoyed the series.

C.B.

About the Author

Chris Bishop was born in London in 1951. After a successful career as a chartered surveyor, he retired to concentrate on writing, combining this with his lifelong interest in history. This is the third book in **The Shadow of the Raven** series, the first, *Blood and Destiny*, having been published in 2017 and the second, *The Warrior with the Pierced Heart*, published in 2018.

STAY IN TOUCH WITH CHRIS BISHOP

Sign up to receive Chris's email newsletter at

www.chrisbishopauthor.com

FOLLOW CHRIS:

 @CBishop_author

---

Find out more about RedDoor Publishing and sign up to our newsletter to hear about our latest releases, author events, exciting competitions and more at

reddoorpublishing.com

YOU CAN ALSO FOLLOW US:

 @RedDoorBooks

 RedDoorPublishing

 @reddoorbooks